TERENCE BAILEY

BLIND
SPOT

THE SARA JONES CYCLE BOOK TWO

Published by Accent Press Ltd 2018
Octavo House
West Bute Street
Cardiff
CF10 5LJ

www.accentpress.co.uk

ISBN 9781786155085
eISBN 9781786153821

Printed and bound in Great Britain by Clays Ltd,
Elcograf S.p.A

For Cambria

Acknowledgements

I would like to thank Greg Rees and Katrin Lloyd at Accent Press for all their help. As ever, I thank Dr David W. Grossman and Inspector Alun Samuel for being on hand with advice, expertise and friendship. Thank you to Annemieke Fox, whose knowledge was invaluable, and to Jo Tyler for reading and commenting on an early draft of this novel.

PROLOGUE

It's the same scene, repeating.

A story that should have happened, but didn't.

A moment when a strange element of chance intervened, and a strand of time – *this* strand of time - changed.

A non-event that has been flashing, unbidden and repeatedly, through Sara Jones's mind.

It starts in the shadows of a small living room. A place lit only by the orange glow from the street – a few household things glimpsed, but indistinct. A brass wall plaque gleaming in the glare from outside; flat-pack furniture and stacks of books; a tea set on a small table.

And from another room, the sound of wailing. A woman in distress. Her tears of frustration overpowered by a man's warning voice. The thud of an open hand against fabric and one single yelp of outraged anger.

The hollow pressboard door flies open. A woman named Fatima Kapadia runs into the living room.

She is in Aberystwyth, Wales.

It is not quite three years ago.

Three very different years ago.

Fatima snaps on the light and braces herself for an attack that does not come. She devotes this pocket of time to composing herself – smoothing her pyjamas, flattening

1

her hair. Waiting for her husband, Navid, to do or say something. No sound from the next room. Fatima summons up all her willpower and speaks into the darkness of the hallway.

'You earn thirty-seven thousand pounds a year,' she states with flat disdain. 'I have to lie to my father. I double your salary, and he still thinks I married a failure.'

This has the desired effect. Navid Kapadia lurches as far as the doorframe. The muscles in his cheeks tremble, his eyes glow darkly. Not with anger, but with humiliation. A far more dangerous emotion.

Fatima and Navid quarrel. She wants to return to Pakistan. He swears that the family will stay here in Wales, and he will keep his under-paid job at the university, and Fatima's rich, corrupt father in Karachi can go straight to hell.

Along the darkened hallway, in the small second bedroom, are bunk beds. Twelve-year-old Jamila and eight-year-old Yusuf try to sleep through another noisy battle.

After an hour, their father lumbers into the room and orders them to wake up, to come with him.

This is the point at which Sara – watching in a different place, at another time – always tenses. It didn't happen like this ... but that never changes the horror she feels.

Navid hustles his children's sleepy forms into the car. Fatima squeals and sobs behind him, but he pulls away, and drives through the amber-lit streets of town. Navid's thoughts are in turmoil – replaying old arguments and older humiliations. He can feel the puzzlement that lies within the hollow silence behind him, on the back seat.

He arcs through the town centre and away, towards a supermarket on its outskirts. By the time he gets there, something has changed in his mood. An inhibition has been lost, or a determination found. He pulls into the petrol station and buys a newspaper and a plastic canister. Calmly, Navid returns to the pump and fills his tank and container. There is no further indecision as he drives up the hill, parks once more outside his house and tells the kids to stay in the car.

'Why?' young Jamila asks. 'What's happening, Baba?'

'Shush,' Navid says.

Navid takes a section of newspaper and rolls it. Thrusts it into the tank. His throat thickens with angry grief as he douses the rest of the paper with petrol and tosses it to young Yusuf on the back seat. He chokes out the words, 'Hold this.'

It is only when Navid wets the front seats with petrol that Jamila lurches forward. 'Baba, what are you doing?' she shrieks.

Navid ignores her, but Jamila tugs at the door handle. 'Ammi!' – Mother! – she screams.

As the car door opens, Navid drops his canister and throws himself against the swinging panel, slamming Jamila back inside. Jamila wails and yanks at the handle. Navid keeps his body pressed against the door, panting, crying, wiping his face on his sleeve. The other side opens with a *thunk*, and Navid turns to see Jamila crawling over Yusuf, tumbling head first from the back seat. He dashes around, skidding on the tarmac, nearly losing his balance.

He kicks.

Navid does not mean to hurt his daughter, but it's a reflex, the quickest way to stop her. Jamila barely makes a sound as her head takes the blow. She slumps to the pavement.

In that other place, Sara flinches.

Anguish washes over Navid as he wails and pulls Jamila up by her nightdress. 'I'm sorry!' he sobs, bundling her over Yusuf, who watches with wide eyes, frozen. Navid manages to half-roll Jamila to her side of the seat, then pauses to control his breath, to fight his tears. Inches away from Yusuf's face, he leans in and kisses the boy on the cheek. 'I love you,' he says.

Navid pulls himself from the car and closes the back door. He forces himself to inhale deeply, and releases a loud, shrill whistle.

'Fatima!' he cries.

A light snaps on in the living room. Seconds later, the porch lamp adds to the pale cast flooding the lawn. As Fatima pushes at the door, Navid sparks his lighter and touches its flame to the newspaper jammed in the petrol tank. Quickly, he opens the passenger's door and slides in, remembering to leave it ajar – fire needs oxygen to burn. He pops the lighter once more and pulls it along the petrol-soaked front seat.

Several impressions tumble through Navid's mind at once: Fatima running towards the car; the driver's seat refusing to catch fire; Jamila back there, motionless.

Yusuf's crying now. Navid curses his lighter, curses the petrol for not burning, curses his wife for making all of this necessary. He cannot let Fatima spoil things now. Desperately, he thumbs the lighter's wheel again.

Inwardly, Sara screams as the wheel sparks, and the story – this missing moment in time – concludes.

As a fireball swells.

And the petrol tank explodes.

ONE

Dr Sara Jones always carried a medical bag equipped with a pre-loaded syringe of pentobarbital. This served as a protective weapon, Sara's final defence against the violent souls any psychiatrist with a tinge of bad luck might encounter. Legally – as Sara's ex-police officer boyfriend often told her – this was an enormous risk. Sara could probably have justified keeping a powerful barbiturate in her possession, but if she were ever caught sticking someone … that was another story. It would certainly be judged medical malpractice, and quite probably common assault. Maybe even actual bodily harm.

But Sara was less worried about the Offences Against the Person Act than about being punched, stabbed, or bludgeoned. She would rather face court than reconstructive surgery, and so she continued carrying the bag that concealed two hundred milligrams of liquid protection. When Sara faced a client, she always kept it within easy reach.

Always.

Until the day when she actually needed it.

That day was a Monday morning in late March, and Sara was in London's Chalk Farm. Although a short walk from both the calm of Regent's Park and the throngs of

Camden Town, the area was an impersonal space, with wide roads that felt like canyons, lined with boxy buildings and brown brick walls. Such drab anonymity made the large council estate Sara was visiting seem like an oasis, with plenty of green surrounding its well-scrubbed 1930s housing. Sara tapped on the door of a ground-floor flat, using her *assertive-yet-reassuring* knock. It was a series of gentle raps with a single knuckle – unthreatening, yet quick-paced enough to be insistent. Immediately, she was assailed by a blast of guttural barking and a body-blow thump against the wood.

The door rattled; she leapt back. The torrent of barks and howls was joined by the scrabbling of long claws. Whatever frenzied creature lurked behind this plank of wood sounded *large*. When Sara was young, she had been bitten by a neighbour's sheepdog. Ever since then, man's best friend had been her enemy. When she'd lived in Wales, she knew a woman with pair of trembling Chihuahuas, and could just about tolerate their bug-eyed presence. Any larger dog turned her into a hyperventilating wreck.

Dogs cannot claw through fire doors, Sara reminded herself. But did she really want to take that chance? Just as she was about to retreat to her car, the barking turned into a series of choking rasps.

'Err … hello?' Sara called.

'Yeah, hang on,' a voice shouted. 'Got him by the collar.' This had to be the young man she'd come to see. Sara hoped he wouldn't open the door while still wielding his drooling, fanged weapon.

'Go on, mate!' the voice inside the flat urged. 'Yummy yum-yum! Go get it!'

There was the clack of claws on linoleum. Sara heard an interior door closing, and then the stiff clunk of an unoiled key. The front door squeaked open an inch. 'Help you?' the voice said.

'Tim Wilson?'

'That's me.'

'Is everything safe now?' Sara asked.

'Oh, yeah,' Wilson said. 'Stanley's locked in the bedroom. He likes salami, does Stanley. I can always tempt him away with a nice chunk of salami.'

'I appreciate it,' Sara said. 'I'm very much a cat person.'

'Ah,' Wilson said, 'the enemy!'

The door opened, and Sara got her first glimpse of Tim Wilson. The twenty-four-year-old's low-rise council block may have been in Chalk Farm, but Wilson himself looked every inch a Shoreditch hipster – all the way from his top-knot down to his skater boy Vans. Sara thought herself broad-minded, but she'd always found something ludicrous about the big-bearded affectation that made London's young men look like effete lumberjacks. Still, Hipster Tim seemed almost sweet as he peered at her.

'You from the council?' he asked.

'No,' Sara replied. 'My name is Dr Sara Jones, and I work for the London Fields Support Service. We're a charity.'

She handed him her card, and he stuffed it in his pocket with a shrug of his muscled shoulders. 'Charity's cool,' he offered. 'Sometimes I shop at Oxfam.'

He invited her in and offered a chair. The room was unsettlingly tidy for a young man's place. Even the dog's bowls looked as if they had been positioned with a set square. It was clean-smelling too – lemon bleach and Air Wick. Sara supposed someone meticulous enough to wrap his hair into a perfect top-knot would also keep a spotless flat. She could identify with that: it took an equal amount of care to keep her own hair that exact shade of auburn, and just the right length to tuft into spikes. She and Tim seemed to share an unhealthy perfectionism. The only thing Sara could find amiss in this room was a jagged crack in the window overlooking the street.

Which was rather dangerous, she thought. Anyone could break in.

'What kind of dog is Stanley?' Sara asked.

'Rottweiler,' Wilson said, sitting. 'They're a tough breed, but this one's a crap guard dog. I swear, he'd sit there and watch a burglar take everything I own. I'd be better off with a poodle.'

Sara smiled. She could probably have coped with a poodle.

'Would you like a drink?' Wilson asked.

'What do you have?'

Wilson moved over to the kitchenette and tugged open his refrigerator door. In it were several bottles of a fluorescent orange beverage and little else. 'Err – not a lot, actually,' he said. 'Unless you like Sunny D.'

Sara smiled apologetically.

'Me, I love it,' Wilson said. 'It's about all I drink. I get through one of these bottles every day.'

'It's a good choice,' Sara said. 'I can't imagine anyone else wants it, so you have it all to yourself.'

Wilson paused, then laughed. 'All mine,' he agreed.

'Tim, let me tell you why I'm here,' she began. 'The clinic I work for helps people sort out their emotions.'

Wilson squinted at her, puzzled.

'In other words, their mental health,' she clarified. 'Usually, clients pay a small fee for sessions, but in some cases, we offer our services free of charge.'

This was not exactly true; providing free therapy was Sara's own side project. In the past eighteen months, she had approached three other people with this same offer, and had persuaded each of them to see her professionally.

Sara hoped that Tim Wilson would join their ranks and make Success Number Four. She watched his brow darken into an expression somewhere between confusion and irritation.

'A mental health clinic?' Wilson repeated flatly. 'What are you saying?'

Sara smiled reassuringly. 'Tim,' she said, 'we both know you have a bit of a temper. I'd like to help you get it under control.'

'Who said I have a temper?' he asked. 'Who told you that?'

'That's not important.'

'Was it my social worker?' Wilson persisted.

Sara raised her hands soothingly. 'What is important,' she persisted, 'is that –'

Suddenly, Wilson was on his feet again, his wooden chair skidding across the linoleum. '*Was it my social worker?*' he shouted.

In the bedroom, Stanley reacted to his master's angry voice. The animal threw himself against the door, growling and barking. The sound made every nerve in Sara's body scream. Within moments, Tim Wilson loomed over her, face purpling, sleeve tattoo bulging with tension. 'Who've you been talking to?' he demanded. Flecks of spittle flew from his lips.

In a flash, Wilson had transformed from a sweet hipster to a threat more extreme than his dog. That was when Sara reached swiftly for her medical bag, and found it wasn't there. As she groped the empty air, panic burst in her chest and Wilson grabbed her by the throat.

Sara felt herself gag.

'It's so easy for you, isn't it?' Wilson snarled as he squeezed. 'Passing judgement, telling me my problems, saying you can help. Just like my fucking social worker!'

His grip tightened. '*Charity*,' he spat. 'That's what

9

you're here for, right?'

He wheezed manically. Sara swooned; her vision spangled like Christmas lights off tinsel. She was losing consciousness – and there was no pentobarbital to save her.

Distraction, she thought as the tinsel-light dimmed into blackness. *That's my one hope.*

'Why ... is your window ... broken?' she rasped.

Wilson stopped and loosened his grip. 'Huh?'

Sara's airways opened. A bright flare pulsed behind her eyes and she sucked in deeply. 'Over there,' she exhaled. 'Some glass ... is missing.' She drew a deeper breath. 'It was cracked ... right?'

'Err – yeah.' Wilson turned to look at his broken window. His fingers slackened further.

'And now the glass has fallen through.'

As Wilson began to curse the building's sluggish maintenance staff, Sara jerked backwards, pulled away, and stumbled to her feet. She swooned and nearly collapsed as her assailant spun towards her.

Don't fall, she told herself. *This is your only chance.*

Sara leapt forward, slapped the door handle, and pulled. Behind her, Wilson shouted. Air cooled her streaming brow as she dashed from the flat and ran spasmodically towards her car. She slammed its door moments before Wilson's Rottweiler came barrelling onto the street.

Neck throbbing, legs trembling, Sara played dodgem with buses and black cabs on the North London route that led south of the river, and home to Brixton. She had opened the driver's window; the steady blast of air helped to reduce her shock. Glancing at the rear-view mirror of her Mini Countryman, she caught sight of her traitorous medical bag lounging on the back seat.

She scowled. *How on earth could I have been so careless?*

As Sara made the awkward turn from Bressenden Place onto Vauxhall Bridge Road, her reverie was interrupted by the saxophone opening to Take That's 'A Million Love Songs' – her ringtone, sounding through the car's speakers. The muscles in Sara's face tightened, and she stabbed a button on her steering wheel. 'Yes,' she snapped.

'Mallorca,' someone said.

Sara frowned. The caller's voice was too distorted by London traffic to identify … but then Sara noticed the background twang of country music. It had to be her closest friend, Ceri Lewis, calling from mid-Wales. Ceri, eight years Sara's senior, was a uniformed inspector on the Dyfed-Powys police force, and had known Sara since she was a child.

Sara took a deep breath to control her trembling. 'Well, well! *Bore da,*' Sara greeted her friend with false cheer.

'Other parts of Spain too, maybe,' Ceri continued. 'Or else Malta,' she added. 'Malta sounds OK.'

'What on earth are we talking about?' Sara asked.

She raised the window. The car was quieter now, and she could hear a lighter flick next to Ceri's mouthpiece; her friend was lighting a cigarette.

'I only have a few years left before I retire,' Ceri said as she exhaled smoke. 'I used to think I'd want to stay here in Wales. But ever since that shit-storm we went through a coupla years ago, I've had second thoughts.'

'You want to retire somewhere else?'

'I'm considering it.'

Ceri had always lived frugally. Sara knew she saved much of her salary and had invested it well. Ceri could afford to retire anywhere and be comfortable – at least for

11

as long as her Marlboros let her live.

'Well, Mallorca's lovely,' Sara said. 'Have you ever been?'

'I've barely ever left Wales,' Ceri admitted. 'But I have the next few years to explore.'

Sara had always thought that Ceri, with her taste for country music, might well thrive in the American south-west. A Stetson and cowboy boots would be an easy fit for her. But maybe Spain was a good alternative – certainly, parts of it looked like Arizona.

'Are you in?' Ceri said.

Sara hesitated. 'In what?'

'I'm going on *holiday*,' Ceri reminded her. 'To Mallorca. Do you want to come?'

'Err – when?'

'I haven't booked yet, but soon. I'm thinking of a few days in Palma, then somewhere on the western side. Not Magaluf, though – too many drunken Brits. I'm bound to have arrested some of them.'

'A holiday would be lovely,' Sara admitted. 'But I've already taken this week off work to get some things done.'

Ceri grunted unhappily. 'You'd let me go alone?'

'You like being alone.'

'I'd rather be with you.'

'Next time, give me some warning,' Sara said.

There was a pause; Sara knew Ceri well enough to *feel* her taking a drag on her cigarette. 'When I decide on the dates for Mallorca,' Ceri said, 'I'll let you know. Look at your diary and tell me what you could do.'

Sara agreed, making sure to sound realistically doubtful. She and Ceri said goodbye.

Rounding the Oval cricket ground, Sara realised their conversation had made her feel better. Sometimes Ceri cast that kind of pleasant spell over her. Yet, Sara's old friend could do nothing to ease her underlying problem. Angry Tim Wilson remained Client Number Four.

And the throbbing in Sara's neck suggested that bulk of tattooed fury would be harder to bring around than his three predecessors.

Sara's South London flat sat on the ground floor of a house near Brixton Hill. The neighbourhood, once largely working-class Jamaican, was becoming gentrified. One day, Sara's street – at least, the portion not taken up by the large council block – would probably have become home only to professionals like herself. Sara hoped to be long gone by then. She enjoyed the variety of accents that still rang from the pavements. Living in such close quarters, residents tended to integrate aspects of each other's dialects, melding them into what some called Multicultural London English. Sometimes Sara listened for, but had yet to hear, her own melodic Welsh lilt being factored into the mix.

Sara lived with her partner, a handsome, copper-fringed ex-police inspector named Jamie Harding. When she got home, it was early afternoon, and Sara found Jamie's Land Rover in their mutually favoured spot outside the house. She drove to a space further down the road, just outside a primary school. As Sara walked back, she noticed Jamie emerging from the house with a shorter man in a grey suit. The man noticed her too.

'Sara, Sara, Sara!' Andy Turner cried.

Andy was a defence lobbyist whose consultancy still worked for the aerospace company Sara's late brother had run. Andy had been fiercely loyal to Rhodri Jones, and when Rhodri died, he transferred his intense devotion to Sara. Andrew Turner & Associates sponsored Sara's position at her mental health charity. Now, Andy skipped towards her with outstretched arms, an eager child in a five-thousand-pound suit. 'I thought you'd be at work,' he said as they embraced.

'Week off,' she replied. 'Why are you here?'

'Playing matchmaker,' Andy said archly. He nodded towards Jamie, who had been joined by a tall, gaunt man Sara didn't recognise.

'Who's he?'

'His name's Gerrit Vos,' Andy stage-whispered. 'You met him at Rhoddo's funeral.'

A small wave of queasiness washed through Sara. She couldn't remember the skeletal figure they approached, but if he'd been at the funeral …

'Don't tell me he works for Thorndike Aerospace.'

'Quite a bigwig, actually,' Andy said. 'Managing Director for Business Development.'

Sara stopped and gripped Andy's elbow. 'Andy – please tell me you're not trying to get Jamie a job at Thorndike.'

'Not a job,' Andy said coyly. 'Just some pocket money. Every young go-getter needs that, no?'

Sara cast her eyes towards Jamie. He radiated an edgy anticipation. From the other man, Sara gleaned a whisper of optimism about Jamie, rising from an older, deeper sadness.

Sara sighed. 'Andy, you're very sweet,' she said, 'but Jamie doesn't need help. Soon he'll get his graduate diploma, and next September he's starting a master's degree in human rights law.'

'This won't interfere a bit,' Andy assured her. 'Just some consultancy. Jamie won't be employed by Thorndike, he'll work for me.' He smiled naughtily. 'I'll just pimp him out to Thorndike.'

'Oh, Andy …'

'Jamie's had so much experience with the Met,' Andy went on. 'It'd be a crime to waste it.'

Sara shut her eyes. This was not the first time Andy had tried to hire Jamie. In Sara's first year of living in Brixton, Jamie had been unemployed, and was considering, but had not yet committed to, studying law. While Sara had taken a job at the London Fields Support Service, and also worked with her special, private clients, Jamie had distracted himself, mostly by wandering aimlessly about London. Eventually even Andy noticed his lack of engagement, and had suggested to Sara that Thorndike would be eager to use Jamie's talents. Sara had refused outright, and began to press Jamie to make a decision about his next move. Did he want to work in human rights law or didn't he? Finally, Jamie had applied to a handful of universities, starting his studies the previous September.

Sara had thought that would put an end to Andy's interests in her partner. Clearly, it had only convinced him to approach Jamie directly this time. Arguing with Andy was impossible, anyway; he always defeated her with enthusiasm.

She looked again at the tall man on her doorstep. Gerrit Vos looked to be in his mid-forties, with thinning hair and deep-set eyes. Despite the early-spring chill, he wore a summer-weight suit in dark cerulean blue. Vos loitered by the door as Jamie moved forward and gave Sara a peck on the cheek.

As he did, she whispered, 'What in bloody hell have you done?'

'Andy called this morning,' Jamie whispered back.

At the sound of his name, Andy took Sara's arm. 'You lovebirds can rhubarb later,' he murmured. 'Now, just smile and say pretty things.'

They approached the house. 'Sara,' he went on, 'you remember Gerrit Vos?'

'Of course,' Sara lied. 'You were so kind to come to

Rhodri's funeral.'

Vos joined them on the pavement. 'Came to the burial at Highgate too,' he said in a deep baritone. 'Didn't get a chance to talk to you. Would've liked to express my condolences.'

'It was an overwhelming day,' Sara replied. 'Did you know Rhodri well?'

Vos frowned. 'Wasn't high enough in the pecking order then. But I always respected him.'

If you respected Rhodri, Sara thought, *you really didn't know him.*

'Damned shame how he went.' Vos shook his head. 'That maniac at the Air Show tipped him right over the edge. Anyone would've gone stark raving mad.'

'Yes, well ... thank you.'

Sensing her discomfort, Jamie cleared his throat. 'I've invited Mr Vos and his partner over for dinner Wednesday evening.'

'Nicole,' Vos said. 'Her name's Nicole.'

'I hope that's OK,' Jamie added.

Sara agreed that dinner with Gerrit and Nicole would be delightful. After a few other pleasantries, Andy tried to shepherd Vos towards his Town Car. Vos restrained him with a raised hand. He turned back to Sara.

'Forgive me, Sara,' he said, 'but something's been nagging at me.'

'Oh?'

He looked at her unwaveringly. 'I'm afraid it's personal.'

Jamie and Andy waited, still with expectation.

'That's intriguing,' Sara said. 'Please go ahead.'

Vos squinted at a spot below her chin. 'I'm just wondering ... what in hell happened to your neck?'

Sara started, and placed a hand to her throat. Her skin was sore to the touch. Jamie twitched into alertness. 'Oh my God,' he gasped. 'Look at that! Sara, what *did* happen?'

'I don't know,' Sara said, faltering. 'Err … please give me a moment.'

She scurried up the path and into the hall that led to their flat. Looking into a mirror, Sara saw four livid marks where Tim Wilson had grasped her. Panic made her nerves pulse. She did not want to have to explain this. Thinking fast, Sara strolled back to the pavement.

'I didn't know they were so obvious,' she said with a dismissive chuckle. 'I work in a mental health clinic.'

Her vague explanation didn't satisfy Vos. He waited for more.

'A client grabbed me,' she explained, as if it happened every day. 'Big fellow. Bit of a temper.'

'This was in your clinic?' Jamie asked.

'There were people everywhere,' Sara said. 'I was never in danger.'

Thorndike's Director for Business Development hesitated. Finally, he squinted again at Sara's neck. 'Looks painful,' he said.

Sara shook her head. 'All part of the job.'

After another moment's contemplation, Vos shrugged.

'And here I was, thinking *I* had a dangerous line of work,' he said.

17

TWO

While Jamie walked his guests to Andy's car, Sara went into their living room and fell onto the leather sofa. Immediately, her elderly Burmese cat, Ego, plopped into her lap. The pressure on Sara's legs made her trembling even more apparent. It wasn't yet mid-afternoon, and this Monday had already wreaked several days' worth of bad luck.

Sara sighed, and looked up at the ceiling, contemplating a brown water stain from the neighbour's bathroom above. Sometimes, when she was feeling down, this cramped flat could drive her spirits even lower. It had once been Jamie's alone, and although Sara had done her best to decorate – covering the walls with some of her favourite Aboriginal paintings and African tribal masks – the place still radiated a sad bachelor aura. Once in a while, she found herself missing the cosy Pimlico flat she had lived in, alone.

A few minutes later, Jamie came in and sank into the leather chair next to her. He dropped his chin to his chest and exhaled slowly, looking overwhelmed. 'Well, that's a first,' he said. 'No one's ever come up to me out of the blue, told me my experience was invaluable, and then offered me a load of money.'

Welcome to Andy Turner's world, Sara thought. 'How

did this all come about?' she asked.

'Andy messaged me this morning,' Jamie replied. 'He just asked whether I'd be home.'

'And then showed up with the Thorndike guy?'

'Yeah – Mr Vos. He's really high up in the company. Reports directly to the Chief Executive.'

Sara nodded shallowly. Absently, she stroked Ego's patchy fur. *Chief Executive* had been Rhodri's old job title. It was so like Jamie to be oblivious to the effect this turn of events might have on her. *Her brother's old friend wants to hire her partner to work at her brother's old company, for a man who reports to her brother's old position.*

On top of that incestuous cluster, there was the fact that Sara had always harboured a distaste for the arms industry. Rhodri's involvement had been one of many things she had overlooked in her brother's life. And even to this day, Andy Turner – an artillery enthusiast to his khaki-coloured core – remained a fixture in Sara's world. That required her to keep certain feelings under wraps.

But Jamie's involvement might just be an entanglement too far.

'Are you going to take up Andy's offer?' she asked cautiously.

Jamie looked at her speculatively, and Sara didn't need to be psychic to read his thoughts. He was worried about her reaction if he were to say yes.

'I don't know,' he replied. 'We'll have him to dinner. See what he wants me to do for Andy's cash.'

'If you're in any doubt,' Sara warned, 'I'd advise against.'

Jamie nodded slowly, a pantomime of equanimity. This only convinced Sara that he'd decided to take the job.

'Let's both reserve judgement,' Jamie suggested.

Angling his head, he added, 'You have to admit, though ... he's pretty sharp.'

'This Vos character? How?'

'He's observant.'

Sara's hand brushed against her throat. She felt the tenderness once again. Vos had noticed the bruising on her neck when Jamie, the ex-detective, had not. A splinter of guilt pricked Sara as she realised she wasn't even surprised. Since their moving in together, she had come to expect so little of her partner. After witnessing Jamie's successful stint in the Met, it was hard for her to accept him as a mature student. And, for that matter, as a house husband. Over the past year, Sara had often thought she was watching Jamie's passion and interests wilt before her eyes.

So then, maybe this aerospace job would be a good thing, she told herself.

Sara had to keep reminding herself that Jamie Harding was no intellectual lightweight. He held an undergraduate degree in Criminology, and one day he would be awarded a master's in law. If Jamie exasperated her every now and then, it was her problem, not his. There were simply things Sara could not share with her partner – such as the psychic powers she'd developed in Wales, and the way they led to occasional, sickening visions of murder. Sometimes, the pressure of keeping such horrors to herself would burst through, suddenly and unexpectedly. Then Sara would shudder so fiercely it felt like hot tar was oozing through her body. Still – it wasn't Jamie's fault she'd journeyed into lands so dark he couldn't see them.

'I'm sorry I made things awkward with Andy and Mr Vos,' she said. 'If I'd known about the bruising I would have covered it up.'

Jamie shifted in his seat. 'How did that happen,

20

anyway?' he asked.

'I told you.'

'Yeah,' he said haltingly, 'but when?'

'What do you mean?'

'It's just ... you were off work today.'

Sara hesitated. 'So?'

'Those bruises are fresh.'

Sara felt herself flush. 'No, they're not,' she said weakly.

'Sara, you're a doctor and I was a cop. We both know about bruising. Day One, red. Day Two, purple. Then green and yellow. Those bruises are red.'

He waited.

'Which means, today,' he emphasised.

Sara grounded herself and smiled reassuringly. 'I didn't want to worry you,' she said, and pressed ahead with a necessary untruth. 'I went to the clinic this morning.'

'They called you in?'

'That's right.'

'To see this client.'

'Yeah.'

'The client who strangled you.'

Sara sighed. 'Look, Jamie, I told you, I was never in danger ...'

Jamie interrupted. 'Were you alone with this guy? Did they ring the police?'

Sara closed her eyes. 'None of that matters. He was out of my office in seconds.'

Jamie was a good partner, she reminded herself. As much as Sara wished he would let this go, he was showing genuine care and concern. 'You can't worry about me every time I go to work,' she told him.

Jamie shifted from the chair to the sofa. Ego stood and stretched with a quiver. 'I do worry. Constantly.' He put an arm around her. 'I just wish there were more I could do.'

Sara laid her head on his shoulder. 'That's sweet,' she said. 'And if you really mean it, there *is* one thing.'

'Name it,' he said eagerly.

'You can get up, take a pizza out of the freezer, and put it in the oven. I'm hungry.'

Later that afternoon, Sara said she'd agreed to meet her colleagues for after-work drinks. She hadn't, but Jamie knew about the clinic's Monday afternoon pub ritual. He assumed that Sara's boss, Jo, would want to talk to her about the abuse she'd suffered from their deranged client.

In a sense, Jamie was closer to the truth than he knew. Although Sara had not told her co-workers about her plan to attend, she did intend to go there. And it was because of Tim Wilson. Since this morning's altercation with the rage-filled hipster, Sara had developed a niggling fear that the young man might lodge a complaint against her. If he did, Sara would have to justify showing up at a stranger's house uninvited, in a professional capacity, and trying to coerce him into taking unwanted therapy.

That would make for an awkward conversation with Jo. Sara cursed herself for having given Wilson her business card. Without it, he wouldn't have known where she worked.

A few minutes after six p.m., Sara entered the large pub in London Fields, just around the corner from her office. Arranging the silk scarf she'd placed around her neck to cover the bruising, Sara joined three of her colleagues in a corner of the cavernous room. The draughty spot had been made more intimate by the artful placing of an ornate screen and a cosy cluster of sofas and chairs. Her co-workers expressed both pleasure and surprise at her coming during her time off, and someone got Sara a large glass of house white.

She sipped. The wine was too sweet for her taste, but she was counting on it to ease the knots of tension that wracked her shoulders. Sara tried to appear relaxed as she asked, 'Did anything interesting happen today?'

Jo, the forty-something social worker who had founded the charity, laughed. 'Just take a look at this lady!' she said. 'Gone for one single day, and she can't bear to be away from the excitement.'

The others chuckled. Sara began to breathe a little easier; Jo's good humour suggested there were no recent complaints from self-righteous hipsters.

'No one asked for me?' she said more pointedly.

'Were you expecting someone to?'

Sara shook her head and tried to relax. Wilson had not contacted the office.

Over the next couple of drinks, a rambling discussion developed about career choices. A fellow counsellor named Rohini asked, 'What about you, Sara? What made you decide to be a psychiatrist?'

Previously, Rohini had been a corporate psychologist with an international firm of accountants. Sara had never discovered what specific eddies of life had made this go-getting young woman drift away from such a big-time career towards the far less remunerative role of mental health counsellor.

'In what way?' Sara asked.

'You were a medical doctor first, is that so?' Rohini asked.

Sara nodded. 'You have to be, if you want to be a psychiatrist,' she replied.

'Is that something a lot of doctors want to do?'

'Good heavens, no,' Sara laughed. 'Most medical students wouldn't talk to a psychiatrist, let alone become one.'

Ellen, the staff solicitor, leaned in. The move brought a waft of the day's cigarettes and traces of White Linen perfume. 'So, you're some sort of medical maverick? Eager to buck the trend?'

Sara smiled. There were reasons she had chosen her profession, but none she wanted to explain. 'That's me,' she said, 'a right rebel.'

'Oh, we like rebels,' chuckled Sara's boss. Sara noticed Jo's Nigerian accent had grown thicker over the course of the conversation – something that happened when she drank. Jo added in a loud whisper, 'We especially like rebels whose salaries are paid by someone else!'

Sara raised her wine glass. 'Then please let me offer a toast to my benefactors, Andrew Turner & Associates,' she said. 'Long may they cover my salary!'

Everyone drank to Andy and his charitable largesse. Ellen took orders for another round of drinks, and the conversation drifted away from Sara. She sipped her wine and pretended to listen to the meandering current of words, all the while thinking about Tim Wilson.

Wilson may not have complained today, Sara thought, but it was no guarantee that he wouldn't do so tomorrow or the next day. Her best insurance against that, Sara decided, was the very thing she had taken pains to keep hidden – the livid mottling under her scarf. Wilson, after all, had attacked her. Complaining about Sara would force him to admit to what he'd done.

Ironically, Wilson's violence may be the one protection she now had.

Jo set the dregs of her rum and coke on the table and stood. She had to leave, she said – she and her wife had tickets to a show. Ellen and Rohini took that as their cue to gather up their things as well. As Jo and Ellen made a quick last trip to the ladies' room, Rohini looked at Sara curiously and said, 'Sometimes I count the number of frowns I see in a day.'

Sara smiled. 'That's an odd hobby.'

'Today,' Rohini continued, 'yours makes forty-six.'

Sara shrugged apologetically. She hadn't realised her gloomy thoughts were so obvious. 'I have a headache,' she said.

Sara realised that this was true. The wine had done little to lessen her stress. She focused attention on her spine and tried to lengthen it, the way her Alexander Technique teacher had once taught her.

'You do seem sad,' Rohini persisted.

Sara feigned surprise. 'Really?'

Rohini studied her with professional speculation. 'May I ask a personal question?'

Sara blew air from her cheeks – an exaggerated reaction to lighten Rohini's tone. 'Oh, go on, then,' she said.

'Do you take antidepressants?'

When Sara blinked, Rohini blushed. 'That was too personal, wasn't it?' she said.

'It's fine,' Sara said. She emptied the last swirl of wine from her glass. 'Frankly, I don't know many psychiatrists who haven't taken them at one time or another.'

'You're not taking them now?'

Sara shook her head.

Rohini let the silence between them express her concern. She laid a hand on Sara's wrist. 'Maybe you should,' she said.

Sara drove from London Fields to Islington, and parked in a tranquil square nestled just behind Upper Street. She stared through the windscreen at the brown brick house that had once belonged to her brother. Sara recalled Rhoddo introducing her to the place not long after his

25

promotion to CEO, and still giddy with his good fortune. 'Over two million quid I've paid for this,' he'd said with a chuckle. 'Can you bloody imagine?'

It would have made more sense to have bought something down on the Surrey-Hampshire border – an executive home closer to company headquarters. But Rhodri had said he liked the buzz around The Angel, with its cool-but-casual restaurants, and its cinemas and clubs.

Not to mention, Sara had thought, *all those brothels clustered around Holloway.*

By the time Rhodri died, the value of the place had more than doubled. As his only beneficiary, Sara could have moved in here with her partner Jamie, or used the profits to buy somewhere more to their taste. Instead, she'd sold the house quickly, giving a large chunk of the money to the family of Maja Bosco, the young woman Rhodri had murdered. Right up there on the first floor.

Sara recalled that night vividly – how she'd leapt from an Uber taxi on this very spot, and let herself through that glossy door. Even now, she could relive the growing trepidation she had felt as she crept up the stairs. Her brother was still alive when she found him, bleeding heavily from his wrists. Rhoddo had changed his mind about dying. He begged Sara to use whatever medical skill or magic she possessed to save his life. Instead, Dr Sara Jones had chosen to let her brother die – a choice spurred by one of her first-ever psychic visions, of Rhodri murdering their parents when they were both only teenagers.

On four occasions since then, Sara had foreseen grisly deaths that would be brought about by strangers she had encountered on the street. A homeless man who would one day commit deadly arson. An alcoholic mother who would kill her child. A troubled young man who would plough his car into oncoming traffic. Sara's psychic mentor, Eldon Carson, would have killed each of them before they could commit their crimes. Sara, however, had intervened by offering these strangers free counselling at her mental health charity.

In all three cases, Sara's trances had told her she'd changed the future. It was as if each upcoming act of murder had been erased.

She was hoping to do the same with Client Number Four, Tim Wilson – because in eight months' time, without Sara's intervention, Tim would commit a bloody murder. That fatal outcome would be set in motion a few days from now, when Wilson would visit a bar in Hackney for a first date with the new love of his life: a kindly older man named Philip Berger. Berger had only recently swapped his wife, kids and home in Chingford for an East End bedsit and liberation. Next September, he would move into Wilson's flat, and in the winter Tim Wilson would fall into a violent rage and beat the man to death.

Sara might have failed to foresee Wilson squeezing her throat this morning, but she was more than certain about the pulpy mess he would make of Philip Berger. She knew she must convince that bulk of tattooed rage to see her professionally.

Sara was disturbed by a rapping on the Mini's glass. She started, and looked up. A traffic warden peered down at her. Sara lowered the window.

'Sorry, madam,' the woman said. 'This street is permits-only. Do you live here?'

'I could have,' Sara said quietly.

The woman gurned uncomprehendingly and Sara turned the ignition key. 'Never mind.'

She was ready to go, anyway. She realised she had

brought herself here to relive these sobering memories, and to ponder what they suggested about her next moves. But now, she had pondered as much as she could. Sara had let her brother die because he was irredeemable – just as she had later helped three potential killers who could be saved. But what if Client Number Four didn't want to be helped? Could Sara bring herself to ignore Tim Wilson's bloody future, and in the process let Philip Berger die? She didn't know the answer.

But she had a pretty clear idea of what Eldon Carson would have said.

THREE

In a well-appointed flat in Mayfair, Gerrit Vos stared out of the leaded windowpanes at the red brick and white stone Edwardian buildings that lined the road. Green Street was a straight, narrow thoroughfare that ran off Park Lane. It had once been the centre of a small Roman town that had been abandoned in favour of land closer to the river. Later a bastion of the British aristocracy, the street and surrounding area were now a second home to wealthy transnationals, and a base for upmarket retail outlets and corporate headquarters. For Thorndike Aerospace, Green Street was a place to house visiting dignitaries. For Gerrit Vos, it was a silent spot for private meetings.

Squinting through the drizzle, Vos noted how the black iron railings in front of every building reflected off the wet grey pavements. It made each straight rail look like a legionnaire's spear, protruding from the body of sand and gravel from which London rose. Vos hoped the man he was waiting for had the nous to arrive in a taxi. Vos disliked the musty animal pong of rain-damp wool. Sheep smell was bad enough, but cashmere was even worse. He didn't want this lovely little room to stink like a wet goat.

He checked his Breitling Chronomat – a gift from the same Saudi prince who leased this flat to Thorndike on the cheap, as part of a complicated barter. The time was 11:51. At least Rootenberg wasn't late. Vos pulled out his phone. 'Yeah, it's me,' he told his partner's voicemail. 'I'm in town. We're due at that guy's flat in Brixton for a stupidly early dinner. Sorry about that – we'll dash as soon as we can. Where will you be? I'll pick you up.'

His reluctant tone was a sop to Nicole. She could not have been looking forward to eating with potential business associates of his – especially when neither of them knew Jamie Harding or his partner. But from what Vos had seen so far, he approved of this ex-police inspector. The guy reminded Vos of himself, years ago – before a whole shit-storm of change had bowled him over. On the whole, that change had been for the best. Still, there was no denying it – when he'd picked himself back up, Vos had found he was a different man.

As he rang off, the flat's buzzer sounded. His guest was early. *The guy's eager*, he thought. *Maybe a tad too desperate to jump back in the saddle.*

'Top floor,' he muttered into the intercom, and wondered whether Rootenberg would climb the stairs or take the lift. And whether he'd be stinking-wet when he got here.

Levi Rootenberg was a small-time arms broker. In that sprawling, deadly community known as the International Arms Trade, no one really agreed on the specifics of such a job title. There were simply too many variables. Some brokers were no more than middlemen who negotiated deals: this much ammunition from China to Iraq, so many AK-47s from Russia to the Afghan Kush. Others offered ancillary services, from finding transport to haggling over insurance. The more countries involved, the bigger the cat's cradle of legislation and mandatory paperwork.

That is, *if* a broker obeyed the law, or tried for the permits. That was another difference between arms middlemen: most went by the book, but a few were downright dodgy. Always, transgressors formed the minority; punishments were harsh and human rights groups kept a righteous eye on global arms traffic. But for those willing to slip through the shadows, remuneration could be high – and some discreet principality or other would always shield the broker's darkly drawn wealth.

This was the world that Levi Rootenberg aspired to join: a society in which devil-may-care rogues traversed the globe, raking in illicit fortunes. To that end, he had once held a valid Trade Control Licence, which made him a broker in the UK, plus a South African dealer's licence and several other bona fides. However, he had also said yes to assignments for which no permits could be obtained. Some were in violation of UN embargoes, others involved recipients frowned upon by Western governments. Levi Rootenberg had never had the luxury of being picky. Truth be told, he'd been at the trade for less than five years, and, so far, wealth had eluded him.

Vos opened the flat's glossy white door and heard heavy trudging. Rootenberg was taking the stairs. Impressive, for such a pudgy little guy. Rootenberg arrived at the top of the stairs panting, but mercifully dry.

'Lee,' Vos said noncommittally.

Rootenberg pumped his hand. 'Gerrit!'

Vos hung up the man's jacket, and they talked about old times as he mixed drinks. With a gin and tonic in hand, Rootenberg settled his back into the sofa cushion. 'This is nice,' he sighed contentedly. 'We haven't spoken since you saved my arse.'

The deal that undid Levi Rootenberg had not involved Thorndike Aerospace; it was far too piffling for Vos even to have heard of, until Rootenberg rang him in distress. Rootenberg had been caught brokering a shipment of

31

Zastava handguns that had been meant to travel from the Balkans to Libya. By the time he turned to Vos for help, the arms broker had already lost his UK licence, and was staring down some serious prison time. Although those ex-Yugoslav service weapons had never touched British soil, the deal had been part-negotiated in London, and that was enough to lead to Rootenberg's arrest. When lawyer's fees had eaten through much of the cash stashed in his Lichtenstein account, Rootenberg turned to the one acquaintance who had the funds, political contacts, and sheer underhanded fuckery to get his case dismissed.

'I'm really grateful for everything you did,' Rootenberg told Vos.

'Yes, I got that batch of Scotch,' Vos said. 'Twenty-one-year-old Macallan. Not bad.'

The truth, Vos reflected, was that he would rather Rootenberg had kept the Scotch and left him the hell alone in the first place.

Rootenberg ran a hand over his bald scalp. 'Next time, I hope be able to afford better,' he said.

Vos raised an eyebrow. 'Next time you're in prison?'

'Next time I have cause to thank you.'

Vos smiled sardonically. Levi Rootenberg had never been a subtle man. He stood and wandered to the window. Opening it an inch, Vos felt a wet breeze blow in. Several floors below, a Burberry umbrella swayed and bobbed down the street. 'What exactly do you hope to thank me for?' he asked, his back to his old acquaintance.

'I've had a thought.'

Vos turned around. The arms dealer was smiling slyly. It made him look like a coy baby.

'I imagined you had,' Vos said. 'You're looking for some sort of payday.'

'My lawyers were expensive,' Rootenberg conceded. 'They were useless pieces of shit, too. You accomplished everything they couldn't.'

Vos returned to his seat, drained his G&T and mixed himself another. 'Lee, Thorndike is a global company,' he began. 'We've got so many eyes on us, *careful* doesn't begin to describe what we need to be. What are we supposed to do with an unlicensed broker?'

'Oh, come on, man,' Rootenberg said. 'You must already have some deals flying under the radar.'

'Nothing I can talk about,' Vos said. 'You know that.'

'You play your cards close to the chest,' Rootenberg observed, 'but you and I both know I'm most valuable in the deals they want to keep quiet.' He smiled. 'After all, it's how we met.'

Vos could feel his eyes narrowing as he stared at Rootenberg. Even when trying to be obvious, there were certain things a person should shut the fuck up about. Vos was beginning to regret agreeing to see this old acquaintance ... but then again, their mutual past was precisely why he had said yes. Vos didn't want to piss the man off. The only way he could trust him to keep his mouth shut was if that mouth continued to be fed.

'What we did in South Africa was for Thorndike Aerospace,' Rootenberg went on. 'Are you telling me Rhodri Jones didn't know about it?'

'Not the details, I'm fairly certain.'

'He promoted you.'

'I got results.'

'*We* got results,' Rootenberg corrected.

'Look,' Vos said, 'Mr Jones did not want to know what we did. That's the point. He was pleased by the outcome, and paid you well for your services.'

'I'm not disagreeing with that,' Rootenberg said. 'What I'm saying is, compared to that, the business I want to propose today will be a walk in the park.'

Vos shook his head wearily. A single arms deal could

33

involve the Ministry of Defence, the Department for International Trade, the Foreign and Commonwealth Office, and sometimes even the office of the Prime Minister. That was a lot of bureaucracy to sneak by.

Rootenberg gulped his drink, then set the empty glass on the coffee table. 'In the short term, the risk is almost non-existent,' he said, 'and long term, it could lead to a relationship that would be very profitable for Thorndike Aerospace. Probably even legal – in time.'

Vos exhaled heavily. This shitty conversation was all part of the deal. He was having to listen to it as payment for the deeds of his past. Vos's years in business had taught him that trusting someone was never a one-time thing. Once you had crossed a line with another person, neither of you forgot it. The very act presumed a new state of intimacy – not to mention complicity – that lasted far into the future. You became each other's responsibilities.

'OK,' he sighed. 'I'm not making any promises, but I'll listen to whatever you're suggesting.'

'That's all I ask,' Rootenberg said eagerly. He waved a hand towards his glass. 'That, and maybe another drink.'

Later, Gerrit Vos's Porsche roared and sputtered through Fitzrovia towards the East End. There, Nicole had been meeting with one of the suppliers to her online shop, and now waited for her partner to take her to a dull dinner in Brixton. As he pushed through the stop-start judder of Central London traffic, Vos thought about Zimbabwe. Fucking *Zimbabwe*, Rootenberg's home turf, and an unwelcome distraction from Vos's day-to-day routine. Rootenberg's argument had gone like this: at the moment, UN, European and UK sanctions were leaving Zimbabwe's defence market open to non-Western competitors, especially the Russians. However, it was Rootenberg's assessment that the shifting sands of international diplomacy – not to mention the inevitable deaths of several elderly African strongmen – would one day reopen the country for business.

At that time, one of two things would happen: either the Russians and Chinese would continue to enjoy their trade monopoly, or the British government would step in and win big-money contracts for the major players in the UK defence industry. As things stood, however, Thorndike Aerospace was unlikely to be among them. The company may benefit from subcontracting certain jobs, as it had always done, but it would not be considered as a prime contractor.

That is, unless it already had a personal relationship with, and track record of sales, to factions within the Zimbabwean military. Fortunately, Rootenberg said, he was on good terms with an element within that very military, who would welcome the chance to purchase much-needed British supplies. 'What I'm offering today is long-term geopolitical insurance,' he had said.

Rootenberg's plan was to start small by brokering some minor arms deals with Zimbabwe, selling items that, he assured Vos, he could get into the country under anyone's radar. This would earn the trust of his friends in a certain faction of the military, and form the basis of a longer-term relationship. 'Thorndike wants to be a prime contractor,' he had said. 'And – correct me if I'm wrong – I think *you* harbour a secret ambition to be CEO. Well, I'm offering a chance to take steps towards both ambitions.'

Vos had said he would consider the proposal. What else could he do, until he had decided how to deal with Rootenberg longer-term? But he felt in his bones that the man's plan was stupid. Vos doubted that even Rootenberg believed in it. Most likely, he was financially strapped, and grappling to rustle up some short-term cash. The whole sordid business depressed Vos, but he had a job to do. He knew Thorndike's best interests lay not with desperate arms brokers and their pie-in-the-sky schemes, but in lobbying Westminster, and working to be allowed to bid as prime contractor on both government and foreign jobs. Make it all perfectly legal – or at least, keep things morally sketchy in precisely the way Whitehall mandarins approved of. The way that allowed cabinet ministers to go to bat for good old British bombs.

On the windscreen, rivulets of rain were being shoved aside by the metronome-sweep of the Porsche's wipers. Peering through the shifting view, Vos could make out Nicole, standing under the awning of Aldgate tube station. He pulled up and tapped his horn. *The poor girl must be dreading the next couple hours of inane chatter*, he thought. Certainly Vos was. As Nicole climbed in and pecked him on the cheek, Vos told himself to look on the bright side. There may well be some way to use the young ex-copper whom fate and Andy Turner had dropped into his lap.

Sara emerged from the bedroom, freshly showered and changed into a blouse and some trousers she hoped looked casual. The smell of onion overpowered the aromas of baking chicken and – was that vinegar?

'When are they coming?' she called towards the galley kitchen.

'Any time now,' Jamie called back.

'Everything ready?'

'Dinner is. I don't know about me.'

Sara nudged back the net curtains and struggled to raise the large sash window. The old painted wood creaked, but the window wouldn't budge. Suddenly, a damp tea towel thumped onto the sill in front of her, and Jamie appeared at her side.

'Why are you opening the window?' he asked with mock offence. 'Don't like the smell of my cooking?'

'Who cooks chicken with vinegar?'

'It's for the sauce,' he said, and shoved open the window. A wet March breeze blew in, and he grinned wide in triumph.

'What are you going to tell him?' Sara asked.

'About Andy's job offer? I don't know. I'll listen to what he has to say.'

'You don't need the work.'

'Actually,' Jamie countered, 'I do. I haven't made any money since I quit the Met.'

'We've been through all this,' Sara sighed. 'I can pay for both of us, And that includes your university fees.'

'Wouldn't it be great if you didn't have to, though?' Jamie said. 'I don't like you having to pay my way.'

'It's only temporary,' Sara reminded him. 'When you're a lawyer, maybe I'll take some time off, and you can support me.'

Jamie laughed. 'Maybe you'd *try* to take a break – for about a week,' he said. 'Then you'd be opening another office on Harley Street.'

'Look Jamie, if you want a job, go get one. But why does it have to be in the arms industry?'

Jamie looked at her quizzically. Sara knew she was about to darken the tone of the conversation, but pressed on. 'The weapons that companies like Thorndike make lead directly to death, maiming, and rape all over the world,' she stated. 'Governments turn British-made arms against their own people. The thought of you being involved in that is depressing.'

'Rhodri was involved,' Jamie noted. 'Did you ever say any of this to him?'

Sara huffed. 'You couldn't say anything to Rhodri – and he wouldn't have understood it if I had. The difference is, you *do* understand. You want to work in human rights law, for goodness' sake! Don't you see a contradiction there?'

Through the open window came the sound of approaching voices, the murmured conclusion of a conversation started in the car. 'Perhaps this is a discussion for another time,' Jamie said quietly.

Sara silenced herself and listened to the rustle of their guests as they neared the front door and pushed the buzzer. It failed to ring, and by the time Gerrit Vos announced their arrival with a couple of sharp thumps on the door, Jamie had already bustled into the hallway. He ushered his maybe-client and plus-one into the flat.

As he entered, Vos asked, 'Will my car be safe out there?'

'Depends,' Jamie replied. 'What make is it?'

'Porsche,' Vos said. 'Boxster Spyder.'

'Oh, that'll be fine,' Jamie said with a grin. 'No one in Brixton's going to touch a car like that. They'd worry it belongs to a gangster.'

Vos introduced Jamie and Sara to his partner, Nicole, a thin, elegant woman in her late twenties with high cheekbones and bright, appraising eyes. Her hair was plaited into perfect cornrows. She could easily have been a model, but Sara thought it likelier she had once been Vos's personal assistant.

Jamie disappeared into the kitchen for wine. As Vos's eyes flicked over the tattered leather sofa suite, Nicole lit on Sara's collection of Aboriginal art. 'Look at these, Gerrit,' she said. 'Aren't they incredible?'

Vos squinted at the wall and called to Jamie. 'You collect this stuff? Who's your dealer?'

Jamie came through the archway with glasses of Chardonnay and followed Vos's glance. 'Oh, the paintings and masks.' He shrugged. 'Not my department,

I'm afraid.'

Expectantly, Vos looked to Sara. She tugged at her spiky hair. 'To be honest, I haven't bought in years,' she said. 'I used to use several galleries. There's a good one in Fulham, and there used to be one in Richmond.'

'They're so interesting,' Nicole said.

Vos shrugged. 'You want a mask? I'll get you a mask.'

'Collecting can be a challenge,' Sara said to him. 'It's important to find out how the works were sourced.'

'Why?'

'It's the only way to collect with a conscience,' Sara replied, emphasising the word *conscience*, and shooting an arch glance towards Jamie. 'For example, you should check whether the gallery has ties to the artists themselves. Maybe through an Aboriginal cooperative.'

'You want to make sure you're not being duped,' Vos said.

Nicole chuckled affectionately. 'She wants to make sure the artists aren't being duped.'

Vos shrugged and grunted.

Jamie began to lay the table. 'Would you like to eat right away,' he asked, 'or should we relax first?'

'Let's eat,' Sara said.

'Hang on,' Vos said, squinting at a small, framed print of a woodcut, hanging low on the wall. 'This picture isn't like the others.'

Jamie glanced over from the table. 'Oh, I bought that for her when we were first going out,' he said. 'It's a plate from an old book.'

The picture Vos stared at was a crude etching of a winged figure surrounded by locusts. 'It's Abaddon,' Sara explained. 'He's an angel of death.'

'Like the Grim Reaper?'

'In a sense, yes.'

Vos grimaced. 'Odd gift,' he said.

39

'I don't think Jamie even knew what it was when he bought it,' Sara laughed. 'He just knew I studied some weird things. He thought I'd like it.'

Vos glanced again at the woodcut. 'And do you?'

'Like it?' Sara said. 'Yes, I do.'

Vos shrugged dismissively. 'No accounting for taste,' he said.

They took their seats, and Jamie carved the chicken. 'Andy Turner's only given me the barest sketch of how we'll work together,' he began. 'I'm intrigued.'

The Thorndike executive appeared not to hear. Jamie offered him the plate and Vos served Nicole and himself, spooning *buerre blanc* from a gravy boat. He reached for the broad beans. 'There's a really good executive restaurant at Thorndike's campus,' he murmured, and glanced at Sara. 'You must know it.'

It was Vos's first reference to Sara's relationship with his former chief executive, her brother Rhodri.

'I've had a few meals there,' she acknowledged.

'Probably more than me,' Vos said. 'I never eat at work unless I'm forced to. Gives me heartburn.' He glanced at Jamie. 'Let's ease my digestion and leave business talk till tomorrow.'

Jamie raised his eyebrows. 'Tomorrow?'

'Come down to Surrey in the morning. We'll talk shop then, OK?'

Jamie's disappointment showed, though he tried to mask it. 'Of course.'

There was an awkward lull in the conversation. Nicole topped up Vos's wine glass, and he took a deep sip.

'What do you do, Nicole?' Sara asked.

'I used to work at Thorndike with Gerrit,' Nicole said. 'Now I run my own business.'

Sara smiled. 'How wonderful.' She'd been right, she

thought – an office affair. 'What business are you in?' she asked.

'I market surveillance equipment online.'

Jamie cocked his head. 'What, you mean spy toys?'

'Oh, they're not toys,' Nicole said.

'Nicole used to work in Intelligence at Thorndike,' Vos said proudly.

'I market to the general consumer,' Nicole said, 'rather than law enforcement or private security. Some companies trade in specialised equipment.' She smiled self-deprecatingly. 'On the other hand, I sell the kind of product you'd expect – covert recorders, that sort of thing.'

'So your customers are trying to catch cheating partners?' Jamie asked.

Nicole nodded politely. 'That's part of the market.'

With effortless grace, Nicole soon shifted the conversation away from her, and onto more general topics. Over the next hour the two couples discussed house prices and London neighbourhoods. If Sara and Jamie planned to stay in South London, they all agreed, East Dulwich was always a good bet. For an up-and-coming area, they might look further south, towards Tulse Hill or even Streatham. By the time they were drinking coffee, London's favourite conversation – itself – had been exhausted, and Vos brought the subject back around to Rhodri.

'Did your brother ever speak with you about his work?' he asked Sara.

'Occasionally,' she answered. 'The question is, did I ever listen? Aerospace isn't really my thing.'

'I think it's fascinating,' Jamie said, and Sara frowned at him.

'It is fascinating,' Vos agreed.

Sara forced herself to smile. She could not imagine

41

that her brother would have got on well with the man sitting across from her, who seemed to be made up of little more than sharp angles and braggadocio. 'Remember that for most of the time Rhodri was with the company, it was a fairly minor subcontractor,' she told Vos. 'I'm not sure he had all that much to tell me.'

Vos snorted. 'Don't bet on it.'

Sara smiled thinly, and looked at Vos's deep-set eyes. He was trying to read her. But for what? For some kind of insight into her brother? Rhoddo had been a monster, that was indisputable – but his villainy had come from weakness. It had been a feeling of powerlessness, combined with an inability to expiate old sins or prevent new ones, that had drawn Rhodri Jones towards people who were gentle and kind. People he could trust, and maybe also exploit.

And what about Vos? He was nothing like her brother. And yet, Sara could not help placing the man in a similar mental category. In Vos, she sensed a depth of something like sadness, or maybe regret – but edged with certain sharper emotions. It was a combination that, she felt, might draw Vos towards the same kind of vulnerability that had attracted Rhodri to his victims.

Was Jamie a potential victim?

And what did that even mean?

Soon, they had finished dinner, and their chatter had grown fragmented and forced. Sara noticed that Vos had not topped up his wine glass again. She smiled and offered coffee and cake. Both Vos and Nicole declined politely, saying they had a long drive home.

Sara and Jamie expressed regret that they wouldn't stay longer. Perhaps Jamie meant it – but Sara felt nothing but relief.

FOUR

Dirty plates and empty wine glasses still littered the table. Jamie and Sara listened to Vos's Boxster roar down the street towards Brixton Hill. Its growl folded into the white noise of South London. Sara carried dishes into the kitchen; Jamie took them and loaded the dishwasher.

'Will you meet him tomorrow?' Sara asked.

'It looks like I'll have to,' he said.

'Why?'

'Well, I didn't say no when I had the chance. And, besides, Andy went to all the trouble to introduce us.'

'Andy will go along with whatever you decide.' Sara frowned, and carried on more harshly than she had intended to. 'For goodness' sake, Jamie, if you're going to go, at least do it because you want to.'

Jamie set down a plate. 'I really didn't know you felt this strongly about the defence industry.'

'It's not even about that,' Sara countered. 'I'm just not sure about this guy!'

'You're not?'

'Are you?'

'He's a bit direct, I'll give you that, but we've no reason not to trust him.'

Sara returned to the kitchen and gathered up cutlery. *Maybe I'm overreacting*, she thought. *Maybe my opinion*

43

of Rhodri since his death has coloured everything I think about Thorndike Aerospace and those associated with it.

But not everything, she realised. She still cared for Andy, and Andy trusted Gerrit Vos. If it were simply Vos's personality she was reacting against, Sara might have over-ridden her concerns. She might have been able to overlook his calling attention to her bruises on Monday. That had embarrassed her, certainly, but it was no reason to stop Jamie from accepting work. What gave Sara pause were the deep pangs of sadness and regret she felt emanating from this man. It was this true self that he covered with bravado. Deep down. Sara sensed Vos was a man who felt guilty – a man who condemned himself. But for what?

Whatever the real reason was, Sara wasn't going to change Jamie's mind about seeing Vos in Surrey tomorrow. But she felt she needed to know more about his potential new colleague.

'I think I'm getting a migraine,' Sara said.

Jamie looked at her with concern. 'You haven't had one in ages,' he said. 'Do you have your medication?'

'I don't know where it is. But it doesn't matter; it will pass.' She gestured towards the table. 'Do you mind clearing up by yourself? I'd like to lie down.'

'Of course,' Jamie said quickly. 'Go to bed.'

Sara kissed him lightly and moved towards the bedroom. Although she had lied about the headache, she did feel a pressing need to lie down quietly. She turned off the lights, undressed and hung up her clothes quietly in the dark. Sitting on the edge of the mattress, she fumbled deep into a drawer of the bedside table, withdrawing the papier mâché pendant she kept hidden there. The disk, which hung on a leather thong, displayed a delicately painted image of an all-seeing eye set inside scales of justice.

It had been made by Sara's mentor, a young psychic named Eldon Carson, during her troubling days in Aberystwyth. Sara had not always been able to peer into the past or foresee the future. She had been trained nearly three years earlier by Carson, who had an ability to see the terrible acts that people would commit before they happened. Carson's response – arrived at through a combination of youthful self-belief and testosterone – had been to murder each of those individuals before they could carry out their awful crimes. This rash solution led to Carson's status as a hunted serial killer, and ultimately to his death – but not before he had passed on his gift to Sara.

The symbol had once been used by Carson as a kind of signature; he would draw it on the bodies of the victims he had killed in order to prevent their future crimes. To Sara, it represented her own psychic powers, and the careful deliberation she needed to use them wisely – more wisely, perhaps, than Carson had. In the days after Sara had left Aberystwyth and joined Jamie in London, she had worn it under her clothing often. Soon she realised what an awkward conversation its discovery might lead to. Now, she kept it secreted away, to be taken out only on occasions such as this.

Sara placed the leather thong around her neck and lay down. She intended to put herself into a deep trance and take a psychic journey into the past of Gerrit Vos.

Vos and Nicole lived in a thatched cottage just south of Wokingham. The place boasted views over open countryside – a feature that Vos seldom got to appreciate. Even in summer, he usually arrived home in the dark. By the time he and Nicole were driving through the Berkshire countryside, the scenery was little more than shades of black, blue and grey. When they got home, Vos parked in

45

their converted barn – downstairs was now a garage, upstairs served as a warehouse for Nicole's surveillance equipment.

Also upstairs, concealed between the joists under a loose floorboard, was a small bag of fine white granules. The package could have been mistaken for any number of Class A drugs, but it was more dangerous than any of them. The bag contained thallium sulphate, a salt derived from the metal thallium. Ingesting even a small amount would affect almost every tissue in a body and leave its victim permanently disabled. A slightly larger dose – say, a quarter of a teaspoon – would be enough to cause a lingering and painful death. The bag under the floorboards held enough of the tasteless, odourless substance to dispatch its target within a day or two.

Thallium sulphate was illegal in the United Kingdom, but working for an international arms firm had its perks. Vos has acquired the powder a few years previously, in those darkest of days when he had planned to kill himself.

He had devised his exit strategy carefully. Thallium poisoning was by no means a pleasant way to go. Its symptoms included vomiting, weakness, numbness, confusion, convulsions and often, just prior to death, coma. However, it had one benefit – it was hard to diagnose. Few labs were equipped to test for it, and deaths by thallium poisoning were so rare that their cause was often attributed to some other disease, such as encephalitis brought on by a viral infection. Even at Vos's lowest emotional ebb, it had been important to him that Nicole not know he had killed himself. A sudden misfortune she could get over; his suicide would cause her distress for ever. For Nicole's sake, he had been willing to endure a couple days' worth of convulsions.

Vos had never actually changed his mind, and made the decision not to die. Rather, days had simply slipped by and he had found himself still alive. Not a great deal happier, perhaps, but at least continuing to breathe. Maybe it had been the grim thought of Nicole finding him coated in vomit and writhing in agony that had stayed his hand. Whatever the reason for his inaction, Vos had eventually concealed the package in the barn. He'd taken some solace from the fact that it was still so close to hand. He felt that same reassurance even to this day; it was a comfort to know that a relatively quick and easily concealed suicide was always an option.

Vos and Nicole entered the cottage through the back door. Nicole dashed away to answer an urgent email as Vos climbed the stairs to the bedroom. Shrugging off his clothes, he stepped into the small en suite. He turned on the shower and made it as cold as he could stand. He needed the jolt – his own personal reset button.

Even the freezing spray could not rinse away his whirring thoughts. Jamie Harding seemed OK; Vos had promised Andy Turner he'd look after him personally, rather than fob him off on one of his executives. Vos had researched Harding's background and had already decided there might be something he could do with him. Enough to keep Andy happy anyway. But the wild card was going to be the guy's partner – this Sara Jones woman. Vos was put on edge by her; she had seemed rather cold. Judgemental. He had hoped that the fact she was Rhodri Jones's sister, as well as Andy's friend, would endear Thorndike Aerospace to her – but she had spent the evening shooting wary glances at her partner.

Vos shivered, and turned off the shower. He shoved open the folding glass door and plucked up his bath sheet. He knew far more about Sara Jones than she could possibly realise. Including something that might damage her reputation considerably. He'd keep that in his back pocket. A man never knew when he'd need an ace-in-the-hole.

'Sorry about that,' Nicole said from the bedroom doorway. 'A query from a client.'

Vos grunted, and towelled himself with swift, violent motions.

Nicole watched him, and her expression turned to one of concern. 'You OK?' she asked.

'Sure.'

'You look tense.'

Vos smiled grimly. 'You always say that.'

Nicole raised a finger – *wait here* – then moved to her dresser. She plucked up a glass bottle. 'Lie down,' she ordered. 'On your stomach.'

'I don't want a massage,' he sighed.

She put on her cutest stern face. 'You're an arsehole,' she said matter-of-factly. 'Lie down.'

Vos huffed, but crawled obediently onto the bed. Nicole uncorked the bottle and slathered him with oil that smelled like a bordello bathtub. A moment ago, she'd been wearing leggings, but when she straddled his thighs, he felt only bare legs.

Nicole's fingers were remarkably strong, and she worked them into muscles in his back he hadn't realised were sore. It was soothing, he admitted. His mind began to drift. He had not imagined that he would ever need to use the information he'd gathered about Sara Jones. It was just a routine part of getting to know about people he'd been forced to deal with ... but after the vibes he'd got from her this evening, who could say what he'd need to do?

'What are you thinking about?' Nicole asked.

Vos opened his eyes and stretched his neck. 'Sex,' he whispered.

'Are you having trouble at work?'

'What makes you think that?'

48

'The conversation I'm having with your back.' Nicole dug a finger into his shoulder muscles. 'This isn't what sexy thoughts feel like,' she said.

He grunted.

'I've helped you before,' she reminded him. 'I'd help again.'

Vos chuckled. 'You don't work for Thorndike anymore.'

Nicole began to pummel his shoulders. 'I'm sure it's like riding a bicycle,' she said. 'If you need me to do something – anything – all you have to do is ask.'

After a while, Nicole's massage softened. Finally, her hands stilled. Vos smiled.

'Sometimes I forget how strong you are,' he said, adding, 'I'm sorry I'm such an arsehole.'

Nicole rubbed the oil from his back with the wet bath sheet. 'Oh, you can't help it,' she replied with affection. 'It's your job. You're a *professional* arsehole.'

Back when Sara had suffered from migraines, they would arrive in clusters. She might sail along for months, head as calm as a summer lake, before a whole storm front of pain would wash in and roil, in sickening waves, for weeks. These tempests had always left Sara feeling as though she were stricken with sea-sickness. She would be queasy for days. Dr Shapiro had given her a prescription for zolmitriptan, but had also suggested the real cause of the storms was stress. 'You're tense – holding your muscles all wrong,' he had said. 'You don't need drugs. You need to learn to use your body better.'

'Easier said than done,' she countered. 'I have a tense job.'

He had laughed. 'You do the same job as me.'

'Yes,' she had countered, 'but you don't chase Satanists with the Metropolitan Police in your off-hours.'

Dr Shapiro had suggested that Sara study the Alexander Technique, a system designed to improve health by learning to adopt better posture and ways of moving. It had taken Sara years to follow his advice. Before she finally did, her only defence had been to pop a pill and lie still – eyes closed, mind unfocused – in a darkened room. It wasn't always an effective ward against the headaches ... but in retrospect, it turned out to be superb training for psychic visions. The techniques were the same: blot out distractions, be still and open the mind. When Eldon Carson had first shown her how to see visions beyond her own time and place, he'd made her focus on a series of random coordinates, as if she were studying an imaginary map.

'Miss Sara, here is your target,' Carson would say. 'The coordinates are four, nine, five, six, one, three, two ... now, go and explore.'

Sara had come to understand that these coordinates were less about locating her actual target than about clearing her thoughts. Although Carson's voice repeating random coordinates often came unbidden to her mind, simply following her old procedure for easing a migraine worked just as well. As she relaxed, Sara would find images drifting into her consciousness. At first, they would be the sort of fragmented psychedelia that could flash across anyone's mind just before sleep – but soon they would coalesce into complete, three-dimensional scenes of what was happening, or had happened, or would happen to someone, somewhere.

As Sara sank into a trance on this Wednesday evening, the movie in her head – the events of four years ago, suddenly happening here, now, before her – starred Gerrit Vos.

FIVE

Gerrit Vos squints against the glare of the South African sun, and pulls out his Ray-Bans. 'Rhodri Jones started out in marketing, right?' he asks, as much to himself as his companion. 'How did a marketing guy end up CEO of this company?'

Vos likes views, panoramas – likes to see the Big Picture. He's at the top of the Magaliesberg mountains, with the Transvaal spread before him. His companion, a pudgy forty-something named Levi Rootenberg, had seemed surprised when Vos asked to ride the cable car up this mountain. Vos knows what this local was thinking: *such a touristy thing to do.* But Vos doesn't care much what other people think – so long as they're useful to him.

'Mr Jones is a smart man,' Rootenberg replies cautiously, his comb-over dancing in the wind.

'No, he's a moron,' Vos counters. 'Only a moron would buy a fucking platinum mine.'

The former Bekker mines – now renamed Thorndike Platinum – lay somewhere below them, out towards Rustenburg. Thorndike's new CEO had engineered a share swap that left the aerospace subcontractor owning a controlling interest in the mines. Rhodri Jones had assumed Thorndike's throne simply crackling with Big New Ideas for his company, and his first manoeuvre left

Bekker's staff, Rootenberg included, answering to the British.

'Thorndike's ownership is the reason I've done well in this company,' Rootenberg says. 'They like the fact that I have experience in both mining and aerospace.'

'A double threat,' Vos says. 'That's why you're with me now, matey.'

Rootenberg smiles. 'There was a logic behind Mr Jones's decision to buy this company,' he says. 'Your manufacturing divisions rely on platinum. It coats your airfoils, it's in your fuel nozzles and heat exchangers. Owning the Bekker mines guarantees supply.'

Vos studies the pudgy man. The reason Rootenberg is here has nothing to do with his understanding of airfoils. Together, Vos and Rootenberg are going to save the company.

'For what your hole-in-the-ground costs us,' Vos says, 'I could coat Head Office in bloody platinum. Right now, half of South Africa's mines are haemorrhaging money – including yours.'

Rootenberg grins. 'It's not my mine,' he corrects, 'it belongs to you English folk.'

Vos scans the flat land stretching below him. 'Did you know this place was a battlefield during the Boer War? The British garrison lay under siege here for months.' He peers at Rootenberg through his smoky lenses. 'Probably by your great-great-grandfather. And now, guess what? We're all under siege again.'

Vos is referring to the strike: an industry-wide conflict that's gone on for many unprofitable weeks. South Africa's two major mining unions have insisted on a one hundred per cent increase in wages, against the mining companies' counteroffer of ten percent. The industry has pointed out that union demands would require a near-doubling of platinum's price per ounce, a scenario that is unlikely at best. For Thorndike Platinum, whose most reliable customer is its own British parent, the breakdown in negotiations makes things even more desperate. Without an affordable deal, the whole company could sink into Rhodri Jones's loss-making metal pit.

'There's one more thing ownership requires,' Vos adds, staring far across the Transvaal, 'and that's a workforce you can control.'

'You'll control them,' Rootenberg says.

Vos peers at the man. 'You sound confident.'

Rootenberg laughs. 'I have to be. Neither of us wants to end up in Pollsmoor Prison, do we?'

Rootenberg drives Vos towards Rustenburg in a company Jeep. Flat grasslands roll past them on either side, under an enormous expanse of sky.

'How long have you worked in mining?' Vos asks.

'Since the early nineties,' Rootenberg says. 'Back then, it seemed a better bet than aerospace.'

Vos chuckles. 'Funny how your past can prove useful again.'

As they leave the highway, they're joined by a heavily armoured vehicle staffed with four combat-ready private security officers. 'Bloody hell,' Vos mutters, 'do we need all that firepower?'

'We are swinging past the site, yes?'

'Sure.'

'Then I guarantee you need all that firepower.'

Soon, the two-car motorcade is kicking up dust along a wide dirt track bordered by electricity pylons. The track leads to a shanty town of breezeblock-and-corrugated iron shacks overshadowed by the chimney of a Thorndike smelter. Today, it bellows no smoke, and the nearby ribbons of conveyor belt stand idle. There are very few men here, but women tote water from communal pumps

53

and hang washing on slack cords. Children play in weeds and rubble. Some glance up as the vehicles pass, but there's little to see. At Thorndike Platinum, armoured cars are the stuff of everyday life.

But when Vos and Rootenberg round a corner, it's a different picture. In the distance, several hundred men occupy a rocky hillock. A ring of police surrounds its base, handguns at their hips, and a few cradle assault rifles in the crooks of their arms. When the miners spy the cars, they rise and bellow, and even within the cocoon of the upholstered Jeep, their roar is formidable. The miners raise sticks in clenched fists, and wave clubs overhead. Police tense and drop their hands to their holsters.

'Stop the car,' Vos orders.

Rootenberg looks wary. 'It doesn't pay to taunt them.'

'What are the cops for?'

'If it comes to violence, they'll err on the side of caution. They got into hot water for killing some strikers a couple of years ago.'

Vos snorts. Everyone knows about that massacre; it set back labour relations more than anything since apartheid.

'The police have been pretty careful ever since,' Rootenberg adds. 'That's why, if you want to control these people, you need to use unorthodox methods.'

Rootenberg stops a couple hundred yards from the strikers. Their roar intensifies, and the security men behind the Jeep leap from their vehicle, semi-automatic assault rifles raised. Vos squints at the crowd. 'Is Kgatla up there?'

'I doubt it. Security should have taken him to the hotel by now.'

Vos frowns in concern. 'Hope nobody saw him leave.'

'No chance.' Rootenberg tilts his head towards the armed men in the vehicle behind them. 'These guys are careful.'

54

On the hill, the crowd parts suddenly. A powerfully built man with mirror shades descends along the newly formed pathway, trailed by a posse of younger lads. Down at the cordon, he selects an armed officer, and places a meaty hand on the cop's shoulder.

'That's Mathaithai Bakone,' Rootenberg says, 'the local union boss.'

Vos's interest sharpens. This man, whose physical strength belies his late middle age, is a controversial figure in these parts. A former Communist organiser and ANC soldier, Bakone inspires devotion among some, obedience among most, and the hatred of a sizeable few. It is Bakone and his small coterie of lieutenants who keep these strikers in line – and although this labour dispute extends far beyond Thorndike Platinum, Bakone is Vos's personal Public Enemy Number One.

Vos and Rootenberg watch as Bakone leans forwards and speaks. A moment later, the police officer's gun lowers as though it were wilting.

'What's going on?' Vos mutters.

The union leader applies soft pressure to the policeman's shoulder, and the officer moves aside like a well-oiled gate. Police on Bakone's other side step back as well, making a wide opening. Bakone and his boys begin to *toyi-toyi*, jogging in step, and the protesters on the hillock take up the dance. Bakone leads the rebellious conga past the police, heading straight for the Thorndike vehicles.

Behind the Jeep, a security man takes quick aim. 'Stop there!' he shouts.

At the fractured cordon, policemen tense. One raises his own weapon and aims it at the Thorndike guard. 'Holy shit,' Rootenberg mutters.

'What the fuck are they doing?' Vos hollers.

Bakone looks straight at the Thorndike Jeep and locks

55

his gaze on Vos. He smiles wide, toothy with triumph. Even through his mirror shades, the man's stare is overpowering. Vos drops his gaze and lurches around to the security men behind the Jeep. He gestures wildly. 'Lower your weapons!' he shouts. 'Get back in your vehicle!'

Rootenberg has already thrown the Jeep in gear; it judders, and they fishtail away in a geyser of dust.

'Sara?'

The dust from the Thorndike Jeep grew thicker, clouding Sara's vision until a tan swirl was all she could see. The roar of the toyi-toying mob faded into a single, hushed voice. It was whispering, 'Sara?'

She eased open her eyes, and could just make out Jamie's form entering the darkened room. Instinctively, she reached around to the back of her neck and eased the pendant over her head. She gripped it in her hand, and slid it under the duvet.

'What time is it?' she mumbled. 'Is there a problem?'

'I dug out your old migraine pills,' Jamie said, and groped for Sara's hand. He dropped a small dot into her palm. 'And, here … I've made you a cup of tea.'

Sara forced herself to simulate gratitude. 'That's so sweet,' she said.

'I hope you weren't already sleeping.'

'Just drifting.' She wriggled her shoulders up the headboard, accepted the mug and swallowed the medication she didn't need. 'Are you coming to bed?'

'Not if it will disturb you,' he said. 'I can sleep on the sofa.'

Sara smiled appreciatively, and handed him back the tea. 'I shouldn't have caffeine right now.'

'Of course. Maybe some chamomile?'

'I'm fine,' she said.

Gently, Jamie kissed her goodnight, and tiptoed out of the room. Sara smiled in spite of herself. He really was considerate; sometimes frustratingly so.

She squirmed onto her back, wriggled her head into the pillow and tried to find that blank space that led back to South Africa, and Gerrit Vos.

'Your families are starving, is that right?'

Vos stares unblinkingly at the slight figure of Phetoho Kgatla, a twenty-nine-year-old union representative from Mine Number Two. Kgatla has none of Bakone's imposing physical presence, but compensates with the scholarly air of a doctoral student. Vos knows this man has the brains to match his demeanour. The two of them sit in a conference room at a spa hotel outside Rustenburg. Management has laid on coffee and a platter of sandwiches, which Vos has thrust aside. He's annoyed that there's no wine.

'Things could be worse,' Kgatla says softly, meeting Vos's gaze with quiet assurance. 'Twenty-five per cent of workers in this country are unemployed. When you think about that ... well, I suppose we miners can tough it out until we get what we want.'

Vos snorts. 'Save the bullshit for your stump speeches. You know it's not going to end that way.'

Kgatla tilts his head. 'And how is it going to end, Mr Vos?'

'The unions will buckle. Sure, they'll get more than the ten per cent the Industry's offering, but not much more. Then, pretty soon, a lot of them are going to be sacked.'

Kgatla moves to hide his surprise, but he's a fraction too late. 'For what reason?' he asks.

'Because platinum mining's a loser's bet right now,' Vos says matter-of-factly. 'You lot have been at it for

57

decades, and now all the easy ore's gone. Hell, we might as well be shovelling rand notes into our smelters; our bottom line would look about the same.' Vos leans back in his chair and stretches. 'The only way any company's going to survive is by shifting production to highly mechanised, shallow mines. And that means slashing the number of workers.'

There's a tapping on the glass door of the conference room. Vos looks up to see Rootenberg peering in. He rises and opens the door, but not all the way. 'What?' he demands.

'Sorry I'm late,' Rootenberg whispers. 'I had to park the Jeep in the other lot.'

Vos shifts to block Rootenberg from Kgatla's view. 'Is your friend here?' he murmurs.

'Not yet,' replies Rootenberg. 'I asked him to meet us in the lounge.'

Vos glances at Kgatla, who studies his fingernails and pretends not to listen. 'Go there and wait for him,' Vos says. 'I've got this.'

'You sure?'

'Just buy the guy a drink when he arrives. Tell him I'll come soon as I can.'

Before Rootenberg has time to acknowledge, Vos has clicked shut the door and turned back to Kgatla; both men listen to Rootenberg trudge down the carpeted hallway. When his soft scuffing has faded, Kgatla cocks his head. 'Your security detail told me you wanted to see me specifically,' he says.

Vos sits. 'That's rather obvious. You're here.'

'They were insistent that I sneak out of camp in a car with blackened windows.' Kgatla snorts softly. 'That seemed a bit odd to me.'

Vos raises an eyebrow. 'And yet you came.'

'Now you tell me we must settle for low pay and job

cuts.' Kgatla raps his knuckles on the table. 'You choose to say this to me. Not to Bakone, not to his deputies, but to me.'

'That I did,' Vos answers levelly. 'Because Bakone's a hothead. Some might even say he's a demagogue. He'll be no good for your people; not in the long run.'

Kgatla clicks his tongue and shakes his head. 'What do you expect me to do, change his mind? I have no influence over that man.'

'No, you haven't,' Vos agrees. 'The two of you hate each other, am I right?'

Kgatla's eyes narrow. 'Is that why I'm here?'

'That, and because you have followers of your own. Truth be told, most miners only kow-tow to Bakone because he scares them shitless. On the other hand, you're respected, Phetoho. Under different circumstances you'd make a fine leader.'

Kgatla blinks, then absently picks up his empty coffee mug. Vos lifts it from his hand and refills it. 'The two unions running this miners' strike are just like Bakone,' Vos says. 'Truculent. Unwilling to see what's coming.'

He leans forward, speaks quietly. 'But what if the workers at Thorndike Platinum broke away? Started their own union? A forward-facing union that understands the needs of the Industry, and is willing to help shape the future rather than resisting it?'

Kgatla sets down his mug. 'A union that won't contest redundancies, you mean?'

Vos frowns in grudging agreement. 'Maybe. But also, one that can negotiate a generous severance package for all workers who leave voluntarily. And a union that could end this strike within days – after agreeing a pay rise of, let's say, twenty-five per cent.'

He lets this sink in, then repeats the figure. 'Twenty-five per cent across the board – while every other miner is still on the picket lines, and feeding his family grass.' Vos shakes his head sadly, as though in sympathy for such short-sightedness. 'Mark my words, Phetoho, when the other strikers finally do settle, the poor bastards won't end up with more than twelve per cent. Is that what they're staying on strike for?'

In truth, Vos has no mandate to negotiate pay rises; he had plucked the twenty-five per cent figure from the air. Still, he's certain his boss will be able to sell the settlement to Rhodri Jones. In fact, Vos knows that if he has success out here, no one will question *any* of his methods.

'I can guarantee,' he continues, 'that when redundancies come about, the workers affected will be well taken care of. Think about it! Any union leader who could make all this happen would be a goddamn hero.' He smiles enticingly. 'And, naturally, that leader would be very well compensated by Thorndike Platinum.'

For a moment, Kgatla's gaze softens as he takes in the mental picture Vos has drawn. But, just as suddenly, his brow furrows and his stare hardens. 'This is a fantasy!' he huffs. 'Bakone would never allow it. I have friends, yes, but would those friends fight for me? Because, I assure you, Bakone's boys will fight for him – with sticks, and clubs, and knives, and their bare hands.'

'Who specifically would fight?' Vos asks, and rises to his feet.

He removes an iPad from his leather satchel, and rests it on the table in front of Kgatla. It shows a surveillance photo of Bakone on the picket line. Vos swipes, and the image is replaced by one of Bakone's lieutenants. 'How about this guy? Would he fight?'

'Oh, yes,' Kgatla sighs.

Another swipe, another lieutenant. 'How about him?'

'Definitely.'

And another. 'Him?'

After several more photos, Kgatla nods softly. 'That's all of them,' he concludes.

Vos snaps shut the iPad's cover. 'Just hypothetically,' he says, 'what if these men were no longer a threat to you? Could I count on you then?'

Kgatla smiles sardonically. 'These men,' he says, 'will be a threat to me until the day they die.'

Vos folds his arms and sits back. Now it's his turn to smile.

SIX

Several years ago, Gerrit Vos had entered into a conspiracy with a young union leader, Phetoho Kgatla, to murder that man's older rival, as well as several of his lieutenants. The murders were arranged by Vos's flunky, Levi Rootenberg – a Thorndike employee from the South African mines. The crimes themselves were carried out by local men, whom the flunky had hired. After the disappearance of those more-powerful rivals, the union leader accepted a hefty bribe from Thorndike Aerospace. In recompense, he broke a strike, and eased Thorndike's path to sacking a large number of their South African miners. Gerrit Vos had returned to Britain a corporate hero. It was the making of his career.

That was what Sara Jones knew when she struggled into consciousness the next morning.

In last night's visions, Sara had not witnessed the murders themselves – but she had felt their spectre haunting everything she'd seen. The foreshadowing of death had come as a sensation, a wash of sickly feelings. They had trickled through every vignette – from the Magaliesberg mountains and the old Bekker mines, all the way to the shiny anonymity of that hotel conference room. Sara finally understood the deep reservoir of sadness she had felt in Vos – it was guilt. Guilt for a terrible crime he

62

had arranged, but could no longer reconcile with his own self-image. The funereal air of the scenes she had witnessed haunted Vos's psyche still. Sara understood the feeling – after what she had seen, she felt them too, like a physical presence in her own stomach.

As Sara came around and her thoughts cohered, they merged into a single, unanswered question.

What about Rhodri?

With her skin pressed against the bed sheet and still sticky with last night's sweat, Sara thought about her brother. Had Rhodri been aware of the way in which his gaunt minion had solved that particular labour dispute? Despite the multiple horrors of Sara's past with Rhodri, she could not bring herself to believe it. Rhoddo had been guilty of so many things, but Sara got no sense – psychic or otherwise – that he'd known about Vos's deadly conspiracy.

Maybe he hadn't wanted to know. Rhodri had always maintained a diplomat's sense of when not to question.

Sara's thoughts were disturbed by Jamie, who slipped in quietly from the shower, a damp towel draped over his shoulders and his hair still wet. He scooted around the bed and eased open his top drawer. Sara watched him select a pair of socks and boxers with exaggerated quietness.

When his gaze finally connected with hers, Jamie grinned wide. 'Good morning,' he said heartily. 'Feeling better?'

Well, look at him, Sara thought. *He's just over the moon about today's Big Meeting.*

She smiled as sweetly as she could. 'One hundred per cent,' she replied, fighting the nausea that continued to twitch in her stomach. 'Thanks for the pill last night. It worked wonders.'

'You should order more.' Jamie tossed the socks onto the bed, slipped into his boxer shorts, and moved to the wardrobe.

The queasiness lurched upwards, and Sara placed a steadying hand against her bedside dresser. She fought down a pulse of bile, then realised it was a losing battle. Accepting the inevitable, Sara rolled out of bed and stumbled to the bathroom. She barely made it to the toilet bowl in time.

Jamie was right behind her. He knelt at her side as she vomited. Placing a hand on the small of her back, he asked, 'Are you sure that migraine's gone?'

Sara retched again. Stomach acid stung her throat. Bending upright, she yanked a few sheets of toilet tissue from the roll. 'I'm all right,' she exhaled as she blotted her lips.

'Is it the headache?'

'Uh-uh.'

Jamie hesitated. 'You're not pregnant, are you?'

She spat. 'God forbid.'

Jamie snorted with relief. 'That's good,' he said, adding hastily, 'I mean, it wouldn't be a tragedy, but still –'

He abandoned the uncooperative sentence. 'You should go back to bed,' he said.

Sara shifted sideways and leaned against the bathroom wall. She appreciated the cool of the ceramic tiles. She tossed the balled-up paper into the bowl. Jamie lowered the seat and flushed.

'Jamie,' Sara said faintly, 'do you remember I said I didn't like Gerrit Vos?'

'Mm-hmm.' He waited for more.

'I still don't,' she continued. 'I'm sorry, but I do not trust that man.'

Jamie sat down and bowed his head. 'I can understand that,' he said indulgently. 'But we have to be honest – you don't know him. Neither do I. That's what today's meeting is all about. To see if there is any common ground between us.'

Sara shook her head. 'He isn't trustworthy.'

'You have no way of knowing that.'

She huffed sardonically. 'What you don't know about psychology would fill a library.'

Jamie tried to wash away her concern with a chuckle. 'Do you really think you understand Gerrit Vos after one dinner with the guy?'

Sara grimaced and pressed her arm against the wall. She tried to stand, but wobbled. Jamie rose, clasped her hand, and pulled. When she was standing steadily, he lifted her dressing gown from a hook on the back of the door. Sara slipped it on.

'One dinner's more than enough,' she told him. 'We make predictive inferences about people after seconds. Research has shown this – we're able to see patterns based on narrow slices of experience.'

Jamie tried to take Sara's arm. She waved him away and pushed past, into the hallway.

'What I'm saying is,' she continued, 'I think I can trust my feelings.'

Jamie followed. 'You're tired, and suffering because of the migraine,' he said soothingly. 'In my opinion, you *can't* trust your feelings.'

Sara snorted and went into the bedroom. She sat on the mattress. Immediately, Jamie perched next to her.

Sara wanted to scream, *I don't have to trust my feelings – I have seen what Gerrit Vos did!*

Instead, she grasped Jamie's arm. 'Jamie, please let me speak to Andy,' she begged. 'I'll ask him to assign you to other clients. You don't need Thorndike Aerospace!'

'You'll feel better after I've made you some toast,' he said.

He patted her leg and rose again. Sara watched him

shrug on a T-shirt and leave the room. She blinked, and patterns of light spangled before her eyes.

I need to know more, she thought. *I can't just leave things like this.*

Once Jamie had left for his ill-judged meeting with Vos, Sara would have some solitude. She knew that she had already decided how to use it – and this realisation made her stomach lurch once more. Sinking back into a trance meant trusting the ebb and flow of its deepest currents. She might set course for a specific sight, but those psychic tides could also sweep her towards a new and turbulent eddy.

Given a choice of destination, Sara would like to witness Vos's return from South Africa – and to see it from her brother's point of view. Those were the coordinates she would aim for. Then she had a chance of understanding how much Rhoddo had actually known about his man-in-Africa's blood-soaked exploits.

Of course, she knew, she could just as easily find herself witnessing the murders themselves.

That's something I don't need to see.

Sara sighed and quietly cursed Eldon Carson for that ominous choice he'd made. The choice to be her friend, to become her mentor. The choice to change her life for the worse.

Sara blinked again. Further flashes lit up her eyes. Her head felt as though it had just recoiled from a rifle blast. She needed to lie down. She shifted awkwardly, and her foot brushed against something that had tumbled from the folds of the duvet.

Sara did not notice when, rolling back, she nudged the pendant, which skittered a short distance across the floorboards. Nor did she hear its soft click as it came to a halt, half-hidden, against the leg of her chest of drawers.

The Thorndike Aerospace campus sat on the western edge of Surrey, offering easy access both to London and to those Hampshire towns so important to the British defence industry. Gerrit Vos's office was on the top floor of Thorndike's executive building, known as Hollybush House. Vos's favourite feature of his office was the view from its window: a striking panorama that looked towards the Hog's Back of the North Downs. Vos had always appreciated views. He'd read once that the physical act of gazing into the distance expanded a person's inner perception. At this moment, though, Vos was looking down, not out – staring at his computer screen. It displayed a live stream from the security cameras at the guard's hut. Vos waited to see an old SUV make the straight drive up the private road from the A331.

What Vos didn't like were visitors cluttering up his office. He preferred to meet people somewhere less personal. A couple of days ago, he had received Levi Rootenberg at the Thorndike flat in Mayfair, rather than invite him down here. Now, he wished he had asked the same of Jamie Harding – but it was too late to alter arrangements. At least Vos could see the younger man in one of the anonymous meeting rooms that sat side-by-side on a lower level of Hollybush House. He picked up the phone and punched in an extension. 'Rashid? It's Gerrit Vos. Mr Harding should be here shortly. Send him to the fourth floor, would you?'

Vos gazed over his large oak desk. For a man who liked to keep his workspace uncluttered, this surface contained an unusual array of knick-knacks. Still, Vos had ensured that each was arrayed in a precise order. Along the far edge of the desk were pieces of surveillance equipment that Nicole sold on her website: a camera watch, a night vision monocular, a remote listening device. In front of them stood a number of painted metal figurines that Andy Turner had given him, including a 1970s Royal Marine, an infantry officer from the First World War, a French Foreign Legionnaire and an eighteenth-century Welsh Fusilier. The Fusilier was the outlier – colourful, where the others were drab. Andy liked his metal soldiers, and seemed to favour the no-nonsense fighting men to more decorative additions. Vos might have quite liked a Scots Guard piper, or maybe a Beefeater, but these didn't fit into Andy's battlefront fantasies.

And it was important to indulge Andy's whims. He may not have been a deep thinker or a strategic whiz-kid, but he could perform a number of useful tasks well; he was especially good at promotional strategy. For that alone, Andy Turner was worth keeping happy – and Vos knew that hiring this ex-cop would make him very happy. Andy was simply part of the furniture here at Thorndike Aerospace. Like Rhodri Jones before him, the company's CEO was overly fond of that PR-man-made-good – or at least pretended to be – and paid Andy's consultancy a hefty retainer without even the slightest wobble. So if Vos had to find something for Andy's new dependent to do, well … it was a cost of doing business.

But there was more to it than that. In some ways, Vos was eager to give Harding a break. Vos had often wondered if his career would have been easier if someone had taken him under their wing ten years ago. Maybe he wouldn't have felt the need to push so hard to prove himself. Maybe he would have found subtler ways to resolve the conflict in South Africa.

Perhaps, Vos thought, he could actually be a good influence, a guiding hand. It might just be the thing Harding needed. Naturally, Vos had done some digging into his new protégé's background. Harding's father seemed to have been a bit of an amoral character, and that was something Vos could identify with. Sometimes business forced a person to do things he otherwise would not choose. How far had Jamie Harding fallen from his family tree? Was he as straight-laced as he seemed? This was something Vos had tried to discern at dinner in Brixton, by raising the spectre of Rhodri Jones with Harding's girlfriend. He'd wanted to see how the couple reacted to ideas – and, of course, business practices – that were less than angel-pure. He still didn't really know. That was at the top of today's to-do list – to glean whether Harding could be trusted to keep calm when operational tactics moved to the margins.

If Harding could keep his cool, maybe this liaison with Levi Rootenberg would be a good trial run for him. That would spare Vos having to spend his time talking illegal logistics with the man.

On the computer screen, Vos saw the vehicle he'd been waiting for. He gathered up his iPad and papers, and strode to the stairwell.

Jamie drove up the long, straight road towards the cluster of buildings that made up Thorndike Aerospace's main office compound, and stopped at the barrier beside the red brick security hut. Even though he was on the visitors' list, the guard insisted he pop open the boot. Only after she had inspected his first aid kit and electric tyre pump did she direct Jamie to a tall glass rectangle of offices flanked by smaller buildings.

Driving past the raised barrier and wheeling around the site's one-way system, Jamie peered at the gleaming pillar of glass, hoping to spot the entrance. It seemed there wasn't one – just a grid of opaque windows. As Jamie stepped from his Land Rover, one of the smoke-hued panels swished open and a uniformed man leaned out.

'Mr Harding,' he called. His voice echoed across the

car park. 'Eight minutes early.'

The man led Jamie into a small lobby. 'No need to sign in,' he said briskly. 'I've done it for you.'

Jamie blinked, perplexed. 'When?'

'Our computer's linked to the security gate,' he explained. 'As soon as you drove through, I printed this.'

He handed over a visitor's pass wrapped in a plastic wallet and dangling from a ribbon. 'Mr Vos likes punctual colleagues,' the man noted. 'You've scored yourself points there.' He raised his chin towards the lift. 'Fourth floor.'

As an afterthought, the man added, 'Mr Vos is linked to the front gate, too. My guess is, he's already waiting.'

As Jamie rode to the fourth floor, he slipped the lanyard around his neck; his visitor's pass dangled over his tie. As the lift doors slid open, he saw Vos standing there expectantly, just as the guard had predicted.

Vos greeted him with a cocked eyebrow. 'Oh, look – there's something we can improve on immediately,' he said. 'Take off that pass. You're not at a sales convention.'

Jamie removed the identification as Vos looked him over. 'Is that the best suit you own?' Vos asked.

'It's about the same as all my others,' Jamie replied.

'Ask Andy Turner for the name of a tailor. Handsome lad like you shouldn't be a poster boy for Primark.'

Vos strode down the hall and Jamie followed, stuffing the ID card into the pocket of his inadequate suit. *Primark, indeed. I bought this suit at Marks and Spencer.* As he scurried behind Vos, Jamie took in his surroundings. Considering the image Thorndike tried to project, he had expected a plush interior. Instead, the building's decor would have suited any business park in Swindon. Rooms on either side of the hallway were formed from flimsy beige partitions that screwed into the ceiling. The floor was covered in grey carpet tiles. *Maybe the disposable look is intentional*, Jamie thought. *That's one thing making weapons teaches you – everything's impermanent.*

Vos led Jamie into an anonymous box with a white pressboard table and some office chairs. Papers, folders and an iPad lay neatly in front of Vos's seat. Jamie sat opposite. 'This feels like a job interview,' he quipped.

'Oh, you've already got the job,' Vos said flatly. In this fluorescent light, the shadows across his deep-set eyes formed a blue-grey mask. 'We both know Andy's done you a favour.'

Jamie's face grew warm and pulsed in embarrassment. Vos may have been abrupt at dinner last night, but he hadn't been rude. The police inspector in Jamie suspected this was a tactic – Vos was establishing his dominance, and reminding Jamie they were now on his turf. Even though Jamie knew this, Vos's ploy was working; he felt the same way he had done when the Dyfed-Powys Police announced a Serious Case Review into the events in Aberystwyth. Jamie had understood the reason why it was happening, but still, it had been like a slap. The way Vos so casually negated his abilities sparked a competitive urge. He wasn't about to let this man play him.

'You say I've got the job,' Jamie said. 'But I haven't asked for it, and I don't know if I'll accept it.'

Vos looked up at him. He seemed rather pleased.

'Maybe I don't want to work for Andy Turner at all,' Jamie pressed on. 'Or maybe I will work for some of Andy's clients – but not for you.'

Vos released a single, amused bark. 'A confident boy,' he observed.

'I've had some successes in my career,' Jamie replied. 'Considering who you are, I'd imagine you already know that.'

'Believe me,' Thorndike's Director for Business Development interrupted, 'you wouldn't be in this office unless I knew that very well.'

He straightened his papers. 'And it's not only your successes I know about,' he added. 'Correct me if I've got any of this wrong ...'

For the next several minutes, Vos recounted what he knew of Jamie's life. He knew that Jamie was the only child from his father's second marriage, and that Jamie's side of the family never spoke to his older half-sisters. Vos was aware that Jamie's father, George Harding, had joined the London Metropolitan Police in 1974. He knew that in the year 2000, George's career had been cut short by a stroke when he was only forty-five. Another stroke had followed in 2013, which had left George's frontal lobe damaged permanently. Vos knew that Jamie's mother, Grace, now lived alone in a Kent cottage close to her husband's nursing home.

Vos looked up from his papers. 'Is that the gist of it?' he asked.

'Impressive,' Jamie replied. 'Just about everything worth knowing.'

Vos smiled thinly. 'Just about,' he echoed. 'But I think we need to lay the more sensitive stuff on the table, too – if only to put it behind us.'

Jamie's eyes narrowed. 'OK.'

He suspected what Vos would say before the man's gaze had even returned to his papers: at the time of George Harding's first stroke, he was being investigated by the Met for corruption. Such a taint was all-too-common for someone who had joined the force in the 1970s; it was no secret that members of the Flying Squad used to tip off armed robbers for cash, or that certain officers in the Drugs Squad were dope peddlers themselves. Some of the bobbies, like Jamie's father, had run protection rackets, shaking down the club owners and pornographers of Soho.

Vos relayed this information with a detached and calculating air. After describing the scale of the investigation against George Harding, he leaned back and folded his arms. 'You attended a private day school until you were eleven, and then went to boarding school in Surrey, am I right?'

Jamie admitted that he had.

'That was expensive, wasn't it?'

Jamie shrugged. 'I was a kid. I didn't think about money.'

Vos looked dubious. 'You were seventeen when the Met began its investigation, right? I'm guessing Daddy couldn't keep it secret from you then.' He leaned forward and tented his fingers. 'Did he ever deny soliciting bribes?'

Jamie lowered his gaze. 'He couldn't, really. I heard too many rows between him and my mother.'

Vos nodded. 'Here's what I'm guessing: he said he'd only done it to put you through school.'

Jamie knew that his silence was an answer. That was exactly what George Harding had said. Jamie's father had always harboured the dream that his only son would attend Oxford, and maybe later read for the Bar. George had known that such a career demanded a better pedigree than a Croydon cop's son could get at the local comprehensive. As it happened, Jamie had not achieved anything like the grades needed for an Oxford college, even with his costly schooling. He ended up reading Criminology at a university not far from London, but quite a distance from the Russell Group.

Vos offered Jamie a rare smile. 'Listen, kiddo,' he

said, 'I don't give a shit about any of this. I only raise it to make a point.'

That you can find out anything you want about me? Jamie wondered.

'The point is this,' Vos continued. 'Your dad wasn't a bad man.'

Jamie snorted. 'No?'

Vos feigned surprise at Jamie's response. 'Do *you* think he was?'

Jamie paused. He tried to decide what he actually felt about his father. 'No, he wasn't bad,' he said quietly.

'That's a good answer.' Vos placed his elbows on the table and clasped his hands. 'Your dad broke the law, and, many would say, betrayed his oath. And yet, you tell me that he wasn't bad.' Vos leaned forward. 'Why would you say such a thing?'

Jamie stared at Vos. 'Why would you?'

Vos smiled with one corner of his mouth. 'Touché,' he said, and added, 'Now you and I are ready to talk about morality.'

Discussions about morals, it seemed, came with refreshments. Vos stuck his head out the door and yelled at the first employee he saw to dash to the staff room and fetch tea and biscuits. As he waited to be served, Vos pursed his lips contemplatively, and then asked, 'Did you ever do anything at the Met that you were ashamed of? You know, the way Daddy did?'

Jamie was certain this question wasn't nearly as casual as Vos made it sound. He straightened his shoulders. In a clear voice – the very same tone he had employed at the Serious Case Review after the Aberystwyth debacle – he said, 'No.'

'Didn't imagine so,' Vos said with a smile. 'And yet, we've established that you don't think your father was a bad man.'

Jamie fought a niggling urge to stuff Vos's tie into his mouth.

'Your dad's reaction to his circumstances is the crux of this issue, my friend. We live in an imperfect world. Some may even call it corrupt.' Vos tapped his finger lightly against the pressboard table-top. 'The rules we pay lip service to – we call them *morality* – tend to fall down in practice. Your dad was set against villains he could never defeat, in a system stinking with corruption. He was told to play by rules that were no more than a public relations smokescreen. If you ask me, he made the only move that was available to him. Hell, it was *expected* of him. The fact that he was later punished is evidence of the hypocrisy built into the system.'

Vos spread his hands in a shrug that suggested he'd just proved something.

There was a tapping at the door. A young male staffer came in with a tray laden with all the fixings for tea, as well as a plate of biscuits. He set it on the table.

'Oh, look,' Vos said flatly, 'Jammie Dodgers. You spoil us.'

The lad flushed and apologised. They were all the staff room had, he said.

Jamie sat silently. He told himself that Vos had said all of that as some kind of ploy to win him over. And yet, Vos was the first person Jamie had ever heard make a solid defence of the things that George Harding had done. Jamie's mother had tried, of course, back when everything had gone pear-shaped. However, Grace Harding's words had been more a plea for Jamie's sympathy and understanding, tinged with a kind of mourning for his father's recent stroke. Vos, on the other hand, made no apologies. He accused the system and blamed society on George Harding's behalf. On the surface, Vos's tortuous logic did offer some sliver of comfort. That fierce defence served as a rebuttal to the ambivalence Jamie had always felt towards his father.

He had always thought of those mixed emotions as a closely guarded secret. No research could have revealed the conflict that had churned in Jamie's mind for nearly two decades. Still, despite the apologies for George Harding that Vos had just made, Jamie knew the ambivalence from which he suffered had nothing to do with any moral confusion. It was very clear that his father had been in the wrong. What Jamie felt was the emotional vertigo of trying to love someone who'd done bad things, and nothing more.

Vos ushered the young employee out of the room. 'Did you notice?' he asked. 'The kid's twenty, and even *his* suit's better than yours.'

'I'll ask Andy about that tailor,' Jamie said.

As Vos poured tea and shoved the entire plate of Jammie Dodgers Jamie's way, he murmured, 'Let's broaden this out, shall we? Let's turn our attention to the global political arena.'

Jamie took a sip of tea. It was a relief to move away from a focus too close to home. 'Sure,' he said.

Vos pursed his lips and stared upwards to the polystyrene ceiling tiles. 'Would you agree that no two governments have exactly the same standards of morality?'

Jamie considered. 'It depends on what kind of morality you're talking about.'

Vos blinked. 'What do you mean?'

'Some standards are internationally agreed upon,' Jamie went on, 'and therefore beyond the interests of any one government. I'm thinking mainly about human rights law.'

Vos chuckled darkly. 'Oh, yeah – the subject of your

forthcoming master's degree.'

'It's important,' Jamie said. 'Governments commit to each other not to practice torture, or to condone slavery, or to conduct executions without a fair trial.'

Vos's chuckle increased in volume. 'And look how well that's been observed,' he said.

'Levels of observation may vary,' Jamie said, 'but human rights laws are fundamental to democracy.'

'Have a biscuit,' Vos said.

Jamie picked up a Jammie Dodger and nibbled politely.

Vos angled his head. 'We could argue that, now and then, any government needs to look the other way,' he conceded. 'But let's not get off-topic. Can you at least agree that, beyond the lofty ideals of human rights, a government's international conduct and the domestic laws it passes reflect its own particular priorities?'

Jamie washed down the sticky jam and dry crumbs with a swallow of tea. 'OK,' he said.

'And that it justifies its priorities according to its own standards?'

'Sure...'

Vos nodded. 'Good. Then let's turn our attention to global trade. Where money is concerned, we can assume that whatever laws a country makes will depend on what it wants to achieve at a particular time. Does that make sense?'

'I suppose so.'

'Governments set laws to help themselves, yet part of the game requires everyone to pretend that the standards behind those laws are sacrosanct. And we've already established that they're not – they're based on expedience.' Vos sighed heavily, as if his own weary shoulders carried the weight of human folly. He levelled his sunken eyes on Jamie. 'So, what are we to do?' he

77

asked.

Jamie returned his unblinking gaze. 'Who do you mean by *we*?' he asked.

'I mean this company,' Vos said. 'Me, you, everybody. We pay lip service to laws that we know are transitory and often wrong ... then, we do what everyone knows needs to be done.'

Vos picked up a biscuit and waved it for emphasis. 'The government knows it, foreign powers know it, we all know it. We also know that if we're caught doing whatever's necessary, we'll be slapped on the wrist and expected to look ashamed. That calms an indignant public. It helps them to forget.'

He dropped the Jammie Dodger onto the table. Its edge shattered into crumbs. 'But, in exactly the same way they treated your poor old dad, it's only a show. For the decision-makers of this world, it's an important show, because it still means mission accomplished. The system carries on.'

Vos leaned forward. 'We're all in the game.'

The two men remained silent for a moment. Finally, Jamie set down his mug of tea and grinned. 'I'm not entirely sure I am,' he said.

'Don't fool yourself,' Vos said. 'You're a player whether you want to be or not, simply by virtue of the fact that you're breathing.'

Vos brushed the biscuit crumbs to the floor and pulled a document wallet from his pile of papers. He slid it towards Jamie. 'The question is,' he concluded, 'do you want to make the game work for you?'

SEVEN

Sara knew all about the connection between the physical and the mental. She understood that the body reacted to emotional upset as a way of telling the brain that things were going wrong. It served as an encouragement to change direction. And if Sara had been advising a client, she'd have said that this morning's vomiting, the headache and feelings of ill-ease, were a clear warning to stop doing whatever had caused those sensations in the first place.

But sometimes doctors make the worst patients, and Sara had no intention of following such reasonable advice. As soon as Jamie left, she showered, put on a clean T-shirt and pyjama bottoms, and returned to bed. Now, she opened the top drawer of her bedside dresser and groped for her pendant. Her hand weaved between the socks and pants, but could find nothing else. She brushed her bare neck. Sara was certain she'd been wearing it recently. But, as it happened, she could not remember putting it back in the drawer. When had she taken it off? Maybe when Jamie came in.

Sara ran her hand under the duvet and brushed its folds – there was no sign of it there either. Impatient, she pulled the duvet up to her neck and thrust her head backwards into the pillow. She didn't need the pendant to see the past and future, she told herself. Eldon's pendant was no more than a kind of security blanket – and wearing it when she was in a trance had become a meaningless ritual.

I'll find it later, she thought.

Right now, Sara was as ready as she'd ever be to discover whatever more she could about Gerrit Vos – and maybe even Rhodri Jones. She relaxed, and breathed deeply.

Imagining Eldon Carson's voice had also become a regular part of this ritual. Now, Sara heard that low-pitched twang saying, *OK, Miss Sara, here are your coordinates.*

And then a series of random numbers: *seven, three, zero, nine, eight, four ...*

Immediately, images form, vague impressions solidifying into distinct shapes. Sara begins to grope her way through them, and finds herself hovering over a neat grid of white and green rectangles glowing in bright sunlight. Far below her, she sees a ribbon of grass, a patch of pebbles, and then the sea.

And Sara finds herself above a caravan park.

She takes it in, and recognises it. It is a place where she spent many summer afternoons: the beach at Clarach, next to Aberystwyth.

What am I doing here? She wonders. *This has nothing to do with Gerrit Vos.*

Sara feels herself drifting downwards, towards a fun fair built alongside the caravans. She zeroes in on a small girl, maybe five years old, running away from a tall plastic slide. The girl wears a pink swimming costume and lime green crocs, and Sara can feel a niggle of unease in her that quickly turns into a pulse of panic. This girl has lost her parents.

The girl looks all around. So many pairs of legs, and none of them Mum or Dad. They had been at the bottom of the slide when she'd climbed up, but when she'd slid down and handed back her burlap sack they weren't there. The girl's breath comes in short gasps and, all of a sudden, she feels very cold. But she doesn't cry, she thinks of the beach across the road. That's where their towels are, and their cooler with Coke and sandwiches. That's where Mum and Dad must be. That's where she'll go.

Sara watches the girl dash across the road and onto the pavement. She scuttles up a concrete barrier and rolls onto the raised strip of grass. She runs across it towards the beach and spots her towels and cooler – but no parents. Now the girl begins to sob. Sara watches as a lone sunbather sits up on his towel …

And realises she knows his name. It is Edmund Haney – another of Eldon's victims, killed before he could molest and murder a five-year-old named Rachel Poole. Rachel Poole is the young girl he is speaking to now.

Why am I seeing this? Sara thinks. *I don't want to see this.*

Before Sara had her vision of Tim Wilson bludgeoning his new partner to death, she had psychically observed another scene of murder. For several nights running, Sara had involuntarily revisited Aberystwyth in her visions, and witnessed Navid Kapadia killing himself and his two young children in a fiery blaze. Those were the very events that Eldon Carson had foreseen three years earlier – the ones that had started him on his deadly spree of murder-for-justice. Sara had not understood why Carson's old vision had nagged at her with such frequency, until she'd had the new one, of Tim Wilson and Philip Berger.

Then it had made a kind of sense. The Kapadia murders were a tragedy that Carson had managed to prevent – albeit in his own homicidal way. With her new vision, Sara realised the connection. Wilson's murder of Berger was something that she could prevent. That was when she had decided that Wilson would be Success Number Four.

But today she wants to see more about Gerrit Vos. What will this vision of Rachel Poole's death contribute to that? What is this sickening scene unfolding before her mind's eye trying to tell her?

'Hey – are you lost?' Haney asks. He is a paunchy sixty-something with thinning hair that he dyes a luxuriant brown. It doesn't match the loose skin and wrinkles of his face. He has a Birmingham accent.

Rachel shakes her head. 'No – there's my towel,' she replies.

He looks. Arches an eyebrow. 'Where are Mummy and Daddy?'

Rachel shakes her head again. She doesn't know.

Haney nods. 'What's your name, darling?'

'Rachel,' she tells him.

'Well, Rachel, my name's Mr Haney, and I'm a teacher. I'm used to helping little girls like you. Would you like my help?'

Rachel nods. Yes, she would.

Suddenly, a blanket of dread rolls over Sara. She is about to witness this girl's rape and murder. *No, no, no, she thinks, I really can't see this happen! I wasn't supposed to see this happen!*

'Is this where you last saw your parents, Rachel?' Haney says.

She shakes her head and points across the road, towards the fun fair.

'At the caravans?' he asks. 'Well, I have a caravan,

82

too,' he says. Haney rolls to his knees and stands. His knees pop as he does. Haney blocks the sun by saluting, peers over at the fun fair and caravans, and then holds out his hand to Rachel. 'Come on, darling – I'll take you over there.'

Trustingly, Rachel reaches for him.

Sara realises she is trembling, sobbing. It is partly the horror she feels at having to witness what she is certain she's about to see, and partly the sense of betrayal she feels at ... at whatever perverse power wants to show her these grisly deaths that Carson prevented.

Hand in hand, Edmund Haney and Rachel Poole walk across the street. Before them lies the fun fair. To their right, row-upon-row of holiday caravans. 'My caravan's back there,' Haney says. 'Where's yours?'

'I don't have one,' Rachel says.

Haney frowns down at the girl. 'Then where do you sleep?'

'At my home in Aberystwyth.'

'Oh,' Haney exclaims. 'Then where did you lose your parents?'

'Over there,' Rachel says, pointing to the colourful plastic slide that dominates the fun fair.

'Well, as a rule,' Haney says, 'you should always stay in the place you last saw someone. It makes it easier for them to find you.'

Haney leads Rachel towards the slide. 'Where were they standing?' he asks.

'Right by those stairs,' she says, pointing again.

'Then let's stand there too, OK?' Haney suggests. 'I'm sure Mum and Dad are looking for you, and they're probably frightened out of their wits.'

Pins and needles tingle through Sara. *What is happening?* She watches Haney gently let go of Rachel Poole's hand as soon as they reach the bottom of the slide's metal stairs. She sees them wait. Haney does not touch the little girl, or even speak to her as he surveys the holiday-makers. Sara tries to read his thoughts, and feels nothing except the focus of someone performing a simple task with all his attention. Haney scans for a couple searching for a lost daughter, and that is all. Sara can sense no passion, no lust – nothing that would lead to Rachel Poole's death by this man's hand.

Will there be a twist to this tale, she wonders, something she cannot read? Sara moves the scene forward a few minutes, until she sees a couple in their early thirties rush towards Haney and Rachel. The blonde woman sweeps her daughter into her arms as Haney points to the beach explaining. Rachel's father nods in gratitude and shakes his hand ...

The family leaves. Sara focuses on Haney as he watches them move across the street to retrieve their towels. That is where Haney wants to go too, Sara senses – back to his towel, to lie some more in the sun – but he doesn't want to follow the family. That would be awkward. Instead, Haney buys a hot dog, and eats it as he watches Rachel Poole and her parents leave the beach with their possessions. Mr Poole pops open the boot of his car and loads in the cooler and towels as Mrs Poole straps Rachel into her safety seat.

'Ceri, I need to ask you a question.'

Sara sat at the dining table, her mobile next to her on speakerphone. She had been brooding over a cup of coffee, lost in a morass of conflicting thoughts. The vision she had intended to have this morning – one that would have revealed more about Gerrit Vos, and possibly her own brother – had not materialised. However, what had shown up was even more troubling

'I know what your question is,' Ceri's voice replied,

'and the answer is yes. You *will* need a swimming costume. Don't bother buying sun cream though – we'll get it there. The same goes for beach towels and floppy hats.'

'This isn't about Mallorca,' Sara sighed.

'Why the hell not?' Ceri said.

Sara pressed on. 'Do you remember Rachel Poole,' she asked, 'the girl Eldon Carson thought he'd saved from that retired headmaster?'

'Haney,' Ceri said immediately. 'He was Carson's fourth victim. The Pooles still live in town; Rachel goes to Plascrug School. They're fine.'

Ego leapt onto the chair next to Sara, and from there onto the table. He rubbed his moulting brown fur against her face. 'That's good to hear,' Sara said, gently pushing away the cat, 'but it's actually Edmund Haney I'm interested in. Eldon Carson was convinced that Haney was going to assault and then murder the girl.'

'I remember.'

'Did Haney have a criminal record?'

'No,' Ceri said, 'but that didn't make him innocent. Whatever the bastard did in his life, he got away with it.' She chuckled. 'At least until he got to Clarach.'

Sara cleared her throat. Over the years, she had grown used to the way her friend jumped to unsubstantiated conclusions. It was a habit Ceri shared with Jamie, and Sara had always considered it a side effect of being a cop. Sara had found it was best handled by ignoring it. There was no point in reminding Ceri she had no proof of Haney having done anything he needed to "get away with."

'Don't get me wrong,' Ceri went on. 'That Carson character was bat shit crazy, and he had no reason to murder Haney. It's just that our headmaster was a bit of a wrong 'un himself.'

Sara took a sip of coffee, which she could barely taste.

85

She plucked a strand of Ego's fur from her lip. 'Haney was from Solihull, wasn't he?' she asked. 'Did the West Midlands Police ever search his home?'

'Of course,' Ceri said. 'They found what you'd expect to find on his laptop.'

Sara paused, and her stomach tightened. Whether it was reacting in dread or hope, she could not tell. 'They found child pornography?'

'Nothing graphic,' Ceri replied. 'Naked little girls, mostly downloaded from naturist websites. You know, frolicking on the beach, that sort of lark. Not illegal, I suppose, but it still gives you pause. Let's just say Haney didn't collect any other kinds of photos.'

Sara tried to rationalise this. It seemed possible that Haney had indeed possessed an unhealthy attraction to girls, just as Eldon Carson had claimed. And yet, the retired headmaster seemed to have done nothing else that was inappropriate. Maybe, Sara thought, she had seen only a precursor to the horror that Carson said he'd witnessed. It was possible that the event she'd watched in Clarach was only Haney's introduction to Rachel Poole. Maybe later he....

But no, Sara told herself. It wasn't possible. Haney's alleged crime would have had to happen on that particular holiday, and Sara had stayed in her trance and followed Haney through the rest of his stay. She had watched the man sunbathe, sleep, read and listen to the radio – right up until the moment she'd seen Eldon Carson creep through the dark and knock gently on the door of Haney's caravan.

That was when she had terminated the vision. Sara had not needed to see Eldon execute an innocent man. And, she had to admit, Edmund Haney had been innocent. Sara had no doubt that Carson believed Haney would kill Rachel ... but Carson's vision had been wrong.

It *must* have been wrong.

'Why are you dredging this up all of a sudden?' Ceri asked.

'I don't know,' Sara sighed. 'Maybe because Jamie's doing some consulting for Andy Turner ...'

'You told me,' Ceri said.

'I suppose it's brought back a few bad memories.'

'Forget them,' Ceri said. 'That's the best thing you can do.'

'I do try,' Sara lied. 'It's not easy.'

If Eldon Carson had been wrong about what had happened on the beach in Clarach, she thought, how could she vouch for the reliability of *any* of his visions? At least, the ones she had not also seen herself.

For that matter, how could she trust her own visions either?

Sara could hear Ceri clicking her tongue – something her old friend did when trying to sound contemplative. 'Well,' Ceri finally said, drawing out the word as if she were about to reveal the wisdom of Solomon, 'if you're having trouble relaxing, there *is* one sure-fire solution. It'll be pleasant as hell and guaranteed to help you forget your troubles ...'

From that moment, their conversation was all about sun, swimming pools, and sangria.

After she'd said goodbye to Ceri, Sara's mood lowered. Ever since Eldon Carson made contact with her at the farmhouse in Penweddig, Sara had believed in his powers as strongly as he did himself. As she grew in her abilities, Sara had come to believe in them as well. Under Carson's guidance, she had witnessed a lone gunman rampaging through the streets of Shrewsbury, exactly as Carson had seen it before her. Exactly as the press had reported too. And Sara knew that the vision she'd had of Rhodri killing their parents had also been true. Her brother had confirmed it, just before Sara had allowed him to die.

This meant that Sara had no reason to doubt that psychic powers existed, or that she and Carson had each demonstrated them. But, she thought, the bigger question was, were they always reliable?

Eldon Carson had once told Sara that the future was not fixed; instead, it was a series of probabilities. In some cases, those probabilities were evenly balanced in favour of more than one outcome. Then, the future truly was unpredictable. In other instances, all probabilities pointed in the same direction – and it was when Carson had a vision like this, in which all probabilities indicated a future murder, that he knew he needed to respond.

And yet, he'd been wrong about Haney. And it had cost the poor man his life.

This line of thought jarred loose another, older one. It was something that had been niggling at the edges of Sara's consciousness for months – a troubling conundrum she had repeatedly swatted away like a midge. Sara's persistent concern was this: Eldon Carson had killed people to prevent the murders he believed, through his use of psychic powers, they would commit. Carson's last intended victim had been Sara's own brother, Rhodri Jones. Had Carson not been stopped by armed police, he would have cut Rhodri's throat at the Hampshire Air Show.

So what murder had Carson been trying to prevent?

It was true that Rhodri had gone on to kill someone that very evening: a young escort named Maja Bosco. It was also true that Rhodri had a history of beating women. However, it was widely assumed by friends, police, and press alike that there were mitigating circumstances. All agreed that Rhodri had committed murder accidentally, after becoming unhinged by Carson's attack. Of course,

Sara knew, this did not excuse her brother. Had Rhodri not been brutal in the first place, that 'accident' would not have occurred. And yet, Sara had nonetheless accepted the basic theory: Rhodri Jones had killed his victim as a result of his confrontation with Eldon Carson at the Hampshire Air Show.

Which meant that Carson had *caused* Rhodri to kill.

Which also meant that, if Carson had not gone after Rhodri in the first place, Rhodri would *not* have committed murder.

Which meant ... what?

Had Eldon Carson not realised that the act he was trying to prevent would actually be caused by his own attempt to stop it?

Had he not seen that, without his intervention, there would have been no murder in the first place?

Sara wondered how on earth Carson could have been so blind.

And, seeing this now, she also wondered whether she could completely trust her own visions. Sara knew she had to allow for the possibility she was equally blind regarding Gerrit Vos.

And also Tim Wilson.

EIGHT

Jamie sat in his Range Rover in the car park outside Hollybush House. He opened the document wallet Vos had given him. The information inside was disappointingly pedestrian. There was glossy maroon-and-white publicity bumph about Thorndike Aerospace – *security on land, sea, air and online* – and some non-classified briefings about Thorndike's recent bids to assorted governments. There was also a black-and-white laser print of a bald, slightly overweight man with puffy eyes. Underneath it, Vos's boxy handwriting identified him as Levi Rootenberg, and included a phone number.

Vos had told Jamie about the man's background at the end of their meeting. Rootenberg, Jamie had learned, spent his early career as an engineer, in both the aerospace and mining sectors. Later, he used the contacts he had made in the defence industry to set himself up as an arms broker. A few years earlier, Rootenberg's licence to transfer controlled goods had been withdrawn by the Department for Business, Innovation and Skills, making him an ex-arms broker. Despite this, Vos had asked Jamie to meet with Rootenberg. Vos would not explain what the meeting was to be about, saying that details would be provided when they met. He had simply told Jamie to act as his representative, and report back.

Jamie suspected that this was the reason for their conversation about morality. If Thorndike wanted to do business through an unlicensed broker, chances were good that the transaction wouldn't be entirely legal. But, Jamie wondered, how illegal would it be? Or, more to the point, how immoral? He knew what Sara would say – she would tell him to drop the whole business. But the truth was, Jamie wanted the work. He wanted to pay his own way. He did not want to rely on Sara.

Jamie decided to find out more about this Rootenberg character before they met. If the man seemed completely disreputable, Jamie would swallow his pride, reconcile himself to living with Sara's support for a while longer, and tell Gerrit Vos and Andy Turner *no thanks*. However, if Rootenberg seemed potentially sound, he would attend a meeting with the man.

If Jamie had still been a cop and Rootenberg the suspect of an investigation, the research would have been simple. Jamie would have started by looking for criminal records in the Police National Computer – the withdrawal of Rootenberg's licence might well be linked to some charge that had been filed against him. If he had found any charges, Jamie would have checked the Met's own Intelligence System. There, officers would have noted any interactions they had had with him. Jamie's status as a detective inspector would also have opened doors at the Department of Social Services, the Department for Work and Pensions and the Passport Office. Without a badge, however, Jamie knew he would need help from someone who had one.

He reached for his phone.

Retired DCI Stephen Ash lived with his wife in a village near Tunbridge Wells. Their house was Edwardian, but at some point had been renovated, its original features lost to deep-pile carpeting and moulded coving. These alterations were not recent; the place had the ragged air of a nest from which the children had flown, leaving only school photos on scuffed wallpaper. Jamie had arrived at midday to find his father's old friend pottering about the house alone. Ash's wife, the man explained, was at the leisure centre.

'Aerobics,' he said. 'Donna can still stretch like a 20-year-old – and I can't even pick up a dropped sandwich.'

He considered, and added, 'Want a sandwich?'

Jamie did not know Stephen Ash well, but his conversation with Gerrit Vos had placed Ash within easy mental reach – the former chief inspector had been a close friend of George Harding. Also, like Jamie's father, Ash had an old-school attitude about things like using police databases for personal reasons. Had Jamie asked one of his own contemporaries, they'd have been horrified by the suggestion of such illegality. So would Jamie have been, until recently. After setting the world to rights with Vos, a small breach like this didn't seem all that bad. It certainly hadn't phased Ash, who had agreed to get on the phone, call in some old favours, and dig up what he could in the couple hours it would take Jamie to round the M25 from Surrey to Kent.

Jamie declined lunch but accepted a bottle of beer. They sat in the living room, chairs angled towards a blank television screen, Classic FM drifting through the hatch from the kitchen. 'I was surprised to hear you'd quit the Met,' Ash said between bites of roast beef on Polish rye. 'I suppose nobody came out of that mess in Wales looking good. Killer had to be taken out by the Hampshire Constabulary. You get any blowback from that?'

Jamie shook his head. 'Nobody filed a complaint. Dyfed-Powys Police held a Serious Case Review, and they commended everyone involved.'

'Really?' Ash chewed and swallowed. 'Then why'd you go?'

Jamie understood why Ash might not be able to fathom his decision. The man had been investigated by the Met in the same corruption sweep that had caught up Jamie's own father. George Harding had suffered the first of his strokes before the investigation's conclusion, but Ash had seen it through to the end. Although he was never charged, the odour of the investigation had clung to his career, and he had never made it to superintendent. On some level that must have irked him, and probably contributed to his confusion as to why Jamie, subjected to scrutiny but offered honest-to-God praise, had walked away.

'There's more than one way to suffer blowback,' Jamie said. 'When I got back to London, everything seemed different. I felt I was in the wrong place.'

'And this aerospace company is the right place?'

'I didn't say that.' Jamie took a pull on his beer. 'But for now ... well, it's interesting.'

'I've looked into your guy,' Ash said. He balanced his sandwich plate on the arm of the chair and reached, wheezing, for a spiral notebook that sat on a nest of tables. 'You're lucky I've still got friends who'll do me a favour in a hurry.' He flipped some pages. 'This Rootenberg bloke was born in 1969 in Salisbury, Rhodesia – now known as Harare, Zimbabwe. He still holds a Zimbabwean passport. As his name suggests, Mr Rootenberg is white. On a not-unrelated matter, his family was forced to sell their farm to the government in the late 1990s. He became a UK resident in 2001.'

Jamie produced his own notebook from his jacket pocket, and scribbled notes as Ash spoke.

'He is registered with Companies House as director and sole shareholder of Rootenberg Global, which lists its main activity as security consultancy. The business may have an impressive name, but Rootenberg's not a big player: his company holds less than ten grand in cash, and is owed another five by debtors. It has net assets of fourteen k and liabilities of about the same.'

'I appreciate your researching that,' Jamie said. 'I did plan to check Companies House myself. What I can't get access to is the Police National Computer and the Met's Intelligence System.'

Ash finished chewing another bite of sandwich. He dabbed some mustard from the corner of his lip. 'My friends checked both of them for me,' he said. 'Even though they shouldn't have.'

Jamie inclined his head – a show of appreciation.

'Still, you're going to be underwhelmed by what they found. On a couple of occasions, the Met took an interest in your man for meeting with certain individuals on their radar. They put him under surveillance, but it never led anywhere. On a later occasion, he was arrested over a shipment of handguns from south-eastern Europe. He lost his export licence, but the criminal case against him was dropped.'

Ash tried to set the notepad on the arm of the chair, but it teetered and dropped to the floor. His waved hand informed the notepad that it could stay there. 'In short,' Ash said, 'this guy seems to have skirted the fringes of what's legal, but he was never Public Enemy Number One. And now, without a licence, it looks like he's out of the picture.'

Jamie tucked his notebook back into his pocket and took another swallow of beer. 'I'm sorry I asked you to put yourself on the line for such little return.'

Ash waved away Jamie's apology. 'You working a private case, or is this something for Thorndike?'

Jamie hesitated. 'I don't want to sound ungrateful -'

'But you can't say,' Ask concluded. 'Don't worry, it doesn't matter. I'm just happy to see you again. It's been too long.'

Ash finished one half of his sandwich and chewed contemplatively. He bobbled his head, as though weighing a new thought. 'But if you really do want to thank me,' he said off-handedly, 'there is one thing you might do.'

Jamie spread his hands in a gesture that said, *Of course, ask me anything*.

'Go visit your father.'

Jamie started. 'I'm sorry?'

'I spoke to your mother,' Ash said. 'She told me you haven't seen George in over a year.'

Jamie realised he was breathing through his mouth. *That's why Ash wanted me to drive over here in person*, he thought. Jamie pursed his lips and swallowed. 'I've seen Mum,' he said. 'A few times, in fact.'

'She told me. George's nursing home is two miles from Grace's cottage. Were you too busy for the extra drive?'

Jamie twitched, as if Ash had surprised him with a sucker punch. He didn't like being bushwhacked by someone he trusted. And Ash wouldn't understand his explanation anyway, Jamie thought. He'd had little to say to his father even before George Harding's decline. Now what could they possibly discuss? George still remembered people and could manage a conversation, but his second stroke had damaged the frontal lobe of the brain. That was the part that regulated inhibitions – the part that had once kept George, like everyone, in check. Without the supervision of an inner censor, his conversation was now uninhibited, and his judgements even more severe than they had been when Jamie was growing up. George Harding had always found his son a mild disappointment. Jamie had not gone to Oxford University, and had not become a lawyer. Instead, he joined the Metropolitan Police just like George, and that had been the ultimate let-down. The truth was, Jamie did not relish giving his father the opportunity to point this out – especially since George had been sheared of the traditional inhibition of tact.

Jamie noticed Ash's hazel eyes peering at him sharply. 'You'll see your dad, won't you, son?' he said.

'Of course,' Jamie replied, and at the same time wondered how clogged the M25 would be. He'd take it as far as the M23, and might make it to Brixton before –

'Now?' Ash persisted. 'You'll go to see him *now*, right?'

Jamie smiled winningly. 'Sure.'

Ash nodded curtly. 'How long will it take you to drive there?'

Bloody hell, what's he up to? Jamie thought. 'Maybe forty-five minutes,' he said.

Stephen Ash lowered the plate to the deep-pile carpet, and struggled out of his chair. He shuffled to the landline on the other side of the room. 'I'm sure your mother will want to join you at the nursing home,' he said, lifting the receiver. 'I'll let her know when to arrive.'

Until 2000, Grace Harding had been an administrator for a sixth form college in Ashford. After her husband's first stroke, she took voluntary severance to become his full-time carer. At first, this involved tasks as intimate as helping her husband eat and being on hand when he was in the lavatory. Later, it meant driving him to physio and speech therapy, and keeping him from getting so bored that his frustration with his new condition boiled over into desperate rage. By that time, Jamie had left home for university. Although he felt sorry for his mother – much more, he had to admit, than for his father – he was also relieved to be out of the house and living the autonomous life of a student. As George improved, Grace spoke about finding another job, but for whatever reason, that had not happened. After George's second stroke, he had moved into the Holly Lodge Residential Care Centre, and the place became Grace's second home.

Now, Jamie waited for her under the building's awning. He peered past the circular driveway towards the road, playing a mental game with the cars that swept past on their way to Ashford. He had been standing there for twenty minutes, and could have gone inside at any time ... but he hadn't wanted to be alone with his father. Finally, Jamie saw his mother's green Ford Focus roll around the drive and into the car park. An unexpected tingle of gratitude rose inside – her presence, he thought, would diffuse the tension of the visit. Then he remembered that he would not have come at all had Stephen Ash not rung his mother in the first place.

Grace Harding climbed from the car. She was a tall woman whose copper hair had been lightened over the years by a dusting of white. She had Jamie's green eyes – or rather, he had hers – and they shared the same quick grin. She offered him one now as she approached.

'Well, look at you,' Jamie drawled, appraising her quilted Barbour jacket, jeans and wellingtons. 'You look like you've been hiking the grounds of your stately home.'

'All ten square metres of them,' she said. 'And it's more of a stately cottage.' She nodded at the door to the care centre. 'You've not been in?'

'I got caught up in a game,' he said.

Grace raised her eyebrows. Jamie answered her unspoken question by pointing to the Maidstone Road. 'A passing white car is worth one point,' he explained. 'So is a blue car. Green ones get two and reds are worth three.'

'So, I'm only a two?' Grace asked.

'Your car's a two,' Jamie replied. 'I'm sure you're worth more. Yellow cars score ten, but silver or black ones cost five points each. Vans count the same as cars, and I ignore lorries. The goal is to reach fifty points without sliding into negative numbers.'

'What's your score?'

'Six,' he admitted. 'There are a lot of silver cars out there.'

Grace smiled and brushed Jamie's fringe from his forehead. 'Your dad will be so glad you've come,' she said.

'He won't,' Jamie replied matter-of-factly.

She let her hand fall to Jamie's shoulder and turned him towards the door. 'Well, whatever he thinks,' she said, 'I'm glad you came.'

Inside, they walked along the carpeted corridor to the heavy door of the secure unit. Designed for residents who required significant care or couldn't be trusted to stay put, the unit was accessible only by swipe card or admittance by one of the overburdened staffers. Grace pressed the bell and peered through the narrow glass window. She waived to the nurse stationed behind a counter, who buzzed them in.

'Morning, Grace,' called the nurse in a thick Jamaican accent. 'Here to take him off my hands?'

'Has he been trouble today?'

'He's trouble every day,' she said good-naturedly. 'There's one in every ward, and in this one, your husband is it.'

Grace offered an apologetic shrug.

'You'll find him in the sunroom.'

Grace motioned for Jamie to follow her down the broad corridor. Jamie imagined that the hallways had to be this wide to accommodate wheelchairs, as well as the occasional emergency gurney. The disproportionate width of the corridors made the unit look like a hospital – which was, after all, the most honest description of the place.

Its true purpose was something that could not be disguised by the well-upholstered chairs, the flower vases or the prints on the wall. Not when Jamie could hear confused shouts and distressed cries emanating from several rooms. He could also smell the tang of disinfectant mingling with the odour of human shit – it made for a pungent memento mori, reminding visitors that death stalked these wide hallways of Holly Lodge.

Jamie hated this place.

George Harding's last stroke had near-paralysed the left side of his body. Although time and physio had helped to restore some of his cruder motor skills, it was unlikely that he would ever speak without a slur, or use his left arm with finesse. George had got to the point where he could walk with a stick, but today he had been wheeled into the sun room, and sat near the window in a wheelchair.

Jamie's mother strode towards her husband with her habitual vigour, almost unobtrusively producing a handkerchief and wiping a fleck of spittle from his lower lip. As she did, she said, 'You've dressed nicely today. Did Doris help you?'

'New girl,' George said. 'Think she's Indian. Nicer than Doris.'

'Doris is lovely,' Grace said.

'Doesn't like me. Says I shout.'

'Sometimes you do shout,' Grace reminded him. 'You can be very rude.'

George grunted and gazed at the trees in the garden. Grace nudged him. 'George? You have a visitor.'

Jamie had been standing in the double doorway. Now

he stepped tentatively towards his father. 'Hi, Dad,' he said. 'Sorry I haven't seen you for a while. I've been busy.'

Slowly, George turned his head and stared at his son.

'George?' Grace said. 'It's Jamie.'

George didn't blink. 'I know,' he replied.

'How are you feeling?' Jamie asked.

George looked up at Grace. 'Take me to my room,' he said.

'George!' Grace admonished.

'Dad –' Jamie began.

'*Take me to my room!*' George shouted. 'You!' he said to Jamie. 'You wait here.'

Grace looked at Jamie and widened her eyes helplessly. Jamie inclined his head: *best to humour him*. Grace frowned with resignation, grasped the handles of the chair and wheeled George around. Soon Jamie stood alone in the sun room. He sat on a plush floral sofa, its cushions trimmed with viscose frills. On a table before him lay an array of periodicals: *Saga, Country Life, Tatler*, and several supplements from the Sunday papers. They all looked unread. Jamie wondered who they were intended for in a ward populated by stroke victims and dementia sufferers. Guests like him? If so, they'd made the wrong choices. He sighed and picked up a month-old *Telegraph Magazine*.

Before he could settle on an article to read, there was a thump against the doorframe. 'Clumsy!' his father barked.

Grace shushed him quietly and pushed him into the room. Jamie was surprised to see that George had a hardcover book in his lap. Something about Fascist Italy. Much too loudly, George said, 'You've got a girlfriend.'

'Err –' Jamie replaced the magazine. 'I have,' he acknowledged. 'Her name is Sara.'

Grace parked George at the edge of the coffee table.

'She's too skinny,' George went on.

'You've never met her,' Jamie reminded him.

With his good hand, George opened the book on his lap and pulled out a folded sheet of A4 paper. He shook it and it unfolded. 'Skinny,' he repeated, and tossed the paper towards Jamie. It missed the tabletop and fluttered to the floor.

Jamie sighed and picked it up. On it was an inkjet-printed photo that Jamie had emailed to his mother shortly after he and Sara had started seeing each other. In it, Sara was curled up in a cane armchair in her Pimlico flat, an African tribal mask glowering behind her. Jamie could date the photo almost exactly: he had taken it on his phone about a week after the tragic conclusion of a case of teenage murder-suicide – the investigation that had brought them together. Neither of them had known it at the time, but Sara had been pregnant then.

'You gonna marry her?'

'I hope to. We already live together.'

'Mum says she's a big-time doctor.'

Jamie nodded. 'A psychiatrist.'

'Why would she settle for you?' George asked. 'You're just police.'

Grace shot Jamie a sharp glance, but Jamie was already saying, 'I'm not with the Met anymore, Dad. I quit the force some time ago.'

George blinked.

'I hadn't told him,' Grace said under her breath.

'You quit?' George said.

Jamie shrugged. 'I was never a very good police officer.'

George considered this. 'You take money?' he asked suddenly.

'Nothing like that,' Jamie reassured him. He slid across the sofa towards the wheelchair and took his father's hand. It lay in his palm unresponsive; he kept hold of it anyway. 'I just wanted to do other things.'

'Yeah?' George said dubiously. 'Like what?'

'He's gone back to university, George,' Grace said. 'In London this time. He's training to be a lawyer.'

George looked at his wife with suspicion. 'That true?' he said to Jamie.

'It's true, Dad,' Jamie said. 'A lawyer – like you always wanted me to be.'

George looked up at Grace with incredulous irritation. 'Why the hell didn't you tell me?'

Jamie decided it was best to leave out the details. No doubt his father wanted to imagine him as a tough, blustering barrister, defending high-ranking criminals before the High Court. Or maybe as a corporate attorney, surveying the City from the floor-to-ceiling window of a thirtieth-floor boardroom. George Harding might have been less sympathetic towards the notion of human rights law, if he could even comprehend what that phrase –

Jamie's thoughts were disturbed by his mother leaning past him, looming over his father. She was close enough for Jamie to smell her perfume – it was Jean-Paul Gaultier. Sometimes Sara wore it too.

'Quiet now, you big old baby,' Grace murmured softly.

Jamie looked up to see her dabbing her handkerchief against her husband's cheeks.

George Harding was crying.

NINE

Jamie stepped out of the lift that had whisked him up fifteen flights to the top-floor café of a central London hotel. Its windows boasted wonderful sights. One side overlooked the pointed spire of All Souls church and the Portland stone prow of BBC Broadcasting House; beyond that, the panorama stretched from Hampstead Heath to South-West London. The other side took in the BT Tower and the cluster of high-rise offices that made up the City. The morning had turned out sunny, and from this vantage point, all of London seemed to sparkle. Despite this, Jamie found Levi Rootenberg at a small table that overlooked neither vista. Even though window tables with postcard views were plentiful in the near-empty café, the man had chosen a seat nestled into an alcove. He was sipping a latte in semi-darkness.

Jamie introduced himself and shook his new associate's hand. 'Shame to waste the view,' he said, still standing. 'I'm sure it's included in the price of the coffee.'

Rootenberg waved his hand dismissively. 'I grew up in Africa,' he said. 'I've seen enough sun to last me a lifetime. That's why I like London. These bright days are mercifully rare here.'

Jamie shrugged and sat. Although Andy Turner was technically his boss, Jamie knew he really answered to

Gerrit Vos. That had been true from the moment he'd accepted this assignment. And if Vos had decided that Jamie should hear Rootenberg's plans for global domination, and Rootenberg wanted to announce them here in the gloom, well … then Jamie's job was to sit and listen.

He ordered coffee. 'Mr Vos is an old friend,' Rootenberg began. 'We have worked together for many years, Gerrit and I. He trusts me.'

Jamie nodded. It seemed important to Rootenberg that Jamie believed this. 'I don't doubt that,' he said. 'Still, isn't it odd that he's asked me to speak to you, instead of doing it in person? Do you know why he might have done that?'

Rootenberg offered a world-weary smile. 'Safer that way,' he said. 'Within any company, certain things need to be handled discreetly. And as for why you specifically are talking to me … well, as I understand it, Gerrit is coddling you as a favour to Andrew Turner.' Rootenberg's hands fluttered modestly. 'Gerrit knows who to turn to for professional discretion.'

Jamie had already had a taste of Vos's discretion. At their meeting, right before mentioning Rootenberg, Vos had informed Jamie that the hours Andy billed for his services would be listed as *consultation on site security at Thorndike offices and manufacturing facilities*. 'With so much terrorism these days,' Vos had said, 'no one's going to question our wanting to beef up security protocols.' He had chuckled and added, 'The downside is, you may actually have to be seen staring at a few wire fences in Lancashire.'

'When you say discreet,' Jamie said to Rootenberg, 'what do you mean, exactly? Immoral? Illegal?'

Rootenberg looked at him with hooded eyes, a few seconds longer than was comfortable. Either he was incredulous that Vos would send someone who'd ask such a question, or else he simply wanted to register mild contempt. 'I mean,' he said with extra-precise enunciation, 'arms deals with my home country.'

'Your country?'

'Zimbabwe,' Rootenberg said. He inclined his head. 'When I was born, they called it Rhodesia. Throughout my childhood, it was a rather troubled place. I personally lived through more than one guerrilla attack. When I was eleven, those self-same guerrillas won, and suddenly we were supposed to call them the government. I found myself in a brand-new country, with a new name.'

'That must have been disorientating,' Jamie said.

Rootenberg laughed. 'That's one word for it. After I left Zimbabwe for university in South Africa, I never really returned. But my family stayed. And then, in the late 1990s, my parents were forced to sell their farm to the government.'

Jamie nodded, as though this were the first time he'd heard this. The waiter placed Jamie's coffee, along with a packaged biscuit, next to him. Rootenberg waited for the man to glide out of earshot. 'So, you see,' he went on, 'my relationship with "home" is a complex one. And yet, I still hold a Zimbabwean passport. And their government still values what I have to offer.'

'I don't know a lot about Zimbabwe,' Jamie said, 'but I do know that, despite the change in leadership, there are UN, EU and British arms embargoes against it because of their human rights record. Is that not right?'

'It is,' Rootenberg agreed. 'And yet, the government used to sell them Hawk jets back in the eighties and nineties. Even in 2000, two months before they banned arms sales to my country, the UK government agreed to sell them spare aircraft parts to use in their war in the Congo.'

105

Jamie thought about Vos, and his talk about the grey hinterlands of morality.

'Even today, the UK allows contractors to apply for an Export Licence to sell controlled goods to Zimbabwe,' Rootenberg said. He added, 'And why wouldn't they? The UN's own charter says every country has a right to self-defence. Last time I checked, Zimbabwe was still a country.'

Quickly, Jamie tried to work out what was really going on in the company he'd just joined. Thorndike was planning to do a deal with a proscribed state, he surmised, and they'd put Vos in the hot seat – not only because Business Development was his purview, but also because of his expertise in sneakiness. Vos had then hired a personal crony with an appropriate pedigree to see the deal through.

'Think of it this way,' Rootenberg continued. 'The government needs the UK's defence industry to succeed. There's not a single cabinet minister who doesn't act as a pimp for British weapons on every foreign trip. Before a minister even leaves this country, they get three separate briefings: one about the actual purpose of the trip, one on the political climate of the state they're going to, and one that gives them talking points the government would like them to raise.' He leaned back. 'You can guess what the key talking points often involve. Defence is a money-maker, my friend.'

If Thorndike Aerospace genuinely was entertaining the possibility of getting an export licence for Zimbabwe, they were dreaming, Jamie told himself. Working through this particular middleman, Thorndike was bound to lose any slight chance they may have had.

'As I understand it,' Jamie ventured, 'you aren't licensed to broker arms anymore.'

Rootenberg smiled sardonically. 'No flies on you,' he

said. 'You're right – I lost my licence over a minor bit of business involving ex-Yugoslav handguns. But then, I wasn't claiming I could obtain legal permission.'

Mentally, Jamie erased all his speculation about Thorndike's motives.

'I'm simply pointing out,' Rootenberg went on, 'that the issue isn't cut-and-dried. Nearly thirty countries have been accused of serious Human Rights violations – and the UK and Europe still exports billions of pounds worth of goods to them.'

Rootenberg drained his latte and raised his hand to the waiter for another. He chuckled warmly. 'Now, let me make you a deal,' he said. 'Why don't I tell you exactly what I'm proposing, and after that, you can tell me what a rotten piece of shit I am.'

Jamie smiled in spite of himself. 'Agreed.'

Rootenberg glanced from side to side, and lowered his voice. 'I have some friends who work in the Zimbabwean military. They are prepared to do me a favour.'

'For payment, presumably,' Jamie said.

'That's irrelevant to you,' Rootenberg replied. 'Whatever happens, such extraneous expenses would come out of my end.'

Rootenberg explained that the initial sale he planned to make to Zimbabwe was small – a consignment of fifteen-millimetre artillery shells. He hoped however that over time – and with Thorndike's unofficial backing – he may become trusted enough to sell his Zimbabwean chums other items. 'Zimbabwe's always in the market for rocket launchers and hand grenades,' he observed. 'Their own manufacturing industry's in the toilet. If we can earn their trust, I have grander visions than artillery shells, believe me. There's big money to be made.'

They fell silent again as the waiter delivered Rootenberg's latte. They offered patient half-smiles as they waited for him to leave. 'I can understand that Gerrit Vos doesn't want to be seen talking to you about this,' Jamie went on quietly, 'but why would he even have to? Presumably, you already know how you're going to transport the shells, and someone at Thorndike knows how to fudge their ultimate destination –'

'Such things needn't concern you,' Rootenberg said. 'It's not about this insignificant consignment of shells. If that were all it was, Thorndike Aerospace would never go near this deal. It's the long-term benefits that the company is interested in. Making friends in Africa right now is smart. Thorndike wants to be in a good position when international relations change.'

'And in the meantime they're willing to risk illegal deals?'

'There's very little risk,' Rootenberg said. 'But there's potentially great reward. That is why Gerrit wants an open line of communication with me.'

'And that open line of communication is …?'

'Yes, it's you. You're a personal messenger-boy between Gerrit Vos and me. That's especially important for a reason we have yet to discuss. This isn't going to be clear sailing – we have a very powerful rival.'

'Oh?'

Rootenberg explained that the rival's name was Strategic Ballistics, and that it was part of the consortium that held a legal monopoly on Russian arms exports. The company also held sway over a number of important figures in Zimbabwean military procurement. Rootenberg said he was relying on factionalism within the military to pave Thorndike's way towards lucrative deals. Rootenberg had formed personal alliances with the enemies of Strategic Ballistics' Zimbabwean supporters.

Jamie couldn't help but feel both bemused and intrigued by the labyrinthine world he had stumbled into.

He was being offered insights into the clash between first-and-third-world politics he was unlikely to get in his law degree. Indeed, he wondered whether this knowledge would prove useful to his education.

'We have to ally ourselves with one side,' Rootenberg continued, 'and there is only one side available to us. That does mean our long-term success will depend on an African country's internal politics – something we can't control.'

He smiled at Jamie. 'But in the meantime, we can at least sell them some artillery,' he said.

Sara took the tube to Green Park and walked up Piccadilly before cutting over to St James's Square and the offices of Andrew Turner & Associates. After yesterday's unsettling vision, Sara had realised that she could not trust her own psychic powers. At least, not until she had convinced herself once more that they were worth trusting.

Tomorrow evening would be the test. One of the details that Sara's psychic foray into Tim Wilson's life had unearthed was exactly where and when he would meet his lover-and-victim-to-be, Philip Berger. In a sense, Sara knew, the two men had already met – in a chatroom online. But their first face-to-face encounter had not happened yet. If Sara's visions could be trusted, that event would take place in a pub in Hackney on Saturday evening. Tomorrow. Sara planned to be there. If Wilson and Berger turned up, Sara would know that her visions of, and concern about, Wilson had some validity. If they didn't …

Well, maybe she would do what she had once threatened Eldon Carson she'd do, and find a way to resign from the psychic club.

In the meantime, Sara had two full days to do something productive. She still needed to find out rather a lot of information, because the problem of Gerrit Vos remained. Had Vos really been responsible for the deaths of union leaders in South Africa? As she could not prove the veracity of that vision with another vision, she had decided to try to discover further details in a more conventional way.

This morning, Sara had waited for Jamie to leave the flat, then rang Andy Turner's private mobile. She had asked to meet as soon as possible. Andy was at work, but told Sara that he was merely shuffling paperwork that day, and had no client meetings. He had offered to drive to Brixton immediately. Sara had not wanted to presume to that extent; she'd come to him, she'd said.

When Sara arrived at Andy's offices, she offered her name to the receptionist. The young woman eyed Sara with curiosity and picked up her phone. Sara glanced about the reception area and thought, not for the first time, how crucial aesthetics were to Andy. Art, design and colour palettes were as important to him as military lore – or even his professional devotion to high-priced defence consultancy. This place, Sara reflected, was painfully perfect in its juxtaposition of modern design and English traditionalism. There was only one objet d'art that seemed incongruous amidst the models of fighter aircraft and modern figurative paintings – a single Senufo tribal mask, that took pride of place on one of the office's most prominent walls. Sara knew, as no other visitor would have, that this was Andy's tribute to her, and her own aesthetic perfectionism.

Within seconds, Andy had emerged from behind the partition that separated the lobby from the offices. Recently, Sara had seen him wearing little other than an array of expensive suits. Today he was dressed for a period without clients, in a black Hugo Boss T-shirt, khaki cargo trousers and jungle pattern Paul Smith trainers. Sara had never thought of Andy as being especially physically fit, but in this outfit, it was hard not to notice his muscular arms and well-developed chest. He even showed a ripple of abs under his slim-cut shirt. Maybe Andy's unrealised childhood dream of joining the SAS hadn't been so far-fetched: he looked ready for an assault course.

Andy kissed her. 'At the moment,' he said, 'my office is a battlefield. I'm absolutely outflanked by hundreds of contracts and reports – and I think the paperwork is winning.' He motioned to a cosy corner of the reception area. 'Let's sit over here. Less of a mess.'

They sat, and by force of habit configured themselves in the way they had once done in Sara's office, during Andy's therapy sessions. Sara curled into a chair that faced him on the sofa. It felt just like old times. 'I have been working to exhaustion,' Andy said. 'Right now, I am organising the minutiae of an Investor Mingle for Thorndike's Investor Relations Team.'

Sara raised an eyebrow. 'A *mingle*?'

'We hold them now and again at some posh wine bar in the City. It's a chance for our investors to chat with the executives. It's never as formal as an investor update event or, God forbid, the Annual General Meeting – but it's important. The company is still struggling to make the move from subcontractor to prime contractor, so image has got to be Job One.'

Before long, Andy was explaining how to handle crowd control at AGMs, and how the company's security guards worked with police to corral the inevitable cluster of anti-war protestors. With typical indiscretion, he revealed Thorndike's tactics against the ones who had bought a few shares in the company, just so they could get inside the hall and disrupt proceedings. All the while, Andy drank mugs-full of Lady Grey tea, as Sara sipped a glass of sparkling water.

It wasn't until forty minutes later that Andy brought the conversation around to why Sara had come. 'I assume,' he said, 'this get-together has something to do with my most recent freelance consultant?'

Sara smiled. 'I've just been wondering where Jamie's new position might lead,' she said. 'I can't get any sense out of Jamie himself – he's so charged-up about working for you – but I do wonder about his relationship with Thorndike.'

'And your concern is entirely my fault,' Andy confessed. 'I should have cleared it with you first. It just happened so fast. Gerrit needed a security consultant, and so I mentioned Jamie and said a few things about his background. Before I knew it, Gerrit and I were in your living room, offering Jamie a contract.'

Sara nodded as if she believed him. Andy would never admit that he'd been looking for some time for a way to funnel money to her partner. She said, 'I suppose I'm just worried about Jamie getting involved with the defence industry, at the same time as he's planning a new career in human rights law.'

'He'd make a damn sight more money in defence,' Andy said. 'Especially with a law degree.'

Sara ignored this observation. 'This morning,' she said, 'Jamie mentioned meeting one of Vos's associates. Who is that?'

Andy frowned. 'An associate? That's the first I've heard of it,' he replied. 'Then again, I don't ask my consultants to report in moment-by-moment. I'm due to meet Gerrit on Monday, so I'm sure I'll find out then.' He sipped his tea and half-shrugged reassuringly. 'But don't worry. Whoever this person is will have been vetted very carefully. They'll be as trustworthy as Gerrit himself.'

That's what I'm worried about, Sara thought. 'Mr Vos

certainly has a long history with Thorndike,' she went on. 'He's been there at least since Rhoddo became CEO.'

'Longer.'

'I know he came to Rhoddo's attention when he sorted out that South African union dispute ...'

Sara hoped that Andy would assume she'd heard what she was about to say from Rhodri himself. 'There was a whiff of scandal about that, wasn't there?' she asked casually.

Sara waited expectantly. Andy furrowed his brow. 'I don't think so,' he said. 'Rhoddo never mentioned anything to me, at least. As I understand it, Gerrit managed to convince one of the community leaders to form a breakaway union. That saved countless jobs and resolved a touchy issue for the company. Gerrit came back a hero.'

'Right,' Sara said.

She wondered whether Andy was lying to her intentionally, or if instead Rhodri had lied to Andy. Or maybe even whether Rhodri genuinely had not known about the terrible crime that Vos had committed in South Africa. 'What I heard,' Sara said, 'was that, just before the new union was announced, some leaders of the established unions went missing.'

Andy raised his eyebrows. 'It wouldn't surprise me,' he said blandly. 'At that time, in that place, people disappeared all the time.' He peered over his mug of Lady Grey. 'Surely, you're not accusing Thorndike of anything?'

Sara smiled. 'Of course not.'

They sat in silence for a moment. When Andy spoke next, he had lost the glibness with which he often spoke. 'Rhoddo was a good man,' he said.

'He cared about you very much,' Sara replied.

Andy set down his mug. 'I should get back to work,'

he said, and stood with a stretch. 'If this union thing bothers you, I could try to find out more from Gerrit.'

'There's no need,' Sara said, rising to her feet. 'I just knew that Mr Vos was involved, and wondered about it, that's all.'

Andy led her back to the front door. They said goodbye, and Sara kissed Andy on the cheek. Just before she ventured back out into the sunlight, Andy put a hand on her arm. 'I would never let anything happen to Jamie,' he assured her. 'You know that, don't you?'

Ego had made a beeline towards his empty bowl before Jamie had even got through the front door. He now stood sentinel over it, peering at Jamie with imperious patience. Every home has a pecking order, and a home owner with a cat knows who's at the top – whether he likes cats or not. Dutifully, Jamie raised the bowl to the counter and opened a pouch of smelly, gelatinous meat product. Ego was already trying to eat it before Jamie had set it on the floor.

All the while, Jamie replayed in his mind the conversation he'd had with Levi Rootenberg. He no longer had any doubts about who the man really was. Stephen Ash may have cleared him legally, but Rootenberg had nailed his colours to the mast when it came to the morality of what he did.

The man had what might charitably have been called a nuanced understanding of international relations. It led him to take legal niceties like trade embargoes with a pinch of salt. So much of Jamie's more-conventional sense of morality reacted against this – but both Rootenberg and Vos had hinted that this exact provincial morality was what caused people to be blinkered. Jamie knew he simply did not have enough expertise within this niche to be certain of his own judgement. He wished there were someone he could go to for advice.

Jamie would have to wait and see what happened. But, he had to admit, Rootenberg's focus on the future – on an African continent whose countries were free from sanctions and open to British trade – was intriguing. Getting in on the ground floor could be the making of a fledgling prime contractor like Thorndike Aerospace.

Jamie wandered into the bedroom and placed his phone, wallet and keys on the dresser. If he could make this consultancy work, Jamie thought, he had the chance to earn rather a decent sum of money. He sat on the edge of the bed to remove his shoes. He had not previously acknowledged to himself how troubled, how *down*, his dependence on Sara had made him feel. He would face life so differently once he could pay his own way ...

As Jamie bent to unlace a shoe, his thoughts were waylaid by the sheen of a small object lying on the floor. It sat next to Sara's bedside chest of drawers, almost obscured by the duvet brushing against the floorboards. Jamie shoved his brogues out of the way and picked it up. It was a piece of jewellery on a leather thong. He peered at it. It had the handcrafted look of a trinket on offer at a car boot sale. It was made of papier mâché and varnished to a gloss. and Jamie caught his breath. Painted on its surface in delicate brush strokes was –

Jamie felt himself blanche. On the homemade disk was a drawing of the occult Eye-in-the-Pyramid symbol, with two scales of justice hanging at its base. The emblem used in Aberystwyth by the serial killer Eldon Carson.

For a moment, his mind grew numb, stunned by the appearance of something that was so out of place. It didn't make sense, appearing here, in his flat. As a sluggish jumble of thoughts started to awaken in his mind, Jamie found himself grasping at tendrils of thought, trying to figure out who might have dropped such a pendant there.

Even as he did, he knew that such a line of inquiry was stupid. This macabre piece of jewellery was right next to Sara's side of the bed, and the only two people in London linked to the image were himself and her.

This is Sara's. It has to be.

But how could she have obtained it? Eldon Carson had drawn this symbol on the bodies of his victims. Jamie recalled that, once, he had also inscribed it at the bottom of a letter to the police. But as far as Jamie knew, he had never fashioned his grisly symbol into a pendant. If Carson had done that, Jamie would have heard about it. And even if he had done so, Jamie thought, Sara would never have had a chance to touch such a thing. As soon as it was found, it would have been locked up as evidence. Wherever this macabre object had come from, there was one overriding question:

Why would Sara have kept it?

Jamie's mind was churning now. It was true that Sara had a tendency to collect things she felt a connection to. There were all the African masks and Aboriginal art for a start. But she also owned a small assortment of occult relics, left over from her days of researching such ephemera: tools for magical rituals, voodoo dolls, devices for divination ... Sara had always claimed to dislike these curios, but Jamie suspected she had a morbid fascination with them, and secretly took delight in possessing such artefacts. If she had come across a pendant once owned by the Aberystwyth killer, maybe acquiring it had been too much of a temptation.

But that didn't make sense. First of all, Sara did not keep her occult paraphernalia by her bedside. As far as Jamie knew, all that stuff was in a box at Ceri's house in Wales. And none was connected to an upsetting personal event, as this one was. Surely Sara couldn't have wanted to own it.

Jamie rose from the bed. He slipped the pendant into this pocket and wondered exactly when – and how – he could raise the issue with Sara.

TEN

The next morning, both Jamie and Sara woke up subdued. When Sara had arrived home the previous evening, Jamie had not been able to find the right way to raise the issue of the pendant he had discovered next to her side of the bed. He'd told himself they'd speak about it in the morning. But now it was morning, and he had no energy to handle whatever emotions would follow after he had raised the issue. Besides, starting a serious discussion now would be tactless – Sara looked like hell.

'Are you OK?' Jamie asked, thinking back to the way she had vomited the previous morning.

'I'm just tired,' she said.

'Would you like some toast?'

Sara sighed lethargically. 'A crumpet maybe.'

As Jamie boiled the kettle and slid a crumpet into each of the toaster's four slots, he wondered what he would say about the terrible artefact he had found whenever he had the courage to bring it up. After all, it was the symbol that the monster in Aberystwyth had killed people by, what he'd drawn on their dead bodies. Jamie thought of that fourteen-year-old kid – the one in the yellow T-shirt who had his throat cut, whose body was battered after death. That symbol was what Eldon Carson scribbled on his corpse. Why would Sara want to preserve something like that?

By the time he had buttered the crumpets and fixed the tea, Jamie had worked himself into enough of a state to believe he really could ask Sara that question. He set their breakfast on a tray, and strode into the next room. Before he could say anything, Sara rose and took the tray.

'I'll be going out today,' she said lifelessly.

All Jamie's righteous determination evaporated. Her voice sounded so hollow. 'Where?'

Sara placed the tray on the coffee table and shook her head aimlessly. 'I just need to get out.'

Jamie nodded understandingly. 'Would you like me to come?'

'Thanks,' she said, 'but I really want to ...'

Her voice trailed away. She wanted to be alone. 'Sure,' he said. 'I understand.'

Jamie didn't know what was eating away at Sara, but he understood that he'd have to wait it out. It seemed laughable that he needed to treat Sara in the same manner as he'd decided to approach Levi Rootenberg – to keep his eyes open, alter his opinions as necessary, and then act accordingly. But, it seemed, that was exactly what Sara needed.

Later, Sara emerged from the tube onto Tottenham Court Road, and walked north towards a certain church basement. There she knew she would find a twenty-eight-year-old named Ken Salter. Salter was the one special client Sara had taken pains to stay in touch with – maybe because he was her first, or maybe because he was an almost-perfect success story. And, now more than ever before, Sara needed to speak to a success story. Ken had been an alcoholic since his teens, and had spent more than two years of his life homeless. Because he tended to be a violent drunk, most of that time had been spent quite literally on the streets; Ken had alienated himself from everyone who could have offered him shelter or helped him to recover.

Everyone except for Sara Jones. With Sara's support, Ken had worked to tame his demons, moderate his drinking, and re-establish contact with the charities that could do him some good. Sara had managed to get Ken on a list for sheltered accommodation and, some months ago, he had moved into a small flat in a complex overseen by a live-in warden. Ken now attended AA meetings, and had stayed sober for five months. He was on benefits and volunteered at a soup kitchen in the basement of the church he had once relied on for meals.

Sara needed to see Ken today. He would lift her spirits, and provide her with a confidence boost before she ventured to Hackney and found out whether she could trust her visions.

By the time Sara arrived at the church, the kitchen was closed. Homeless women and men milled around the pavement outside as Sara descended the stone steps and rapped on the locked basement door. Ken, dishcloth in hand, answered and let her in. Grinning, he handed her a bottle of disinfectant. 'You spray, I'll wipe,' he said.

'Which table?' she asked.

'They're all filthy – pick one.'

Sara hadn't seen her former client for a couple of months. They cleaned tables and made small talk, listening to the rattling of pots in the kitchen behind them, until Ken peered at Sara with narrowed eyes. 'You're flustered,' he said.

'Sorry?' Sara replied.

'Uneasy. I can tell. You're not yourself.'

She smiled. 'You can read minds now?'

Ken set down his cloth. 'In a way,' he said. 'One thing being homeless does for you, is it teaches you to size up someone fast. Your life may depend on it.' He gestured to a black plastic chair. 'Sit down,' he said. 'Tell me what's wrong.'

Sara thought back to her first meeting with Ken on Oxford Street. She remembered the way he'd looked, talked and smelled. It was quite a contrast to the pleasant-looking man with thinning ginger hair and a slight paunch who stood before her now. The fact that Ken wanted to hear her troubles made her happy. Sara didn't actually think he could be of any help to her, but his concern felt like a further step in his amazing progress.

She sat. Obviously, she could not tell Ken the literal truth. However, she did manage to construct a vague story that didn't stray far from reality: a violent client whose future she worried about, a listless boyfriend grasping at a job she didn't think was right for him, and the low-level buzz of tension in those quieter moments between them.

Ken nodded understandingly. 'So you came here.'

'I was going to visit you anyway,' Sara said. 'We haven't seen each other for ages.'

'But it just so happens that you feel down,' Ken observed. 'I'm guessing you knew you'd find me well and reasonably happy. You know that has everything to do with what you've done for me, and you wanted to reassure yourself that you haven't been wasting your life.'

Sara raised her eyebrows. 'You should do this professionally.'

Ken offered her a grin. 'You've told me before that there were other charity cases after me,' he went on.

'A couple.'

'Do you visit them too?'

'No,' Sara said.

'Why not?'

Sara thought. The truth was, she hadn't liked the other two in the same way she liked Ken. When Sara had befriended this tragic person, and then managed to turn his life around, she'd felt a sense of gleeful triumph. Maybe it had been naive to expect the same miraculous results from subsequent patients.

There had been nothing wrong with the results she had obtained. Despite her more recent doubts, at the time Sara had been certain of the terrible crimes those patients would have committed, and equally sure that she had prevented them. But that was where things had ended. She had felt no particular warmth for Clients Two or Three – Ellie Giddings and Conor Lowe.

'I suppose,' Sara replied finally, 'you're just the special one, Ken.'

She expected another smile, but Ken pursed his lips. 'And what about this violent patient – is he a charity case too?'

Sara blinked. Ken was a surprising man; even when she remembered how perceptive he was, he could still say something that blindsided her. 'As a matter of fact, he is,' she said with a nod. 'But I haven't managed to bribe him the way I bribed you,' she said.

'He doesn't need money?'

'Everyone needs money. He hasn't let me offer it to him.'

Ken raised an eyebrow. 'Maybe you've been too honest with the guy.'

Sara looked at him sharply. 'What do you mean?'

Ken offered a friendly, mocking smile. 'Maybe you haven't lied to him as carefully as you lied to me.'

Sara recoiled. 'Ken!' she said. 'I never lied to you.'

He laughed good-naturedly. 'You're lying now ... or else you've forgotten. When we first met, you told me you worked at this canteen.'

Sara remembered – she had said that.

'I came here for tea that very afternoon. Asked about

you. Obviously, nobody had ever heard of you.'

'So you knew from the start that I told you something that wasn't true?'

'Sure.' Ken shrugged. 'But I didn't care. You gave me money and promised more. You could've said you were the Queen of Sheba and I'd have stuck around.'

He fiddled with one of the damp cloths. 'But it did make me curious. Once I started getting better, I visited the library.' He chuckled. 'You're easy to Google.'

'You researched me?'

Now Ken looked positively smug. 'Every time we met, I'd know a little more about you. That psychology book you wrote about magical thinking? I reviewed it on Amazon.'

'You didn't!'

'I never read it, of course, but I gave it five stars. And that investigation you were part of in Wales – that must've really been something.'

Sara tried to smile. 'It was,' she said.

'I want you to promise me one thing,' Ken told her. 'Some day – only when you feel like it – you'll take me out for coffee and tell me the whole story.'

Sara made a gesture of agreement. *Maybe not the whole story*, she thought.

'Only when you're ready,' Ken repeated and shook his head. 'You know Sara,' he added, 'I think I've made a hash of things.'

'How's that?'

'I asked you to sit down because you looked out of sorts, and I think I've made you worse.'

'I'm just surprised,' she admitted. 'I spent our time together trying to learn about you. I had no idea you were learning about me.'

'Only because I knew how much you were doing for me,' he said. 'Maybe I didn't catch on to that at first … but I came to understand. I owe you everything.'

For the first time ever, Ken Salter reached out and took Sara's hand. 'I'm glad you didn't give up on me,' he said. 'But I'll tell you something else – if I'd ever been violent towards you, you would have had every right to walk away. Not only that, but you should have.'

Ken locked his eyes onto hers. 'If there's any chance, however small, this guy's going to hurt you,' he said, 'give up on him. Whatever his problem is, it's not worth putting yourself in danger to fix.'

The Black Swan on Hackney Road looked like any East End boozer, save for the strings of coloured lights flashing around the bar and the eccentric collection of knick-knacks behind it. Back there amid the bottles, superhero dolls consorted with religious figurines, while above them, glass shelves displayed cookie jars, taxidermy, gargoyles, snow globes, feathers, oversized plastic rosary beads and Mexican Day of the Dead skulls. When Sara arrived, she chose a table in the corner, and claimed it with her jacket and a copy of the *Guardian*. She was relieved to find the place empty enough to keep an eye on most tables, but full enough for her not to be conspicuous. If needs be, she could hide behind the newspaper, like a spy in a Cold War film.

Sara's caution was, in itself, an act of optimism; she had no idea whether Tim Wilson would show up or not. If he didn't come, it would serve as evidence that she may have been deluding herself about the extent of her psychic abilities. Indeed, it would be *powerful* evidence, because she had never felt anything as strongly as her certainty that Tim and his new boyfriend would have their first date here, this evening … and soon.

Sara ordered a glass of Chardonnay at the bar and took up her position. The small crowd spread before her was mostly young, but otherwise mixed. There were both men and women, and few seemed especially aligned to any particular tribe. Many sported the smart-casual anonymity favoured by Gap advertisements. Sara had assumed that everyone here would look like Tim, but The Black Swan was no hipster hangout. It seemed more like a bolt-hole for those who wanted to avoid both the super-clubs of Vauxhall and the sterility of Soho nightlife. In fact, Sara decided, this pub was the perfect no-man's-land for a young urbanite on a first date with his newbie boyfriend – that is, when the boyfriend in question was a mature estate agent from Essex.

Sara was halfway through her wine when Tim Wilson entered the pub alone. She heard herself gasp out loud, and a tingle of elation pulsed through her: *he's here!* She remembered to raise her newspaper in front of her face, and took stock of what Wilson's arrival actually meant. It meant that she had been right when she had seen that he would come here this evening. Sara peered over the top of the paper and watched Wilson order a pint. He stood at the bar, a foot on the rail, with his gaze focused on his phone. What happened next, she knew, would be the real decider.

Her visions had been quite specific. She had seen Philip Berger in detail and, although they had never met, she knew every line on his pleasantly bland face, and every short, tidy hair of his receding hairline. After her vision, it had not been difficult to track down his business – and Berger himself, member of the National Association of Estate Agents – on Google. That had been Sara's first proof that Berger was more than just a phantasm created by brain chemicals and faith. He existed out there, in the real world.

The question was, would he show up here, in this pub?

Several minutes later, Philip Berger stepped haltingly into the room. He wore a chain store blue suit, crisp white shirt, red tie, and brown brogues. Once again, a strong emotion pulsed through Sara – but this time it was not excitement or vindication, but fear. She knew that Berger's presence here meant that, even in the face of her doubts, she would have to proceed as though all her visions about the couple had been accurate - including the final, bloody one …

She watched Berger scan the small crowd and single out his date. He moved forwards, and gave Tim Wilson a small touch on the shoulder. The younger man spun around, pocketing his phone, and embraced Berger – a man he had only met online – in a hearty bear hug. Sara noticed that the older man looked uncomfortable with Wilson's effusive display of affection. As much as she was able to discern his emotions, she suspected that Berger was feeling bemused, being here in an unfamiliar bar, trying out a new, unpractised ritual. Sara decided his bemusement was appropriate. She did not really understand this suburbanite's attraction to a London hipster fifteen years his junior. Maybe, she thought, there was a wild side to Philip Berger he kept deep under wraps. Or maybe he thought he might enjoy mentoring a young man with a daddy fixation.

Either way, Sara understood her job: to make sure that this attachment didn't overheat into a violent act of symbolic parenticide.

Already, Wilson and Berger were deep in conversation at the bar. Sara felt confident enough to lay the newspaper flat on her table. She reached into her handbag and pulled out her favourite Mont Blanc fountain pen; on a corner of the newspaper, she inscribed her mobile number and waited. Before Berger arrived, Sara had watched Wilson down two pints. Now, he was working on his third, as his date nursed a shot of Scotch. Soon, Wilson would need to head to the loo. To the extent that Sara had any kind of plan, Tim Wilson's distended bladder formed part of it.

Finally, Wilson drained his glass, ordered another round and gave Berger a friendly pat before disappearing through a door that led downstairs. Sara knew she could count on maybe two minutes alone with Mr Right, but no more. She grabbed her bag, tore off the corner of her *Guardian*, and hustled towards Berger.

She sidled up to him and he shifted politely to his right. The bartender set down a fresh whiskey and a pint, and Berger paid for the round. The bartender looked towards Sara, and she sent him away with a quick shake of her head. She stared directly at her quarry.

'Mr Berger,' she said in her most professional voice, 'can I have a minute?'

Although he had barely acknowledged her arrival, Berger now looked sharply at Sara. 'Do we know each other?' he asked.

'I know you,' she said, 'because I know Tim.'

He looked her over dubiously. 'You're friends?'

'I'm affiliated with his social worker. You do know he has a social worker?'

Berger angled his head, perplexed. 'I'm sorry – you say *affiliated* ...'

'This is important, Mr Berger. Tim has a violent temper, and it's got him into trouble before. That's why he has a social worker. He seems sweet, I know – and he is, until he gets angry. You look like a nice man, and I wouldn't want to see you hurt.'

'Who are you?' Berger demanded. 'Did you follow me here?'

'I'll answer all your questions,' Sara promised, 'but not now. It wouldn't be wise to let Tim see us talking.' She slipped the torn corner of newspaper towards him.

127

'You need to ring me. I'll meet you wherever you like …
but please do me one favour. Until you've heard what I
have to say, don't tell Tim about our meeting.'

Before walking quickly from the pub, Sara laid a hand
on Philip Berger's shoulder, and fought the urge to say,
Take care of yourself.

She didn't need to. She knew for a fact that Philip
Berger was perfectly safe.

At least, until next winter.

ELEVEN

All the way home, Sara had braced herself for a phone call from Berger. She'd realised her hyper-alertness was silly; she had only just given the man her number, and he was out on a date. Almost certainly, he would not ring her so early. Still, she had entertained the hope that the man would find an excuse to slip away from Tim Wilson, perhaps troubled enough by her warnings to want to hear more. Sara knew she had a lot resting on this optimistic outcome. Getting Philip Berger to reject Tim Wilson now, when the two men were still relative strangers, was her simplest way to avoid the bloodshed that was to come.

When Sara arrived home, Jamie was already in bed. He had been reading, and had fallen asleep with a hardcover history book propped open on his chest. Sara tucked his bookmark between the pages, placed the book on the table, and switched off the bedside lamp. Jamie mumbled something to her as he rolled over, but quickly began to breathe in a deep, regular pattern. Sara released a breath she hadn't realised she'd been holding, relieved that Jamie hadn't woken up. The last couple of days had felt heavy with tension between them that was even greater than usual. It was her fault, Sara knew. Jamie's dalliance with Thorndike Aerospace would have been enough to push her into a sullen funk, even if she hadn't also known the unpleasant history of Gerrit Vos. Add to that her pressing concern over Tim Wilson, and she must have appeared to Jamie like a thundercloud hovering darkly in his line of sight, blotting out the light.

Worse still, Sara wasn't sure whether she would be able to behave any better tomorrow, or the next day, or even next week. Ken Salter had suggested she abandon her violent client – but then again, Salter had no way of knowing the consequences of such an abnegation of responsibility. Sara could not abandon Philip Berger without feeling responsible for his murder. And she now accepted that Berger's death at Tim Wilson's hands was otherwise inevitable. Had neither Wilson nor Berger walked through the door of that pub this evening, she almost certainly would have tried to forget them. She'd have disregarded that vision as a random glimpse of an unlikely possibility. That was what Eldon Carson's visions of Edmund Haney had turned out to be.

The difference was, Carson had been over-confident. He had not tested his visions as Sara had done. This meant that the responsibility to prevent Philip Berger's murder still rested on her shoulders. And yet, the temptation was still to give up. If Wilson was unwilling to be helped, and Berger was as good as collaborating in his own murder, then what was the point? Sara wondered why she shouldn't simply let destiny take its course. But she knew the sin of omission was sin, nonetheless. It wasn't Philip Berger's fault that he was attracted to an unstable young man. And, Sara had to admit, it wasn't Wilson's fault that he suffered from surges of rage either. The lad needed therapy, not punishment. But, damn it, what could she do if he refused it?

These concerns over future death and present duty swirled through her mind as she lay next to Jamie. Despite the still-cool weather, Sara felt too warm; she shoved the

130

duvet aside, scrunched up the feather pillow, and fought the buoying drift of wakefulness.

When the weight of disturbed thought finally pulled her down, Sara sank into a recurring, terrible dream.

Philip Berger has done wonders with the flat since he moved in. First of all, he has managed to get the broken window in the living room sorted. He's done this by informing the maintenance staff that one of two things was about to happen. Either they would replace the window pronto, or Tim and Philip would hire the most expensive glaziers they could find, and then sue the council for the cost. Of course, that would require a notarized statement from the head of maintenance, Philip had told them. It'll be read in court, so it should explain why the broken glass hadn't been repaired in a timely fashion. Philip admits to Tim that everyone realised he was bluffing, but that it didn't matter. The fact that this crazy couple was willing to bluff so intently meant they'd be easier to appease than ignore.

'People like that maintenance guy just want a quiet life,' Philip tells Tim after the job's been done. 'Really, who doesn't?'

Once the staff has hopped to it and solved the window problem, it's easier to get them to fix the dodgy thermostat and replace several squares of curling linoleum. This is one of the things Tim loves about Philip – he knows how to get stuff done.

Of course, there are things that annoy Tim about Philip, too. For one, he's really messy. He leaves his tie on the bedroom chair. Sometimes his shirt as well, which really pisses Tim off. And Philip sheds worse than Tim's dog. Tim's always finding strands of hair from Philip's head, his pubes, and God knows where else. Tim notices them strewn across the shower tray in the morning, all slimy with soap scum. Philip never rinses the fucking shower. Tim has asked, again and again. *It's just gross*, he says. *Please*, he begs. But Philip – the thicko – forgets. Tim has taken to scrubbing the moulded plastic every day, once Philip has gone to work. Then he dumps caustic soda down the plug hole. By lunchtime, things are clean.

But there's only so much a guy can take.

The final straw has to do with Stratford. Philip's estate agency is located there, and Philip thinks they should move. He's been keeping an eye out, seeing all the best properties before they're even listed, and he's found something he likes. It's a two-bedroom terraced house, a five-minute walk from Westfield Shopping Centre. The place is a steal at just over £400,000, he says. Negotiate, and they'd get it for under four. It's basic, no question about that, and a lot of its original features have been stripped – but location is everything and the house's potential is huge. They could put a third bedroom in the loft. Or maybe a massive bathroom. Open shower, hot tub …

Tim says he can't afford to buy a place, but Philip promises to take on the burden himself. Philip and his wife are selling their house in Chingford, he says, which means a certain amount of cash will be coming his way. Not half, by any means – a judge has determined a sixty-five/thirty-five split in the wife's favour, but still – he'll see some profit. And with Philip's salary and commissions, things really aren't all that bad. Finances will still be tight, he admits, because there will be child support to pay for years, but when an opportunity arises –

Tim hates these sales pitches. They make Philip sound like *such* an estate agent. The thing is – and this really is the bottom line, the honest-to-God deal-breaker – Tim likes Central London. Who wants to live in Stratford? It's practically Essex.

'On the other hand,' Philip counters, 'it's practically *Hackney* as well. And Hackney is cool. We could never afford to live in Central London.'

'We're already in Central London!' Tim says every time they discuss it, his voice growing edgier with each conversation. 'We'll just stay here.'

'In this council flat?' Philip gasps. 'I would rather die.'

Of course, there's no irony in the phrase when he says it. But when Sara views these scenes that have yet to play out, Philip Berger's words are deeply ironic and grimly funny. That is, until Sara gets to that winter night in the bedroom, with the two men side-by-side on Tim's futon, Stanley the Rottweiler curled at its edge. On that night, Tim's trying to sleep, but Philip wants to talk. It's the same old conversation.

'Interest rates are low right now,' Philip says. 'But I'm guessing they'll rise. If I can lock myself into a five-year mortgage soon, this is do-able. If we wait, maybe not.'

This is the most vivid part of Sara's vision. She's so close she can smell the lingering aroma of the day's aftershave, still clinging to Philip's neck. It blends with the dry-grass whiff of Tim's tatami mat. Sara can hear Tim's breathing, too. It's growing more laboured.

'I don't want to move,' Tim huffs, his voice muffled by the pillow over his head.

'Well, we can't stay here,' Philip says.

'We can.'

'You can. I will not.'

Tim's pillow rolls away and smacks against the wall. 'What are you saying?' he demands. 'That you'd leave me for a fucking terrace in Essex?'

'Stratford is not in –'

'I don't care where it fucking is,' Tim shouts, *'it's not where I fucking want to be!'*

Stanley raises his massive head at this, and, when

Tim's muscled arm shoots out and lands a blow against Philip's chest, he barks.

'*Shut up!*' Tim screams at the dog.

Philip gasps from the impact of Tim's forearm. 'Give him some salami,' he wheezes. The word *salami* comes out as a sneer, some sort of ill-defined put-down against Stanley. That is a huge error in judgement, but Philip's biggest mistake is to accompany those words with a shove to Tim's shoulder.

It's a mild push, but Tim twitches as though he's been smacked in the head. '*Fuck you,*' he bellows.

Tim's next blow lands, full force, in Philip's face. Philip's head rears back, and impacts with the wall, just below Tim's favourite poster – the duo Daft Punk looking like cyborgs from a film, surrounded by a pristine metal frame. The frame matches their gleaming helmets.

Now Tim is rolling over, straddling Philip's torso, assailing him with blow after blow. Philip's punching too, but his are weak shots to Tim's chest. Really, they're no more than shoves, but they make Tim pummel harder. Stanley's barking wildly, leaping forwards and back, and Tim's screaming 'Shut up, Stanley, *shut up*' as he punches and punches.

Blood sprays over Tim. It dots the futon, the pillows, the duvet – and spatters over the Daft Punk poster when Philip's head lolls at a funny angle. Tim keeps striking until he's exhausted. Then he slides prostrate over Philip's body, covering it. Tim's sticky and crying.

There are already sirens wailing in the distance. Fucking neighbours must have called the cops. Tim can hear them because Stanley has stopped barking now.

Then Tim feels Stanley nuzzling the small of his back with the judgement-free compassion of a true soul mate. Tim loves Stanley, and soon they will be separated, and this makes him cry all the harder.

TWELVE

On Monday morning, Gerrit Vos was back in the Green Street pied-a-terre, brewing tea – fucking *Lady Grey* tea – for Andy Turner. Vos had had to buy that shit specially once, during their first meeting here. Now he kept it on hand for those rare occasions when they met in this flat, rather than in Surrey, Hampshire or St James's. Vos wondered what kind of guy could both regret not having been in the SAS, and also drink something as effete as Lady Grey tea? Bergamot was an interesting fruit and it made a pleasant oil – Nicole sometimes dribbled it into her bathwater – but it did not belong in fucking tea. And anyway, what kind of guy could know so much about third world despots and also wear those particular socks? Hell, half the psychopaths Andy Turner had dined with would flog their own peasants for wearing socks like that. Andy was a man of contradictions, that was for damn sure.

'Sugar?' he asked.

'As it comes,' Andy said.

Vos hoped that Andy Turner would not bring up the subject of Jamie Harding. Vos had not told him exactly what tasks he'd assigned to the ex-inspector. The less Andy knew about cockamamie schemes to sell munitions to proscribed countries, the better. Of course, it was possible that Harding had briefed his nattily dressed paymaster directly, but Vos tended to doubt it. Harding's comings and goings probably didn't even register on Andrew Turner & Associates' radar. Andy was showing Harding a kindness, throwing him a financial bone, and probably wasn't all that bothered about what he did for the money. One of Andy's great talents was not knowing things – or else forgetting them if he'd been unlucky enough to learn something unhelpful. Selective amnesia was a lobbyist's skill. Whenever people engaged in acts of propaganda – which included all lobbying, marketing, or persuasion of any sort – the first targets they had to brainwash were themselves. It was likely that Andy Turner *wanted* to believe his protégé was doing no more than checking out factories for security flaws. Knowing anything contradictory would play holy hell with the *vérité* of his narrative.

Besides, the fewer conflicting facts people held in their heads, the smoother they slept. Vos set the tea on a Thorndike-branded coaster in front of Andy, took in his pleasant, benign expression, and bet he slept like a baby.

'Ta,' Andy said.

Vos knew that Andy met regularly with the heads of several divisions at Thorndike. He had a limited set of issues to cover with each. If meetings ran long, it was only because some of the executives were soft enough to let him ramble. Andy spent so much time in the lands of irrelevant discourse, Vos suspected he must own property there. Early in their relationship, Vos had squashed all of Andy's attempts to speculate, reminisce, or roll out favourite anecdotes. Now their meetings were short and business-like. It took only that one cup of tea to despatch the items on their agenda, and Vos was preparing to stand when Andy said, 'One last question, Gerrit.'

Vos glanced at his Breitling. 'Yeah?'

Andy reclined and crossed his legs. 'I've been thinking about South Africa.'

Vos looked up. 'Thorndike Platinum? Why?'

He decided he'd give Andy enough time to say something interesting. Either that, or cut him short and say goodbye. Although Vos himself made regular trips to the Transvaal, ensuring local security kept a tight lid on operations there, Andy Turner's company didn't have a great deal to do with the platinum side of the business. It was mildly intriguing that Andy had brought up South Africa at all. Worth five more minutes to find out why anyway.

'I've been thinking about that union dispute a few years ago,' Andy continued.

Suddenly Vos's skin prickled. 'Oh?'

'What was behind the scandal?'

Vos stared into Andy's peaceful, innocent face. Anyone else and he'd be fearing a trap right about now. 'There was no scandal,' he said flatly.

Andy shrugged as if, scandal or no scandal, it was all the same to him. 'Some union leaders – coincidentally, ones that opposed Thorndike – went missing.'

What the fuck? Vos thought. His mind whirred. Had Jamie mentioned Rootenberg to Andy? If he had, it wouldn't have taken much effort for Andy to follow the link back. *Where is this going?*

'Political leaders in South Africa do that from time to time,' he observed dryly.

Andy chuckled. 'That's exactly what I said,' he agreed.

Vos twitched. 'What you said to whom?' he demanded.

Even as he asked, Vos was constructing scenarios. Maybe it hadn't been Jamie. Maybe Andy was describing an old conversation he'd had with Rhodri Jones. That

137

would suggest that Jones had known more about what had happened than he'd let on. It would also mean, for fuck's sake, that he'd felt free to share such delicate information with his old mate Andy Turner. If that were true, it rewrote several events in Vos's own past. It cast new light on all his dealings with Thorndike's former Chief Executive Officer, and also with Andy himself.

But hang on ... when Vos thought about it, that wasn't necessarily a bad thing. If this interpretation were true, it suggested that the powers that be had not only known what he had done, but *approved* of it. Maybe they promoted him not only for sorting out the miners' dispute, but for showing the balls to do it in a decisive way.

And yet ... if both Rhodri Jones and Andy Turner had understood the truth about what transpired back then, then who else might know?

'Sara Jones,' Andy concluded.

'What?' Vos said.

'It's what I said to Sara. We saw each other last week, and she brought it up. She mentioned there'd been some scandal in South Africa, right after the resolution to the strike, and a few union bosses went missing. I said that sounded fairly normal.'

Vos felt his brow knitting. Sara Jones – he had hoped she was on board. After all, her brother had been Thorndike's CEO. He rubbed his forehead. *OK,* he thought, *Andy doesn't know anything.* Maybe he'd heard whatever was in the public domain – certainly, the basic facts had hit the news in South Africa at the time – but he wouldn't have been privy to anything especially incriminating. Or, if he had – and Vos wasn't stupid enough to think that Andy didn't have his own sources – he was being especially coy. No – that wasn't likely. Feigning coyness wasn't a move in Andy's playbook. Vos looked at him sipping his Lady Grey. It was safe enough to assume that this PR whiz was genuinely ignorant of the full facts.

On the other hand, there was Sara Jones ...

Now, Sara too, might just be responding to old news. But even if she were, why would she bring it up? The only answer was, because she suspected something. There was no other reason to fish for more information.

'Good tea,' Andy said. It was only then that Vos realised he'd continued to stare at Andy, while also keeping him waiting. He grunted – *fuck him*. Andy could wait a few seconds longer.

'Pour yourself some more,' he said.

Sara Jones's interest suggested three questions. One: did she know anything more than she could have read online? Two: if she did know more, how much more? And finally, three: where had she got that extra information?

If she knew more, then the third question had an obvious answer – she must have heard things from Rhodri Jones. In the past, Sara would have had no reason to be troubled by her brother's indiscreet confidences. Some enemies had been killed in South Africa, and Rhodri suspected some of his own security people. So what? Sara would have had no reason to act on that. But now, something had changed – her boyfriend was working for Thorndike Aerospace. More than that, he was working for Gerrit Vos.

And that suggested that Sara Jones understood, or at least suspected, something about his own involvement in the event.

'It's odd that Sara brought it up,' Vos said finally, as casually as he could. 'Did she explain why?'

Andy made a shrugging frown. 'She's been thinking about Rhoddo, I suspect,' he speculated. 'She's still creeped out by the way he died. She misses him.'

'Yeah, that's probably it,' Vos agreed. He decided to make sure Andy was in no doubt about the party line. 'As far as I know, all of Thorndike's business in South Africa was conducted with complete integrity,' he said with emphasis. 'That's the way Rhodri Jones operated.'

Running the risk of sounding like a corporate promotional video, Vos added, 'And it's still the way Thorndike Aerospace presents itself to its partners, both internal and external.'

Andy chortled. 'On land, sea, air and on line.' He stood, and added, 'Thanks for your time, Gerrit. Rest assured, everything you've said is what I think too.'

Of course it is, Vos thought with a mental sigh. *One of your talents is not knowing any uncomfortable facts.*

Sara Jones on the other hand, might well know a few too many.

The clinic where Sara worked occupied the basement of a deconsecrated church not far from London Fields. Her office was in its the dimmest corner. Sara had spent the first part of the morning seeing clients in the fluorescent-lit gloom. She had just spent half an hour with a recently divorced and surprisingly inarticulate man who had arrived with his far-too-articulate advocate. Trying to pull information from the client was exhausting, and handling the advocate's endless stream of inconsequential quibbles even more so. In the end, Sara had determined that the client needed practical help rather than counselling. She had sent him and his advocate down the hall to talk to her colleague Ellen about housing. It would have been wonderful if that had been the end of this particular case – but Sara also knew that clients' problems were never cut-and-dried, and practical issues tended to overlap with emotional ones. She realised she must reserve a time this week for herself and Ellen to discuss a care plan for this homeless divorcee.

Usually, Sara was able to shunt her personal problems into the background during sessions with patients, but today she could not ignore the queasiness that still lay coiled inside her. Even as she dealt with the client and his advocate, Sara had reflected on how Eldon Carson once referred to the burden of psychic knowledge as 'an awful thing'. That burden felt particularly heavy today.

Maybe I'm just tired, Sara told herself.

Sara's vision of Tim Wilson bludgeoning Philip Berger to death had recurred not only on Saturday night, but last night as well. *Damn it*, she thought – if only she'd been able to warn Berger away from Wilson on Saturday, that bloody future could not possibly happen. But she had failed in that attempt, and knew she could do nothing until Philip Berger rang her.

Or failed to ring, she thought.

What will I do then?

Not for the first time this morning, that question led Sara to relive a conversation she'd had with Eldon Carson almost three years before, during that terrible summer in Aberystwyth.

It had been a day in mid-August. Sara had known Carson for less than a fortnight, but he had already convinced her of the reality of his powers – and also the vast potential of her own. At that time, Sara had a clear goal. She planned to master the arcane skills that Carson had to teach her, and then use them to understand – finally – the awful mystery of her past. Such was the extent of her ambition, and the line she drew on the use of her fledgling psychic abilities. On that day, they sat in Sara's living room in the small coastal village of Penweddig. Sara had drawn the blinds against prying eyes and the late-summer light. They discussed a burden that Sara had still believed to be

Eldon Carson's alone.

'Let's assume you're right,' Sara had said, 'and every one of your victims would have committed the crimes you expected them to commit.'

His grin had been both compassionate and taunting. 'You can safely assume that,' he had drawled.

'Well, I'm a medical doctor,' Sara said, 'and despite my research into fringe subjects, I'm a fairly skeptical one. I believe the human brain is no more than a physical entity. The chemical processes that occur within it create what we call the mind.' She sat forward in the love seat, and leaned towards Carson. 'I strongly suspect there's nothing else – no disembodied spirits or sentient forces inhabiting us.'

Carson shrugged. 'I have no problem with that,' he said. 'We both know that psychic powers are as real as this coffee table. There needn't be any mystical mumbo-jumbo involved at all. We may not know exactly how these abilities work, but since they do, we can assume they're natural.'

'I'm not referring to psychic powers,' Sara had countered. 'I'm talking about the freedom to make choices.'

For a moment, Carson's habitual air of cocky certainty had faltered. He hadn't understood what she was getting at. 'Go on,' he'd urged.

Sara chewed her lip, wondering how best to relay complex ideas to this bright-but-undereducated young man. For a moment, she felt as though she were back in the lecture rooms of UCL, delivering a first-year introductory course. 'An individual,' she began, 'may believe she's made a particular decision out of her own free will. But neuroscience has shown decisions appear in our conscious minds fully formed. In other words, they're made deep in the *un*conscious – often seconds before

142

we've become aware of them.'

Carson blinked. 'So?'

'So, looking back on some action, people might assume they had the potential to change what they chose to do at the time. We might say to ourselves, "why didn't I just do X instead of Y?"' She spread her hands. 'But how could we have? The decision to act had already been taken by the time we became aware of it.'

He frowned skeptically. 'You're saying there's no such thing as free will?'

'I can't be quite that definite … but I am saying that it's hard to imagine how true free will could exist, considering what we know about how the mind works.'

Carson offered a small shrug. 'OK Miss Sara,' he conceded, 'I reckon you've made some kind of point. What I'm not so sure of is what it's got to do with you and me.'

'It hasn't got anything to do with me,' Sara said. 'Only you. If your victims had no other choice but to do what they did – or, what they would have done, if left to their own devices – then you're punishing them for something they cannot control.' She shrugged. 'That hardly seems fair.'

Carson pondered this, and then nodded as though he now understood. 'I get it,' he said, 'you're saying that, if people don't have any real free will, then it's not actually their fault if they go and kill someone. They had no choice. And I'm a monster for trying to stop them.'

'I never called you a monster,' Sara reminded him.

He laughed. 'You're one of the few.' Quickly, his mirth evaporated, and he added, 'Still, there are problems with what you're saying. First, let's take the word "fair." I define it as treating people equally – and I do. If you're going to commit an atrocity, then I'll kill you before you can do it, without any concern over who you are. That's fair, isn't it? But, frankly, I'm more concerned with *justice* than fairness. Justice is about doing what's morally right – such as stopping someone from murdering another human being. That's why your argument is a red herring. I don't care if any of those folks could've made a different decision. The fact is, they were going to commit atrocities, and I had the power to stop them. Free will or no, what I do is administer justice.'

Sara was shaken from her reverie by her mobile's saxophone ringtone. She looked for the caller ID, but the number had been blocked. Hoping it was not a telemarketing robot, she answered.

'Sara,' the voice said with unwarranted cheer. 'It's Gerrit Vos calling.'

Sara's stomach lurched. A robot would have been preferable. 'Mr Vos,' she said neutrally.

'I never thanked you for dinner,' he said. 'It was delicious.'

'Oh, I can't take credit – Jamie was the cook,' she replied, trying to add some warmth to her tone. 'The most I did was load the dishwasher ... and, come to think of it, Jamie did that, too.'

'You want to keep him,' Vos said with a chuckle. 'Nicole's lucky if I rinse out my coffee mug.'

'What can I do for you, Mr Vos?' she asked.

'I'd like to chat with you,' he said. 'I'm in town today. I was hoping you'd be free.'

'As it happens, I'm at work,' she said.

'Of course,' he demurred. 'Stupid of me. But it's almost lunch time. You do take time off for lunch, don't you?'

Sara considered telling him today was entirely out of the question. In truth, she had no clients booked that afternoon, but she did have other things to do. However,

144

she also felt morbidly curious about what Vos could want from her. 'When are you free?' she asked.

'Two o'clock,' Vos suggested. 'How about Highgate?'

Sara made a quick mental map. Over to the Holloway Road and straight up. 'That's quite convenient from here,' she acknowledged. 'What restaurant do you have in mind?'

'No restaurant,' he said. 'The cemetery.'

Sara started. 'I beg your pardon?'

'Highgate Cemetery,' Vos repeated. 'I've been meaning to pay my respects to your brother for ages. Nothing would please me more than to do it with you.'

THIRTEEN

Highgate's East Cemetery had been accepting residents since 1860, when the body of the sixteen-year-old daughter of a local baker became its first internment. One of its more recent burials had been Rhodri Jones, Chief Executive Officer of Thorndike Aerospace. Rhodri's grave was located just off a main path, some distance from Karl Marx's, but quite close to a 1980s television celebrity. His memorial was a simple rectangle of grey granite, carved with a Welsh dragon just above the words *Er coffadwriaeth am Rhodri Huw Jones*, and his dates. That inscription read "in remembrance of" – a neutral epitaph chosen by Sara at a time of conflicting varieties of grief, when more personal sentiments would have seemed hypocritical. Despite such diffidence, Sara still visited this tranquil place regularly. The cemetery trust required the family of the interred to keep both grave and memorial presentable. On the way up, Sara had stopped at a small garden centre and purchased a pot of daffodils. She had just placed it on Rhoddo's plot when a deep voice rang from behind her.

'Twenty thousand quid?' it said.

She rose, turning. Gerrit Vos stood before her in a dark blue summer blazer, light blue open-necked shirt and tan cotton chinos. He carried a Panama hat. Vos's eyes were masked by Ray-Bans. 'To be buried here,' he elaborated. 'Something like twenty thousand?'

'Slightly less,' Sara replied.

'Still … a fair whack.'

'It's worth it, if it's what you want,' she said. 'It's what Rhodri wanted.'

Vos tilted back his head and examined the sky; twin suns reflected in his grey lenses. 'Andy said he suggested scattering his ashes over Wales from a helicopter.'

Sara smiled. 'That was never going to happen.'

Vos nodded. 'This is more tasteful.'

On the way up to Highgate, Sara had wondered whether this man was trying to bond with her through her late brother. She quickly dismissed that benign interpretation: although Vos had not said what their meeting would entail, Sara had received a few distinct impressions, which had radiated through the phone lines and pierced Vos's casual bonhomie. Thinking back on the conversation, Sara realised Vos had been feeling suspicion and fear. She knew there was only one reason he would be afraid of her – the suspicions she'd revealed to Andy about the events in South Africa. And the only way Vos would have known anything about them was if Andy had actually said something. Sara believed with all her heart that Andy would never betray her intentionally. He may have been in Thorndike's pocket, but he was not Vos's snitch. Still, Andy did like to talk.

'So, Mr Vos -' Sara began.

'Gerrit,' he countered.

'Gerrit,' she repeated. 'Why are we here?'

Of course Sara had realised Andy might inadvertently say something to this man. *Maybe you actually wanted a confrontation*, she told herself. She brushed against Vos's mind, and sensed he no longer felt afraid. He was resolute, confident. But why the change?

147

Vos ignored her question. 'I like your boyfriend,' he said.

Sara forced herself to smile. 'He's alright.'

'Human rights law,' Vos went on.

'That's where's he's heading.'

Vos nodded. 'It's an important field. Especially in today's world.' He ran his fingers over the top of Rhodri's gravestone, gently brushing against the Welsh dragon. 'Can I be blunt?'

Sara shrugged in a way that said, *you always are*.

'Jamie said yes to Andy's offer – and agreed to work with me – because he wants to save his pennies for university.'

That much was true. Sara waited for more.

'I imagine you already had financial resources before your brother died ... but you sure as hell have more of them now.'

Sara raised an eyebrow. 'You know the details of Rhodri's will?'

Vos shrugged. 'Would you respect me if I didn't? What I'm saying is, paying Jamie's university fees isn't exactly a stretch for you. Jamie knows that – so why is he so keen to make his own money?'

Vos paused, but it was clear that he didn't expect Sara to answer. He was savouring the drama of a prepared speech. 'I'm guessing Jamie has felt rather emasculated, the way he's been living off you. It's quite a come-down after all – from police inspector to household pet.'

Sara must have reacted unconsciously, because Vos smiled. 'That's not a good self-image,' he went on. 'Jamie would rather pay his fees himself, so he can show he isn't reliant on you.'

'Jamie contributes to our lives in other ways,' Sara said. 'He owns the flat, for one thing.'

'A spit in the ocean,' Vos said. 'Anyway, we're

talking about his feelings.'

In truth, Sara knew Vos's analysis was fairly accurate. She had been aware of Jamie's feelings of inadequacy, perhaps even of being trapped, for some time. But she wasn't about to admit that to Vos. 'I can't read Jamie's mind,' she said, and took pleasure in the irony of the statement.

Vos grunted. 'Let's assume I'm right. That would mean Thorndike Aerospace is more important to Jamie's emotional well-being than to his financial security.'

'OK,' Sara said neutrally, 'let's assume that.'

'You want him to feel good about himself, right?'

'He already does.'

'I don't think that's true,' Vos countered, 'and I suspect you don't either. Your partner is a mass of insecurities – about his father, about you, and about what he sees as his failure to get anywhere in life.'

'That's a bit harsh.'

'Again, I'm not talking about what's true. I'm saying it's what Jamie feels. And his doubt is so unnecessary.' Vos gestured to the ground under which Rhodri lay. 'Whatever you think about your brother's approach to life, or the business he left behind, let me assure you that Thorndike Aerospace is committed to being a good corporate citizen.'

He put on his Panama hat and slipped his Ray-Bans into his pocket. Fixing Sara with an unwavering stare, he said, 'I'm going to speak to our CEO about funding Jamie's master's degree next year. All the fees, as well as some sort of retainer, so he can afford to live. That way, he won't have to scrimp and save. He won't have to rely on you, either. As for what Thorndike gets out of it, we'll be giving Jamie a sense that he's important to the company.'

Sara was already shaking her head. 'Thank you Mr

Vos, but I really don't think –'

'When he graduates,' Vos interrupted, 'Jamie will have an area of expertise that will become increasingly important to Thorndike. Combine human rights law with his background in the Met, and I think our CEO would jump at the chance to offer him a full-time position. Well-remunerated of course. Jamie will have his own money, a good career, and he'll have the dignity that, frankly, being your dependent doesn't offer him.'

Sara wondered whether this was the reason Vos had shifted from fear over the phone to a kind of cocky confidence now. Did he really think an offer to buy Jamie would silence Sara's doubts?

'Mr Vos,' Sara began, 'you're fond of what you call bluntness, so let me be blunt right now. I really don't want Jamie to get too deeply involved with Thorndike Aerospace. He may have some issues with his self-esteem, but they're temporary. Situational. Once he's got his master's degree, he'll be fine.'

Vos shook his head. 'I'm offering him a better career than he could get anywhere else,' he said. 'Why are you so against it?'

'The aerospace industry deals in death,' Sara stated. 'It's all about weapons, after all – and weaponry's only function is to kill.' She shrugged. 'Forgive me if I don't like that.'

Vos smirked at her naiveté. 'The defence industry,' he countered, 'is about the prosperity of this country. It's about the development of knowledge and skills – which are essential to the economy, not to mention Britain's self-reliance. Exports mean jobs. 150,000 of them rely on the aerospace industries, many of them high-tech. A strong defence capability is also a signal of our political commitment to our allies. Then there's our freedom to act independently in an unstable world. What exactly are you against, Sara?'

Vos paused, smug in his mastery of the argument. Sara steadied herself. She had already decided that, if it came to it, she was willing to play what followed as an endgame.

'OK then, let's bring it closer to home,' she said. 'I am against what you did in South Africa.'

Vos's expression betrayed his shock. He had not expected Sara to come out and say what had been lingering in the cemetery air. He squinted at her, then reached into his pocket and covered his eyes with his sunglasses.

'You shouldn't be surprised that I'd bring it up,' Sara went on. 'You know I asked Andy Turner about it.'

Vos inclined his head in acknowledgement. 'And he had nothing to tell you,' he said. 'That's because there's nothing to tell.'

Sara could feel Vos radiating wariness. His senses were heightened. There was a sudden, queasy steeling of his muscles. She pressed on. 'I know exactly what happened,' she said.

Vos stared at her without expression. Still, Sara knew what he was thinking. Gerrit Vos had finally concluded that Rhodri Jones had known about his actions at Thorndike Platinum – and imagined that Rhodri had told Sara everything. What was he feeling about that?

She concentrated. Vos no longer felt fear. Not quite anger, either. His emotions added up to something more like unhappy conviction. The sensations a person gets when a certain marker has been passed.

Slowly, Vos licked his lips. 'Whatever you think happened – and indeed, whatever your brother may have suspected – it isn't true,' he said steadily. 'But I'll tell you what is true: Jamie needs Thorndike Aerospace. In fact, he needs it more than he needs you. So, regarding any unfounded suspicions you have about me, my advice would be to keep them to yourself.'

Vos gestured to Rhodri's grave. 'It is precisely because of this man, and the fact that he loved you, that I took a gamble with Jamie. It paid off – I like him. He's got a future. For Jamie's sake, I had hoped your rarefied little world could find a way to exist alongside mine, as once it did with his.'

'Jamie doesn't work with murderers,' Sara said.

Vos straightened his jacket and looked in the direction of the East Cemetery's exit.

'What did I do to make you think so badly of me?' he asked.

He began to stride away. A moment later, he stopped, turned and called, 'If it comes down to a choice between your world and mine, your boyfriend is going to choose mine.'

Sara snorted and shook her head. 'He won't,' she said.

Vos grinned sardonically. 'Trust me,' he said. 'I'll make sure he does.'

Sara wandered the grounds of the cemetery, her heart thudding. A spike of self-recrimination made her cheek muscles spasm.

How could I have been so stupid?

Although Sara had watched Vos's back until he'd disappeared from sight, she still suffered waves of trepidation in this public space. She felt too exposed on these well-tended paths. She diverted herself onto a verge of grass. From there, she waded deep into a patch of tall trees. In this solitary spot of shadows and dappled sunlight, overgrowths of ivy sprawled across the woodland floor, and crept up the clustered Victorian gravestones. The stones' weathered shapes jutted at odd angles from this tangle of greenery. Beyond them, an old brick wall separated the East Cemetery from the steep, narrow lane on its other side.

Sara felt better-protected here, more able to think. She settled onto a sloping altar tomb, silently asking its long-dead inhabitant to forgive the disturbance. The stone felt damp, even through the wool of her business suit. Sara inhaled the wet must of foliage, and tried to imagine the rich oxygen stilling her quivering muscles. Even though she might calm her body through an act of will, she could not quite manage to soothe her teeming mind. Part of it still screamed that she'd made a rash move in revealing her hand to Gerrit Vos.

I've shown him the extent of his problems, she thought. *And I've seen for myself how that man solves problems.*

Sara pressed her hand against the rough stone of the tomb, concentrating on nothing but its solidity. Its coldness numbed her fingers. She forced herself to picture Vos in her mind's eye. A mental haze enveloped her as she tried to form a connection with him, to get a solid impression of what he was thinking and feeling. What she received was no more than that which she herself was experiencing – the sense of something coiled, twitchy, and tinged with regret. *We're both feeling the same thing,* she thought. Sara knew that in her case, the regret was over showing Vos too much, too soon.

In Vos's case it was regret for – what?

What he'd done in South Africa?

Or maybe what he might do next.

That was the crux, Sara knew, the one difference between the emotions that she and Vos shared. Although she could not read exactly what his plan entailed, she had the firm impression that Vos had options.

Sara, on the other hand, had no idea what to do next.

As Gerrit Vos drove towards the M4, he could feel the

muscles of his arms and chest quivering. It was not the result of anger, or even fear of exposure – it was the fight-or-flight impulse that told him he would now have to act. That understanding caused numb despair to run from the tensed muscles of his face straight down to his gut. Vos had gone to Highgate unsure of how much Sara Jones understood about his past, and hoping the woman might see reason. Now, he knew she was unable to entertain any thoughts beyond her own prissy presumptions.

Fucking hell, he thought, *wouldn't it be nice if things ran smoothly once in a while?*

He would need help now, Vos knew. He had tried to bribe Sara Jones on his own, but had failed. Any further steps would require more than he could accomplish by himself. Certainly, he could rule out Levi Rootenberg. That bastard was already a millstone around his neck, and Vos didn't need to be any deeper in his debt. Besides, when it came to dealing with Sara Jones, Vos would never use the kind of service he knew Rootenberg could arrange. He would not be able to solve this problem in the way he'd dealt with those union men in South Africa. Putting a contract out on an ex-copper's partner would be a rookie mistake, opening him up to more potential blackmail.

Even allowing the idea of murder to cross his mind made Vos's stomach lurch and caused those hated memories from South Africa to press forward, trying to reveal themselves once again. Seeing those ghosts always made Vos think of the relief that might come with a single swallow of thallium sulphate. It waited for him in the floorboards of his barn…

Vos grimaced away the thought. He needed a subtle approach to Sara Jones, and someone he could rely on completely. And there was only one person who fitted that description. But in order to recruit Nicole into this, he would have to tell her something about his past. Not all of it, maybe, but something more than the official Gerrit Vos-as-Thorndike-hero version. Just enough honesty to help her understand the potential shit he was in.

The worst part of his encounter with Sara Jones had not been finding out she knew his secret, or even having to tell Nicole some sanitised version of the events in South Africa. Rather, it was those unpleasant memories their confrontation had shaken loose. As he wondered how much to tell Nicole, Vos pictured meeting Rootenberg's paramilitary chum for the first time, in that hotel lounge outside Rustenburg. He recalled seeing the guy sitting there, looking all weathered and rustic. Vos could picture him again now, plainer than he could see the North Circular Road stretching before him. Old-school Afrikaans, he had been – the man's paramilitary khakis looking entirely out of place in the midst of the bar's international swank. Vos could remember adjusting his suit jacket before sitting down – an odd little detail to recall. He'd ordered wine, then had that uncommon conversation that would change his life …

Vos glanced down to his phone on the dashboard mount. He scrolled through the screen until he found Nicole's number. When she answered, he said, 'Where are you right now?'

'I'm at home today,' she replied. 'Why?'

'I'll be there in an hour.'

'You're coming home?' she asked, as though he'd said aliens had landed on Parliament Square. 'What's wrong?'

'Nothing,' he said. 'Just don't go out, OK?'

Vos hadn't seen that old Afrikaner again until Rootenberg gave him the call. Directions to somewhere remote – the breezeblock shell of an abandoned shanty. Vos had driven there himself. Even today, he could call to mind the sharp crunch of gravel under the jeep's wheels.

He had taken a moment to put on his game-face before sauntering into that Spartan space, which was crumbling from years of skirmishes and neglect. In his mind's eye, Vos could see the weathered Afrikaner standing in the derelict hovel. Once again, he'd worn fatigues, and he mingled with a cluster of similarly clad colleagues. All were white. Each was armed.

Those men, Vos thought. *They're the reason I'm now taking blowback from Sara Jones. The reason I have to have that fucking difficult conversation with Nicole.*

How grim those men had looked, how solemn. But also pumped with self-righteous anticipation. In front of them, strapped to chairs, sat Bakone and his lieutenants, already bloody and gagged. Puffy eyes, broken cheekbones. Vos remembered looking over the captives, and gesturing to Bakone.

Someone lowered his gag.

Vos had spoken softly. 'Sorry we didn't get to meet a fortnight ago,' he'd said, 'when you and the lads did your little dance. I remember you smiled at me. Seemed eager to say something. What did you have to tell me?'

Bakone had responded with curses, and launched a gob of bloody spit through his split lips. Vos recalled leaping to the side so Bakone wouldn't stain his trousers. A couple of the paramilitaries had laughed at his clumsy pirouette, but the chief Afrikaner silenced them with a frown. Then the man had knocked Bakone to the floor with the butt of a Kalashnikov. The chair went with him.

As Vos sped up the ramp that led to the M4, he surged with a residual sense of the power he'd felt at that moment, watching Bakone fall. The feeling shamed him now, in a way it hadn't then. He remembered staring down at Bakone for a long time, until the old Boer said, 'Well, boss, it's your call.'

Vos recalled how, even then, he'd swallowed sour

phlegm as he sauntered to the crumbling door of the shanty. About to take his exit, still wanting to look casual … but unwilling to witness what was about to happen.

'When you're finished,' he had said, 'mop up and then contact Rootenberg.'

That was part of the story he could never tell Nicole, even though the scene was so vivid in his mind. Vos could picture himself so clearly, walking into the blinding glare of the gravel forecourt. Hearing his heart pounding wildly in his chest, and grateful that nobody else could.

He hadn't even made it to his car before the shooting started.

Vos arrived at his thatched cottage to find Nicole on the landline; around her lay packages destined for the Post Office. She looked up and raised her eyebrows.

He gestured to the phone. They'd talk when Nicole had finished. Vos went into the kitchen and put on the kettle. He could smell the lingering aroma of a cooked lunch; when Nicole wasn't forced to eat dinner for social reasons, she preferred to have her main meal in the middle of the day. He checked the fridge and found a plate containing a slab of ham, some mashed potatoes and peas. All still lukewarm – Nicole hadn't eaten very long ago. He stuck the food into the microwave.

Nicole appeared in the doorway. 'Why are you home?' she asked. 'Was there an attack on the Thorndike campus? I can't think of much else that would convince you to leave.'

'Actually, I was in London,' he replied. 'Just didn't make sense to head back to the office.'

Nicole offered an impressed whistle. 'Maybe you're developing some perspective in your old age.'

'Don't count on it,' he said, removing his food from

the microwave. He remembered that he'd boiled the kettle. 'Want tea?' he asked.

'Sit down and eat,' Nicole said. 'I'll make it.'

Vos climbed onto a stool at the breakfast nook and cut into the slice of ham. Absently, he watched Nicole re-boil the kettle and fill a tea ball with loose English Breakfast. She poured the steaming water into a teapot. This ritual was a nicety that Vos seldom bothered with – he tended to drop a bag into each mug.

'Will you want biscuits?' Nicole asked.

'Sure,' he said absently.

Nicole set a mug of tea in front of him, and one on the other side of the thin counter for herself. She slid onto a stool and laid a plate of biscuits between them. Vos had never understood why Nicole went to such extents to make his life easier. Maybe she saw in him things he didn't see himself. He wished he didn't have to exploit that sentiment now. By enlisting Nicole back into his world, Vos was aware, he may be doing damage to the fragile bindings that held their lives in place.

'Can I ask you a question?' he said to Nicole.

'Of course,' Nicole said.

'Last week, you said you'd help me if I wanted you to. With all this Sara Jones shit, I mean.'

'I did,' she agreed. 'And I will.'

Vos took a gulp of tea, and sighed to himself quietly. 'Did you know,' he said, 'that she hates the defence industry?'

Nicole frowned. 'Sara Jones?'

He grunted.

'That seems unlikely,' she said. 'Isn't she Rhodri Jones's sister?'

'Yeah,' Vos said. 'A contradiction for sure. Maybe some old sibling rivalry's coming into play. But whatever her reasons, Sara Jones's attitude is becoming a problem.'

'How?'

'She's a negative influence on Jamie Harding. I like the kid, and I think he's got a future. I don't want her poisoning him against us.'

Nicole had been about to bite into a biscuit. Now she set it back on the plate. 'How could she do that?'

Vos put down his mug. 'She's putting a particular spin on the union thing.'

Nicole raised her eyebrows. Vos did not have to explain what he meant – although the South African mining dispute had happened before they met, Nicole knew the official version of how Vos had resolved it. That story was legendary in the company: through masterful negotiating, Vos had managed to convince a secondary union leader to form a breakaway union, take most of the strikers with him, and marginalise all the hotheads at Thorndike Platinum. The company was back into production when other mines were still paralysed by labour disputes.

'I don't know if I ever told you about the aftermath of that incident,' Vos said, 'but shortly after I talked Kgatla into starting the new union, some of his rivals went missing.'

Nicole furrowed her brow. 'You think Kgatla had something to do with it?'

'It's possible,' Vos said.

She stroked his hand. 'And that makes you feel guilty,' she suggested. 'Having elevated a man who would do something like that.'

Vos shook his head. 'It's unsurprising, actually,' he told her. 'Rivalries have been solved like that before. But that's not what Sara Jones thinks. She's threatening to spread other rumours.'

'Such as?'

Vos drew a deep breath, making sure to look both

awkward and pained. 'I met her today. She suggested I might have had something to do with those disappearances.'

Nicole's face contorted. 'What?'

'I know,' Vos said, 'it's crazy. But in a way, it's also believable. Everyone knows Sara Jones was close to her brother. If there *had* been some sort of ugly plot, and Rhodri Jones and I were involved, it's possible he would have confessed it to her.' Vos twitched his hands helplessly. 'At least, that's what people might think.'

'But that's ridiculous,' Nicole breathed. 'You're no murderer.'

Vos looked her square in the eye. 'No,' he said, 'I'm not.'

And in a sense, he believed it. Vos had never once thought of himself as a murderer. Truth was, he wasn't someone who enjoyed strong-arm stuff. And, after all, he hadn't pulled the trigger on those union men himself. He couldn't have even if he'd tried. For years, Vos had thought carefully about all that had happened, and had offered himself many justifications for his actions. He was merely taking a position on behalf of the company, he'd told himself. The choice had been impersonal, detached. A mere executive decision. It was people like Rootenberg and those Afrikaners – men who didn't mind getting dirty – who bore personal responsibility. Rootenberg had made the calls. The paramilitaries had done the wet work. Once again, Vos reminded himself that he wasn't even in the room when it happened ...

'But why?' Nicole asked. 'Why would Sara accuse you of such an awful thing?'

'I told you,' he said. 'She hates the defence industry. She doesn't want her boyfriend involved. She knows I think highly of him – hell, I'm lucky Andy Turner introduced us. But I suppose she imagines if she threatens me with rumours, I might let him go.'

Nicole sat silently, pondering this new information. Suddenly, her expression hardened. 'Then you should,' she said. 'Let him go, I mean. Sack him. Gerrit, even if you like the guy, he's not worth the trouble. Just tell Andy it didn't work out. Then Sara will have what she wants and she'll leave you alone.'

Vos shook his head. 'Can't do that,' he said. 'Even if I wanted to get rid of Jamie, I made a promise to Andy. I intend to keep it.'

That sentiment sounded noble, but Vos knew it was a smokescreen. Releasing Jamie Harding would not help matters, and might even make them worse. After all, Andy Turner was a close friend of Sara's. If Vos sacked Jamie, Sara might tell Andy everything – if only to explain the sudden change in circumstances. And once Andy Turner knew a morsel of gossip, everyone knew it. If that rumour spread, would anyone believe that Vos *hadn't* ordered the murder of those men in South Africa?

Nicole raised her eyebrows and fixed him with a steady stare. 'OK,' she said, 'That's your call. What do you want me to do?'

Her steadiness soothed him. This was why he loved her – no matter how much shit hit the fan, Nicole never flinched. Vos picked up his fork, speared a chunk of ham, and mopped up a streak of mashed potato. As he chewed, he wondered whether putting the two women into contact would be a good idea. Nicole was a trustworthy presence. She could at least find out what Sara Jones might do next. But was it also possible that Sara might convince Nicole of her version of events? No, Vos thought – Nicole was loyal to the core.

'Call Sara and ask to see her,' he told Nicole. 'When I left her, she was rather hot under the collar. I couldn't get any sense of what she planned to do with her silly suspicions. Once she's had a few hours to calm down, we may be able to find out. And I'm sure she'd rather talk to you than me.' He grinned sardonically. 'You might even be able to convince her that she's wrong about me.'

'That would be a long shot,' Nicole guessed, 'but I'll do my best to make her my friend.' She reached over and took Vos's hand. 'It's horrible to be falsely accused.'

Vos smiled heroically, and Nicole asked, 'What if I can't get her to tell me anything?'

Vos's smile vanished and he looked at Nicole sternly. 'Then you ring me immediately. Ring me regardless of what happens. I know more about Sara Jones than I've let her realise. There are other things I can do.' Vos forced himself to relax and gave Nicole's fingers a squeeze. 'Don't worry about what I'll do,' he said. 'Just talk to her, and let me know.'

He forked another slice of ham into his mouth. 'Actually, there's one more thing,' he said, chewing. 'Pop into the barn and find a GPS tracker. That waterproof kind you sell – the one with the big magnets in it. When you see Sara, find out where she's parked. Stick it under her car.'

Nicole arched her eyebrow.

Vos shrugged. 'Why the hell not?' he asked. 'That way, if she goes anywhere odd, at least we'll know about it.' He put down his fork and pushed aside his plate. 'It would be stupid not to take precautions, don't you think?'

FOURTEEN

Sara's Monday evening had been full of edgy self-recrimination, mixed with trepidation about what Vos would do next. She sensed he was as unsettled by their confrontation as she had been, but could get no firm impression of his intentions. It was early on Tuesday morning when she received a call at work, from Vos's partner, Nicole. Nicole wanted to know whether Sara would be free for lunch.

It seemed typical somehow that Vos would send his partner to try to make things better.

Sara had suggested a popular delicatessen built into a railway arch, which was near her clinic and just up the street from the London Fields Overground station. The café itself was a cramped box of fashionable tiling and exposed pipework, but it also offered tables on the pavement outside. The street they faced was as quiet as anywhere below a railway line could be. When she arrived, she found Nicole already sitting at one of the metal tables, with two menus in front of her.

'Where do you park around here?' Nicole said as Sara sat down. 'Every space seems to be permits-only.'

'It's not easy,' Sara said. 'I should have warned you – sorry. There is a small car park up on Amhurst Road.'

'I missed that one,' Nicole said. 'I ended up at the

Tesco car park – I hope they don't tow me.'

Sara shrugged. 'Buy some milk when you get back.'

A waiter arrived and took their orders. Once he had retreated into the deli, the two women shifted in their seats and smiled awkwardly at each other.

'So –' Sara began.

Nicole cut her off. 'Mostly, I'm here to apologise,' she said. 'I know you met Gerrit yesterday, and he annoyed you.'

Sara parted her lips but wasn't sure how to respond. Both of those things were true ... but was Nicole really naïve enough to think *annoyance* had been the problem?

'It's a funny thing about Gerrit,' Nicole went on. 'He's a smart man, and he has a really subtle mind. And yet, when he talks to people about important things, he can sound stupidly blunt.' She raised a finger. 'I'll tell you what it is – it's shyness. I know he seems confident, but really, he's socially awkward.'

Sara blinked, then gazed absently at the modern, blonde-bricked houses across the street. 'So you're not apologising for his attempt to bribe me,' she said quietly, 'just that he did it awkwardly.'

Nicole frowned sadly. 'Sara,' she said, 'Gerrit wasn't trying to bribe you. This is exactly the point I'm trying to make – sometimes, he expresses things clumsily. Gerrit was trying to tell you how highly he thinks of Jamie, and how much Thorndike Aerospace could do for Jamie's career.'

Nicole snapped her fingers, as though she had just remembered something. 'I want to give you this,' she said, but the rest of her words were muffled by a passing train overhead. She raised her hands in comic exasperation and waited for it to pass. As it did, Sara glanced back at her appraisingly. Vos's partner seemed so upfront, so sure that she could spin what had happened yesterday into a case of mere social awkwardness. Obviously, Nicole had been briefed by Vos prior to coming here today – but how much did she actually know?

Nicole listened to the fading rumbles of the train, and then held up a finger. 'As I was saying … I brought you something. She reached into her jacket pocket. 'After that lovely dinner at your house, I felt so inspired. As a result, on my way here this morning, I visited a gallery.'

She produced a bronze figurine about an inch-and-a-half tall. 'And I picked up this little fellow,' she said, and set in on the table before Sara. 'It's for you.'

Sara peered at the green-grey effigy. It was a sculpture of a crouching man, its features worn and mottled by age. 'West African?' she speculated.

'They told me it's from Mali,' Nicole said.

Sara nodded. Nineteenth-century, most likely. It would probably have been placed in a shrine, to represent a spirit or ancestor. They were fairly common in London's specialist African galleries – but still, it would have set Nicole back several hundred pounds. *That's quite an apology*, Sara thought. She smiled in a way she hoped looked appreciative. 'Thank you,' she said, 'but this is too much. I really can't accept it.'

Nicole nudged the figurine closer to her. 'I bought it for you,' she repeated. 'What would I do with it?'

The waiter arrived and set their food before them. Sara was forced to pick up the figurine and place it to the side. The mere act of touching it seemed too much like acceptance. Nicole watched her set the figurine next to her plate and chuckled. 'If it makes you feel any better,' she said, 'Gerrit paid for it. I put it on one of his credit cards. Every time you look at it, you can think of that.'

Sara chuckled appreciatively and watched the waiter retreat. Then she shook her head. 'It just makes me feel a bit awkward,' she said quietly, 'considering what actually happened yesterday.'

Her eyes moved from the figurine to the newly delivered plate of avocado on toast. She realised she had little appetite. 'The disagreement I had with Gerrit,' she said, lowering her tone, 'wasn't about how things were phrased. I assume he heard I'd been asking difficult questions. And I have been – to Andy Turner. I wanted to know more about what happened in South Africa.'

'Well, you chose the right guy,' Nicole replied. She took a bite of brioche as though nothing were wrong. 'If anything out-of-the-ordinary had happened back then, I'm sure Andy would know about it.' She arched an eyebrow. 'And Andy can't help sharing a good story. Am I right in assuming he didn't tell you anything?'

'Nothing,' Sara admitted.

'There you are,' Nicole concluded. 'That's because there's nothing to tell.'

'My questions to Andy unnerved Gerrit,' Sara said. 'That's why Gerrit asked to see me. He started telling me about all the ways he could help Jamie. That suggests he felt threatened.'

Nicole smiled. 'Wouldn't you?' she asked pleasantly. The lightness of her attitude belied her words. 'I mean, if someone were making unfounded accusations?'

Sara frowned. 'Despite what you say about his social awkwardness,' she went on, 'Gerrit's offer can only be seen as an attempt at bribery. And when I wouldn't take the bribe, he threatened to turn Jamie against me.'

For a moment, there was silence – and then Nicole began to chuckle softly. Sara realised she must have looked annoyed by this response, because Nicole quickly stifled her laughter. She placed a hand over Sara's. 'Look, I believe you,' she said. 'I'm only laughing because it's so like Gerrit. Sometimes, when he doesn't get his way, he

166

responds with some silly threat. It happens when he feels out of control.'

She gazed deeply at Sara. 'Please don't take him seriously.'

'I'm afraid I have to,' Sara said. 'I can't un-know what I know. Men were murdered at Thorndike Platinum back then, and Gerrit was involved. I'm afraid that's the truth, Nicole. If Jamie wasn't working for him, it would be none of my business. But he is.'

Nicole's face tightened. 'Whatever you heard,' she said, 'is a lie.'

'Gerrit told you that?' Sara asked.

'Yes,' Nicole stated emphatically, 'and I believe him. Your brother was mistaken. Of all people, Rhodri Jones must have known how volatile South Africa was at that time. It was never as simple as management against the unions. There were rival factions among the miners too – power struggles that your brother and his subordinates could never have controlled. Why didn't he tell you about that, rather than speculating about Gerrit?'

Sara pursed her lips. This confirmed the suspicion she'd had in the cemetery – clearly, Gerrit Vos thought Sara had been given inside knowledge by Rhodri. It certainly sounded more rational than the way she had actually come by the things she knew. 'I know how much you care for Gerrit,' she said. 'And I know how eager you are to believe what he says. In a similar situation, I'd take Jamie's side too.'

'I believe him because I know it's true,' Nicole said.

Sara smiled sadly. 'We shouldn't argue. Neither of us is going to change our minds. Can I suggest we declare a stalemate? I want Gerrit to tell Andy Turner he no longer wants to work with Jamie. Or, he can ring Jamie and do it directly. That's all I ask. And if that happens, I'll say no more about it.'

Nicole looked at Sara neutrally. She really had done a remarkable job of keeping calm, Sara thought. Nicole had sat here, listening to a near-stranger accuse her boyfriend of murder, and yet kept her emotions in check. When they had dinner together, Vos mentioned Nicole had once worked in Intelligence. Sara imagined she had been very good at it.

'I can tell him what you've said,' Nicole replied cautiously, 'but I can't guarantee how he'll respond.'

Sara nodded. 'Of course not.' She looked down at her plate, and realised she had barely touched her food. 'I have to get back,' she said.

Nicole signalled for the bill, and insisted on paying. When the waiter had pulled Vos's debit card from the machine and retreated back into the deli, Nicole reached over, picked up the bronze figurine and placed it in Sara's hand. There was no more point in arguing; Sara tucked the small sculpture into her pocket.

'I have to go back up to the Tesco,' Nicole said. 'But let me walk you to your car first.'

Sara blinked; the woman was truly remarkable. She was smiling as though they were the best of friends.

'Actually, I left my car at work,' Sara said. 'As you found out, there's no point in driving around here if you can avoid it.'

'Of course,' Nicole said. 'Then I'll walk you back to your clinic instead.'

Vos had rung Jamie that afternoon. Just after tea-time, Jamie peered onto the Brixton street, wondering what his client wanted to discuss. He watched for Vos's Porsche, observing neighbours from the estate several doors down. They were holding an ad hoc party on the pavement, complete with clouds of fragrant smoke and thumping music. Vos was fifteen minutes late, which was unusual

168

for him. Sara had been lying down for an hour now; she had arrived home from work early that Tuesday afternoon with another headache. Jamie did not want to wake her until he absolutely had to. He hoped she was managing to sleep through their neighbours' impromptu DJ set.

Maybe Vos had a new opportunity for him, Jamie thought. As far as his current work for Thorndike Aerospace went, things seemed to be falling into a rather sluggish groove. Not much had happened for a few days. The most regular part of the job seemed as though it was going to be the deposits Andrew Turner & Associates would make into Jamie's Barclays account. Considering how little he was doing to earn the money, it felt almost like stealing. It was true that Jamie had met Levi Rootenberg again, to receive a report on the progress of talks with his Zimbabwean friends. Rootenberg had developed a plan to ship Thorndike's artillery shells to Zambia – quite legally, he claimed. Because he lacked a Trade Control Licence, the End User Certificate and other paperwork would be administered by Thorndike themselves. From there, Rootenberg would handle the sale onward to Zimbabwe. The only thing Rootenberg was waiting for was a go-ahead from his team of defence insiders within the country. The timing of that depended on rivalries within the Zimbabwean government and the political party that controlled it. Rootenberg had reminded Jamie of the ultimate goal, to compete long-term for Zimbabwean business against a Russian-government puppet company. And, with hope, to do it in a future where sanctions were a thing of the past. 'Keep your eyes on the prize,' he had said.

After that conversation with Rootenberg, Jamie had rung Vos to deliver a summary. Otherwise, he had done nothing but go to the university. Little had happened that might justify his pay cheque – and Vos had seemed happy enough for things to linger in this way. But that afternoon, out of the blue, Vos had requested an evening meeting at Jamie's home. And, stranger still, he had asked that Sara be there.

Jamie heard Vos's Boxster power its way past the revellers on his street before he saw it. Quickly, but as quietly as he could, he edged into the bedroom and touched Sara lightly on the arm. Immediately, she opened her eyes.

'He's here?' she said.

'You weren't asleep,' Jamie observed.

'No luck,' she replied.

Sara rose immediately. Jamie left her waiting in the living room as he opened the front door for Gerrit Vos. Vos nodded, but said nothing until they had both joined Sara.

'Mr Vos,' Sara said with a tight smile. 'I had a lovely lunch with your partner today.'

Jamie felt that he might have imagined it, but Vos and Sara seemed to hold eye contact for slightly too long, as though a second conversation was happening that he was not party to. Jamie offered drinks, which Vos refused as he sat down in Jamie's leather armchair. Vos balanced a small case on his knees with solemnity. Jamie, still standing, shot a puzzled glance Sara's way, and she wrinkled her brow. He gently steered her towards the sofa, and they sat.

'This is a touch awkward,' Vos announced. 'I'm not here specifically in relation to our mutual business, Jamie, but in my larger capacity as Thorndike's Director for Business Development. Part of my job is to mitigate risk to the company's reputation.' He looked pointedly at Sara, and added, 'Out of necessity, I have to get involved in certain aspects of intelligence gathering.'

It was unlike Vos to be so halting in his tone, and so

formal in his words. His manner flagged that this meeting was important, and also delicate. Jamie glanced at Sara. She seemed less puzzled than angry. Her eyes gleamed, and she stared at Vos with distaste.

'Go on, then,' Sara said in a flat voice. 'What have you got?'

Vos blew air from his cheeks, as though what he was about to say caused him pain. Sara replied with a derisive snort.

'Sara,' Jamie said under his breath. 'Do you know what this is about?'

She shook her head, but her eyes suggested she didn't expect it to be good. Vos opened his small case and withdrew a manila envelope. 'I also have digital copies of these,' he muttered, 'but I thought it might be best if you saw actual photographs.'

He slid out a small stack of seven-by-five-inch photos and handed them to Jamie. Jamie looked down. The images were grainy, and each was time-and-date stamped in the corner – security camera stuff. The first showed a London square at night, and a car Jamie didn't recognise sitting next to the pavement. A figure could be seen emerging from the passenger's side. Because it had been taken in the dark by a low-resolution camera, the photo was indistinct, and the individual unrecognisable. Jamie squinted, then passed the photo to Sara with a shrug.

The next image was taken from inside a house. The large black front door was partly open, and what may have been the same figure was entering the foyer. In this picture, it seemed evident the person was Sara. Jamie felt himself frown as he handed it to her. 'Is that you?' he asked.

She didn't answer.

The following few photos featured Sara in the same entrance space. The final one showed her mounting the

171

stairs to the next floor. Jamie took the stack back from Sara and shuffled through them a second time. 'I don't understand,' Jamie said to Vos.

'Check the date,' Vos said.

Jamie looked.

'Mean anything to you?'

Jamie thought. The date stamp suggested that these were taken about the time when -

'Oh, for goodness' sake,' Sara snapped, 'why don't you just come out and say it?'

She was speaking to Vos, who stared back at her with hooded eyes. 'You want to explain it to Jamie?' he asked. When Sara remained silent, he added, 'The house she's in belonged to Rhodri Jones.'

Jamie looked again. He hadn't noticed before, but it was Rhodri's foyer. He noted the tell-tale mosaic floor and, just at the edge of the frame, Rhodri's umbrella stand, which had toppled over. The date that was stamped on the bottom would have been...

'That was the day Rhodri died,' Sara said with a weary sigh. Then she added a question that Jamie didn't understand. 'Would you be doing this if I'd been more cooperative at Highgate?'

Jamie may not have understood, but Vos seemed to. 'Nope,' he said pleasantly.

For a moment, Jamie felt paralysed, the result of too many thoughts and sensations rushing in at once. 'You were there, the night he died?'

'Evidently,' Vos drawled. 'What your partner didn't think about was security cameras.' He looked at Sara. 'You must have known Mr Jones had one outside.'

She blinked. 'I suppose I knew. It never really crossed my mind.'

Vos snorted. 'You didn't know about the one in the foyer, though, did you? Small pinhole jobbie. Easy to miss.' He chuckled. 'Now, given that you inherited the place, you really should have discovered it. But, then, you were so eager to sell up quickly. Never did take the time to do a proper inventory, did you?'

'OK, I was there,' Sara said to Vos. She turned to Jamie and clarified. 'The night Rhodri died.'

Jamie squeezed his eyes shut until he saw stars. 'But why?' he said.

Sara ignored him. 'What are you trying to prove, Mr Vos?'

Vos leaned back in Jamie's chair. 'Pity Thorndike didn't hide cameras in more places,' he mused. 'It would have made your movements easier to follow.' He cocked his head speculatively, and said, 'Then again, I suppose Mr Jones didn't want that, given his recreational tastes. Anyway,' he went on, 'the camera in the foyer was enough to show where in the house visitors were heading. Did they turn left into the sitting room, or go towards the laundry room in the back? Or – as in your case, Sara – did they turn right and go upstairs? That alone tells us a lot.'

Jamie looked at Sara. 'You went to his bedroom.'

Vos left a significant pause before continuing. To Jamie he said, 'Considering the time those photographs were taken, we can surmise that Sara found her brother dying or dead.' His gaze hardened. 'Oh, yes – and with a woman's corpse on the bed.' He swivelled towards Sara. 'And yet you said nothing.'

Jamie's mind buzzed in a jumble of confused thoughts, and he fought to make sense of them. Why was Sara even there? *How* was Sara even there? Rhodri had killed himself after being attacked at the air show in Hampshire. Jamie and Sara had both been in Wales then. Jamie tried to piece together what he could recall from that day. It was Ceri who'd told Sara that Eldon Carson had targeted her brother. At the same time, Jamie was driving to Sara's

173

farmhouse. He'd got a call from the Ministry of Defence Police, saying Carson had been killed as he tried to cut Rhodri's throat. Sara went into hysterics at the news, despite her brother being – at least at that point – safe. She'd blacked out; Jamie and Ceri had spent the next half hour reviving her. Once Sara came around, she'd sent them away. She'd planned to take a bath, then ring Rhodri.

Was it possible she'd changed her mind and driven to London once they'd left?

He picked up the first photo and stared at it again. It showed Sara outside Rhodri's house, emerging from an unfamiliar car. Now that he thought about it, Jamie had never again seen Sara's BMW after that evening. Later, she told him she'd sold it. For the rest of her time in Wales, Sara had relied on a rental, and then had bought the blue Mini here, when she moved back to London.

'You're wondering about the car,' Vos said. 'Sara got into a fender-bender near Madame Tussauds and abandoned it on the Marylebone Road.' He glanced at Sara. 'That's the gist of it, isn't it? I have traffic-cam photos on my iPad if you'd like to look.' Turning back to Jamie, he continued, 'She signed the car over to the lady whose van she'd hit, then called an Uber. That's the car you're seeing there.'

Stupidly, Jamie said, 'You gave away your car?'

'I had to get to Rhodri,' she replied softly.

Vos reached over and slid the photos from Jamie's fingers. 'It's best you don't keep these,' he said. 'They're not the kind of evidence you want lying around.' He placed them in his case. 'Obviously, the traffic accident is a matter of public record,' Vos said to Sara. 'It establishes that you were in London on the evening of Rhodri Jones's death. But that in itself is no crime. As for breaking into your brother's house ...'

Vos paused and looked thoughtful. 'By the way, was Mr Jones dying or already dead when you got there?'

Sara closed her eyes. 'Go to hell.'

Vos huffed. 'Well, anyway. Moot point. Only Thorndike Aerospace has the video files from the house. I'll keep them safe for you.' He smiled. 'You know – to protect you. It could get messy if people started asking questions. After all, whether Mr Jones was dead or alive when you got there, the place was already a murder scene.'

Vos turned to Jamie and said, 'What do you think, Inspector? Would the police charge her with perverting the course of justice? Assisting an offender? Maybe even assisting a suicide?'

Jamie felt himself shrug. He was numb, dazed. He wanted to scream, to question Sara, or to go to sleep and blot out this new reality. 'They'd speak to her,' he confirmed. 'Certainly take a statement. But, unless she confessed to something, there'd be no charges. Insufficient evidence.'

Maybe he was imagining it, but Jamie though he'd felt Sara flinch when he'd said the word *confess*. Perhaps because it presumed guilt. He looked at Sara, who was smiling grimly at Vos.

'If you wanted to protect me,' she said, 'you could always delete the files, couldn't you?'

Vos stood. Casually – but in a tone that made his request sound like a boss's order – he said, 'Jamie, walk me to my car.'

Jamie rose immediately, then stared down at Sara. Her face was flushed with anger and possibly shame. Lips pursed, she tugged on a spike of hair. 'I'll be back,' he said. He had tried to sound neutral, but his voice was wavering.

'One of us has a story to tell,' Sara muttered, 'and it's

not you.'

Jamie hesitated.

'I'm not talking to you,' she said to him.

Jamie furrowed his brow, then followed Vos outside. At some point, the street music had stopped, and most of the revellers had returned indoors. The two men walked down the pavement to Vos's Boxster Spyder, and Vos leaned against the car.

'Told you it was awkward,' he began.

Jamie shook his head helplessly. 'I can't …'

'Look, kiddo,' Vos interrupted, 'I don't have any explanations for you. I can understand Sara's instinct to find her brother, considering the shit he'd gone through that day in Hampshire. Still, damned if I know why she'd keep quiet about what she found. Who wouldn't call the cops?'

'She panicked,' Jamie said. 'She must have.'

'Maybe,' Vos said. 'That would explain her running away at that moment. But Sara was on good terms with the Met. She'd been one of their consultants. There must've been someone she could call after the fact, once she'd escaped from that awful place.'

Jamie's mind reeled as he groped for a way to make sense of the accusations. 'In her last days consulting with the police,' Jamie said, 'her closest contact was me. She hadn't really dealt with anyone else for months.'

Vos looked as though Jamie had said something significant. 'Then why the creeping fuck didn't she tell you?' he said. 'I don't even mean as a detective inspector, for God's sake – just as her friend. Why has she hidden this from you for all these years?'

Jamie wondered that too. Why had Sara not felt able to talk to him about it? Him, of all people. The fact that she hadn't unsettled Jamie even more than her lying about where she got those bruises. Or, for that matter, even more than finding that weird Eye-in-the-Pyramid symbol.

'Face it, chum, your girlfriend's got a few secrets,' Vos said. 'That's not so strange; I've seen plenty of dysfunctional relationships.' He placed a hand on Jamie's shoulder. 'You want my advice? Talk to her about it. Go easy on her, sure – if she feels threatened, she's only going to lie again. But do try to get some answers.'

Jamie nodded. 'I will,' he said. He felt himself breathing more heavily than he wanted to.

'If you want to take some time out,' Vos went on, 'just to think things over, I've got a place you could stay.'

'Thank you, but I don't think it'll come to that.'

'It's here in town,' Vos went on. 'You wouldn't have to go far. It might be wise to detach, to consider your options. It's sure as hell what I'd do. But, hey – it's your call.'

Vos walked around the car to the driver's door and opened it. 'Just let me know.'

In their time together, Sara had seen Jamie in many moods. She had watched him navigate difficult situations with a cocky confidence he really shouldn't have felt. She'd seen him mimic bravado when she knew, inside, he was quaking with uncertainty. She had observed him pacing the room with excitement, and also collapsed into his chair, despondent. But Sara had never before seen Jamie in this particular state of confused anger. He wasn't shouting or out of control. If anything, his blush, combined with his darkening expression, looked like humiliation. He stood in the centre of the room, breathing heavily, his muscles twitching as if he wanted to run. When Sara reached out and touched his emotions, she felt a burning incomprehension – the emotional maelstrom of a man who sensed he'd been cheated but didn't know how.

'Why didn't you tell me?' he asked. 'Why didn't you say you were there? You never bothered to inform me you'd run off to London. You didn't admit you were in his house. Or that you actually saw the dead woman. Or that you watched him, while his life was draining away –'

Suddenly, Jamie drew in a sharp breath and his head fell forward onto his chest. He released a guttural groan, and Sara saw tears welling in his eyes. She had been sitting on the sofa, hoping he would sit down, too. Now she leapt to her feet.

'Jamie,' she said, her voice trembling with shock and concern. She reached out a hand. Hyperventilating, he shook her away.

'What did you …' he stammered. 'Why would …?'

She grabbed his arm roughly, and tried to force the pleading from her voice. Maybe the only way Jamie would hear her was if she met anger with anger. 'Listen to me,' she said. 'You're not thinking clearly. You need to remember what that night was like.'

Jamie drew a steadying breath. His eyes, red and wet, met hers.

'You told me about what had happened to Rhoddo. About Eldon Carson trying to kill him. Then, you and Ceri wanted me to rest,' she continued. 'As if I could, knowing Rhoddo had been attacked. So, yes, I humoured you. Got you out of my house so I could go to him.'

Jamie was panting. 'But when you got there …'

Sara bit her lip. *How much can I tell him?* She cursed herself for not having rehearsed this. She should have guessed that Jamie might find out about her trip to London – unlikely as that had seemed to her. It was stupid not to have run through some scenarios, just in case.

'The woman – Maja Bosco – was already dead,' she said slowly, quietly. 'Rhodri wasn't. Not yet. He was bleeding, dying. Probably beyond saving.'

'Probably?' Jamie said.

'Jamie, I was in shock! I should have rung the police, or dialled 999, but I didn't. I left the house. My car was gone, and it was too late to get a train. I stayed in a hotel near Euston Station. I didn't sleep that night, I just listened to the traffic on the Euston Road. The first train was just before seven the next morning, and I was on it. London to Birmingham, Birmingham to Aber. A taxi from there. I was back at the cottage in Penweddig by early afternoon. In the cold light of day, I couldn't tell you what I'd done – or rather, what I'd failed to do. I certainly couldn't admit that to Ceri. You both thought I'd been sleeping the whole time.'

She reached out and held his arm. This time, he did not shake her away. 'You didn't even notice the car was gone,' she said with affectionate mockery. 'Not for a week. A bright red BMW.' She smiled, and attempted a chuckle. 'Some copper you were.'

Jamie sat still for a moment, in thought. Then he stood and disappeared into the bedroom. He returned within seconds. 'On Friday,' he said, 'I got home just before you did. I went into the bedroom and took off my shoes.' He raised his hand and opened his palm. An object on a leather thong dropped and dangled. 'Then I found this on the floor.'

Sara looked up. When she saw what was swinging in front of her, she was surprised to feel her whole body relax. Relief washed through her. In fact, she felt almost giddy. She reached up and took in her fist Eldon Carson's papier mâché Eye-in-the-Pyramid pendant. Sara realised that she had subconsciously been dreading this moment ever since she had moved back to London two-and-a-half years ago. It was true that she'd had no idea that video images of her from the day Rhodri died existed, but this – this she had been waiting for. Still, Sara had not spent much time considering what she would say if Jamie ever found the pendant, and had certainly never entertained any thoughts about getting rid of it. But now Sara understood how much stress its concealment had caused her. Now that stress was gone.

In a soft breath, the first thing she said was, 'You've damaged it.'

Jamie looked down. His anger seemed to drain away, leaving only puzzlement. 'What?'

Sara held it out. 'You must have rubbed it. You've worn off the gloss. And look – the edge has crumbled away.'

Jamie reached for it to have a closer look, but Sara pulled it back. She held the disk protectively. 'It's only papier mâché,' she added.

The calmness of her response, and maybe her wistful reaction to the damage, appeared to increase Jamie's confusion. He really didn't seem to know how to respond. Still, Sara had only bought a moment of flummoxed silence. She would need to tell him something. But what? Was she willing to admit to her clandestine relationship with Eldon Carson in Aberystwyth – a secret conspiracy Jamie might view as a kind of treason? More than that, one that would add another layer of complicity to her visit to her dying brother's house. Could Sara find the strength to explain that she was, in fact, psychic?

That wouldn't be strength, she thought. *It would be foolishness.*

If anyone had asked Jamie whether Sara believed in psychic powers, he would have said no. She had once told him that most people who claimed to have them were either deluded or lying. In fact, at one time, Jamie would have been likelier to accept the existence of psychics than Sara was, even with all of her academic knowledge of the occult. No – she couldn't tell her partner any of her

180

deepest secrets. They were much too strange. Too far removed from the Sara Jones Jamie thought he knew, and maybe even loved. Such knowledge would have the strength to shatter their relationship. Before Jamie had time to ask Sara where she had got the pendant, she spoke.

'I made this,' she said quietly.

Jamie's blank expression shifted slowly into something like disgust. 'You made it? For God's sake, Sara – why?'

Sara lowered her gaze, licked her lips, and thought rapidly. She looked back up towards him, and actual tears welled in her eyes. Even though she was about to lie, she didn't need to fake her emotions.

'That's the question, isn't it?' she said in a trembling voice. 'Maybe before you climb on your high horse, you might try to answer it. For you, Aberystwyth was nothing more than another investigation – and maybe, as a bonus, the chance to reconcile with me. But for me, Jamie … for me, it was linked to so much more. To my home, to my childhood community, to my best friend – and even to my parents' murders. And in case you've forgotten, it all ended with my brother's suicide. That summer in Aberystwyth cast a different light on everything I've ever experienced. And if there's one image that symbolised the whole of what happened, and whatever it all meant, it is this. This bloody Eye-in-the-Pyramid that the killer made his own.'

At some point in her speech, they had locked eyes. Jamie's were guarded, watchful. Waiting for her to go on. To explain. To justify.

'If you could ever understand that,' she said, 'you'd realise why I had to run to London after Rhodri was attacked. And, afterwards, why I couldn't bring myself to explain what I'd seen.'

'You recreated the killer's symbol because you watched your brother die?'

'I made it so I won't forget. Believe me, it's a tempting option – to accept everything I have now and not look back.' She lowered her eyes. 'But I need to remind myself of where I've been, and what has changed.'

Sara dangled the damaged pendant by its leather thong. 'I am a psychiatrist,' she added. 'I know about confronting the past. If I choose to use this awful symbol to do that – to make sure I never slip into some sort of self-satisfied dream state – then who are you to say I can't?'

Jamie was silent for a long while. Sara was surprised that – even though she had meant to deceive, or avoid, or at least to distract – much of what she'd told him had been true. Especially about her desire to forget. The idea that she could find some sort of cosmic reset button to take her back to a time before Eldon Carson was alluring. It would be wonderful to lose all memory that she had ever been psychic, and not to be plagued with uncertainty over any vision that flashed before her mind's eye.

'It's going to take me time to work out what I think of all this,' Jamie said.

'Of course,' Sara agreed. She reached out and brushed her fingers lightly against his thigh.

'And I can't do it here,' Jamie added.

Sara stopped mid-stroke. 'What?'

'I think I'm going to leave for a while,' he said.

'To go where?' she asked.

'Somewhere I can think,' he said.

Jamie backed away from her reach. 'This past week, we've been going in different directions,' he explained. 'You don't want me working with Vos – and I think I want to.'

'Vos,' Sara said with more vehemence than she'd

intended, 'just tried to threaten me.'

'That's not how I see it,' Jamie said. 'He was pointing out how vulnerable your carelessness has made you. He was showing you how useful he can be. You need to decide if you can accept that.'

He turned towards the bedroom, to pack. 'And I need to decide if I can accept ...'

Jamie looked about the room, focusing on nothing. 'If I can accept all *this*,' he concluded.

FIFTEEN

In Holly Lodge, the smell of a fried breakfast still hung in the air. It mingled with the ubiquitous odour of disinfectant and, today, a waft of lilac blossoms through the sunroom's half-open window. Down the hall, a woman wailed. Not, Jamie guessed, for a particular outcome, but from some existential dread. He flipped through a several-months-old copy of the *Oldie*, trying to distract himself from that noise, as well as the clatter of dishes in the dining room, and the myriad other individual cacophonies that echoed through this residential home's corridors.

Before long, a new tone joined the soundscape – Jamie heard Doris-the-nurse's voice murmuring words of encouragement in the hallway. The sound was accompanied by the rustle of fabric and the occasional clack of a walking stick against the wall. 'Goddamn it, let go of me. I can walk,' he heard his father say.

Doris made a dubious hum. 'You can fall over, too,' she said. 'You want to do that?'

Doris led George into the sunroom holding his arm, her hand underneath his elbow. When they stopped, she placed her hand around George's back, resting it on his hip to steady him. George looked to Jamie and rolled his eyes. 'It's like we're dating,' he muttered.

Jamie smiled at Doris. 'You make a lovely couple,' he said.

'Jesus help me,' Doris replied, and eased Jamie's father into a chair. 'He's all yours,' she sang, and retreated swiftly.

'You're speaking quite clearly today, Dad,' Jamie observed.

'Where's your mum?' George asked.

'I didn't tell her I was coming. I wanted to talk to you alone.'

George frowned. 'She ill?'

'Mum never gets ill,' Jamie said. 'She's healthy as a horse.'

It was Wednesday morning, and Jamie had spent the night in a nearby hotel. Although his mother's cottage was close to the nursing home, Jamie had not wanted to visit. He knew that choice would have led to her presence here, this morning – and Jamie had wanted to be alone with his father. 'This is about me, Dad,' he said. 'I wanted to ask your advice.'

George Harding frowned, as though his son might be playing a trick on him. Jamie explained that he had been financing his law degree by doing some consultancy for a defence company. This alone seemed to raise Jamie in George's estimation – he nodded seriously and leaned forward in the floral-patterned chair. 'So, what's the problem?' George asked.

Jamie explained that he was involved in a business transaction that wasn't entirely legal. He thought it might be a test, he said, to see how he would handle himself in such a situation. Jamie assured his father that the level of illegality was minor, and that he personally was in little danger. On top of that, he said, he did not intend to continue working on the wrong side of the law, even with the support of a major defence company. But in this instance, he thought it best to go along with the plan, and establish a reputation as a trustworthy player.

'No danger?' George clarified.

'I don't think so. I'm really just relaying messages from one party to the next.'

'And it's well-paid?'

'It is.'

George blew air from his cheeks. He used his right hand to ease his troublesome left arm into a more comfortable position. 'You said they're testing you,' he noted.

'I think so.'

'And you need the money, right?'

'Sure.'

George Harding pondered, wiping a fleck of spittle from his lips with his good hand. Finally, he said, 'Nobody gets hurt?'

'No.'

'OK,' George said, leaning back in his chair. 'Then I'll ask again. What's the problem?'

Jamie sighed. 'My partner.'

George furrowed his brow.

'My girlfriend,' Jamie clarified. 'The one you have the photo of.'

He explained to his father that Sara had qualms about the arms industry in general – and, specifically, about Jamie's involvement in illegal deals. He did not tell him how, yesterday evening, he had fled the flat with no intention of going back any time soon. Nor did he tell George how he had switched off his phone because Sara had rung several times in the night, and Jamie had found it too painful to keep declining her calls.

'You're the only person I know who's had to face this,' Jamie said. 'When you were investigated by the Met, how did Mum react?'

186

'Fine,' George said curtly.

'Really?'

'Your mother's supportive. Always has been.' George Harding's eyes drifted away from Jamie and looked into the distance. Something in them softened. 'Did she know about it before I got caught? I don't know. I told her we could afford to send you to that school, and she chose to believe me.'

Jamie brushed his hair from his eyes. 'Sara's not like that. She always needs to know the truth.'

George shrugged. 'Not always a good thing.' He arched an eyebrow. 'You love her?'

Jamie hesitated. Of course he did – but it was more complicated than that. Finally, he gave a short nod. He did not say that, recently, Sara had been hiding things from him, or that he was beginning to doubt he knew her as well as he'd thought he did.

'Well, I don't know what to tell you,' George sighed. 'She sounds like a do-gooder to me. You know, the self-righteous sort. Holier-than-thou. If you love her, then, hell – you're going to have to put up with that. But you've also got to do what you think's right. Life's not black-and-white, you know – not the way people like your girlfriend seem to imagine it is.'

George Harding looked down, and added, 'Sometimes you do the wrong thing for the right reasons.'

Jamie nodded. 'Thanks, Dad. You've helped.'

'What are you going to do?' his father asked.

'Take some time to think,' Jamie replied.

'Smart,' said George.

Jamie stood, and told his father he'd ask Doris to help him back to his room. George asked for a wheelchair – he was feeling tired.

'And, Jamie,' he added, 'Keep coming to see me, OK? We don't talk enough.'

Jamie said he would – and for the first time ever, he meant it.

Sara had spent the last hour of Wednesday morning in Ellen's office, discussing the ways in which the housing requirements of a client interacted with his mental health needs. It had felt good; wrapping herself in the routine of work was like placing a soft gauze over Jamie's absence. There were so many things that could have caused Sara to feel out of control if she allowed them to distract her. Far more than simply not knowing where Jamie was. She could have worried about whether her explanation about the pendant had been enough to waylay his suspicion and disgust. Worse, Sara could have felt unbalanced by the sudden shift in power Gerrit Vos had achieved over her. If she had truly allowed herself to confront that reality, she knew she would fall into another spiral of self-recrimination – *Why did I tell Vos what I knew about South Africa? And why did I trust Andy to keep his mouth shut?*

As Sara walked along the dank basement hallway towards her own office, she met her fellow counsellor, Rohini. In the fluorescent glare, Rohini met Sara's eyes with quivering compassion. 'Sara, I'm so sorry,' she said.

Sara blinked, and adopted a neutral expression.

'If you want to talk about it,' Rohini went on, 'I have some time.'

'Wonderful,' Sara said. She realised she could not maintain a charade of comprehension. 'Talk about what?'

For a moment, Rohini's expression blanked, then she blushed. 'Oh, I'm so sorry,' she breathed. 'I didn't realise that you ...'

Without warning, she moaned and clasped Sara in a tight hug. Sara held herself awkwardly, staring at a spot on the wall where a patch of old plaster had crumbled away.

'Find Jo,' Rohini said softly into her ear. 'Talk to her. Then, if you want someone to share with, you'll find me in my office.'

Rohini detached from Sara, holding her at arm's length, and offered a sad-but-reassuring smile. 'A little heart-to-heart, *na*?' she said.

She turned and fled down the hallway. Sara watched her go, then cocked her head. What on earth was wrong? She concentrated …

And an impression washed over her in answer. It felt as real as the crumbling plaster, and far more solid.

I have just lost my job.

Sara felt certain of it. And yet, the mere idea was ludicrous. She'd had no warning that anything was wrong here at the clinic. In fact, things had seemed to be going very well -

It's Vos, her senses told her. *He's leaned on Andy.*

Of course he had. Andy's company funded Sara's position, for goodness' sake. And it was at the beck and call of Thorndike Aerospace, its biggest client by far. When push came to shove, Andy's loyalty to Sara could never outweigh the health of his business, nor the wellbeing of the people who relied on his paycheques.

Sara noticed her pulse was racing. She forced herself to breathe slowly. Why get upset about being sacked? Money wasn't an issue, she told herself. In fact, she had always been willing to offer her time for free; it had been Andy who'd insisted her job come with a salary. If Andy had withdrawn his funding, Sara could always offer to work as a volunteer. Then Gerrit Vos would have no control over what she did with her time.

Although, Sara sensed, Jo might have some qualms about accepting charity from an employee she had just let go. Sara began to consider alternatives: maybe she could take a break, let things calm down, and then return after a suitable pause. That seemed a good plan. It would give her time to sort out the other, many, looming problems in her life.

Sara, you're getting ahead of yourself, she thought. *Jo hasn't even sacked you yet.*

Then, as Sara walked the final few steps to her office, she felt her phone vibrate. She thumbed the icon and looked at the screen. On it was a text from Nicole. It read, *Gerrit says you'll get a message from him soon.*

Sara snorted grimly and opened her office door. When she found Jo sitting sad-faced in the chair next to her desk, she wasn't at all surprised.

Within three hours of Jamie's telephone call to Gerrit Vos, both men were outside the Green Street flat. Jamie took a step backwards and looked up. He hadn't even known Thorndike had a place like this. He found himself wondering whether Sara knew about it, before stifling the thought. 'I wasn't aware you were in Hampshire this morning,' Jamie apologised. 'You didn't need to come all this way so quickly. I could have wandered the West End for a while, or even got a hotel room.'

'Don't be an idiot,' Vos interrupted bluffly. 'I said you could ring yesterday evening. Frankly, I was expecting it.'

Jamie did not mention he'd spent the night in Kent, or had sought his father's opinion before dialling Vos's number. He had rung from Holly Lodge's car park, and Vos had given him the Mayfair address. Jamie hadn't arrived at the building's front door too long before Vos. As soon as Vos got there, he asked where Jamie had parked. Jamie said his Range Rover was in the Park Lane car park, and he hoped the old banger felt special – it was costing him twenty pounds an hour. Vos gave Jamie a resident's permit. 'Rescue your car as soon as you can,' he advised, 'or Andy will need to pay you more just to cover your parking.'

Despite what he'd just said, Vos immediately led Jamie upstairs. Jamie got a brief tour of his new, temporary home – where the linen was kept, where the thermostat was. 'I won't be here long,' he promised as they moved from feature to feature. 'I'm just giving Sara some time to think.'

'Stay as long as you like,' Vos said, turning on the bathroom tap. He tugged the plunger that switched over to the shower. 'As I said last night, it's the wise choice.'

He waved a hand to the flow of water. 'That's how the shower works,' he said.

Absently, Jamie watched steam rise and form beads on the tiles. 'Sara's just got the wrong end of the stick,' he told Vos over the hiss. 'I know you were trying to help.'

Vos twisted the tap, and the spray drizzled to a stop. 'Those photos exist,' he said matter-of-factly. 'I'm not the only one who can put two-and-two together. That's why it's important for me to keep them under wraps.'

'I know. She'll come around.'

Vos peered at Jamie through hooded eyes. 'You think she will?'

'Yeah, I do.'

Vos squeezed past him and moved into the hallway. 'How can you be so sure?'

Jamie followed. 'I trust her.'

Vos smiled without mirth and opened the front door. He led Jamie down the stairs and back onto the street. 'There's a grocery shop around the corner,' he said, and then waved to his Porsche. Somehow, he had managed to park it in a space that had been occupied when Jamie drove past it not long before. 'Go get your car,' Vos said. 'I'll hang around until you're here. Otherwise, you may never get a spot.'

Before Vos climbed into his car, he said, 'Look, kiddo – I know you want to trust your partner. Who doesn't? But remember how important it is to have a basis for your trust. You've got to know why you're doing things.'

He popped the locks and opened the door. 'You've bought yourself time to think,' he said. 'Be sure to use it.'

Later, alone in the flat, Jamie thought about Vos's reaction to Sara. It was obvious that Vos didn't trust her – and didn't think Jamie should, either. But Jamie's time as an inspector had shown him how many domestic disputes were caused more by miscommunication than malicious intent on either side. The heat of yesterday's anger had cooled, and in the silence of the flat, he was newly able to wonder whether he hadn't overreacted. He still did not understand why Sara had kept secret her visit to Rhodri's house on the night he died. But, Jamie told himself, maybe that was the point. *He did not understand.* He could not comprehend the trauma Sara had suffered. Sara had endured a life of it – from the murder of her parents by Rhodri's troubled friend, Glyn Thomas, to the loss of their baby, to the horrors of the Aberystwyth investigation – which had concluded with Sara having to witness the aftermath of Rhodri Jones's crazed act of murder-suicide. With the weight of so much horrifying baggage on Sara's shoulders, could Jamie really condemn her behaviour? Should he be outraged by her tasteless choice of pendant when she found solace in it?

Jamie had damaged the pendant. Rubbed it raw, crumbled its side. He should have apologised, rather than condemned. He wondered what Sara was doing now.

I could walk to Oxford Circus in less than ten minutes, he thought. *Take the Victoria line south, be home in half an hour …*

But, no. There were problems with returning home with nothing resolved. He had left badly, and couldn't guess how Sara would react to his sudden return. And, he admitted to himself, he would feel foolish slinking home so soon. Jamie told himself that he and Sara both needed time to heal. But Jamie also sensed they would not be apart for ever. There would be a time, soon, when going back to Sara would be right, and they could both forgive.

And when they did, Jamie wanted to make a gesture – to give Sara something meaningful. Something that said he empathised, even if he could not fully understand her point of view. Jamie pulled out his phone and Googled the address of a jeweller's shop on Oxford Street.

He knew just the thing.

Sara arrived at the offices of Andrew Turner & Associates unannounced. The place was bustling today. Well-dressed staff glided over the plush carpet with papers clutched in their hands and phones pressed to their ears. There was a hum to the office – not just a metaphorical energy crackling in the air, but the literal humming of printers, air circulation systems, and the background burbling of people going about their workday. It had been quieter on Sara's previous visit, when she had sat in that plush chair, right over there, and listened to Andy's assurances of his loyalty. Now the receptionist, whom Sara did not recognise, explained that Mr Turner was in a meeting and couldn't possibly be disturbed. The woman stated this fact with the disdainful air of the young functionary who knew she was doing the boss' bidding, and imagined she carried all his authority, too. Sara smiled pleasantly. She announced that she'd wait. She sank into a chair and watched the receptionist pick up the phone and speak to someone in hushed tones.

Within two minutes, Andy appeared. He did not

venture into the Reception area, but hovered half-behind the partition that separated the receptionist from the company's inner sanctum. He seemed to feel any public conversation with Sara would prove overwhelming; his wary expression suggested uncertainty about the attitude he might expect from his friend. Andy made eye contact with Sara, and angled his head towards the glass offices in the back. She rose immediately, smiled at the peeved-looking receptionist and followed. Andy led her to the only private office in the open space behind the partition – a large glass cube set into a corner.

Andy shut the door. 'Andy,' Sara began. 'I just wanted –'

Andy raised his finger, silencing her. She followed his gaze through the glass, to the open-plan where several staffers were sneaking surreptitious gazes in their direction. One young man was staring more openly. 'Your assistant?' Sara murmured.

'M-hmm,' Andy said, and pressed a discreet button on the wall. Blackout blinds began to creep down the glass panels of the office. The two of them waited mutely, listening to the motor's soft electronic hum, until the grey fabric was brushing the nap of the carpet. Only then did Andy turn to Sara. He stared at her appraisingly, taking a barometric reading of her emotional weather. Finally, he lurched forwards and wrapped his arms around her. 'Sara, I am so, so sorry,' he whispered. 'I feel just awful about – well, about everything, really.'

'Andy –' Sara said.

Andy stood back and raised his hands in surrender. 'No, no,' he went on, 'I've been a spineless little turd, and I know it. I should have told Gerrit to roger himself with a rocket casing ... but I didn't.' He hung his head dramatically. 'I just couldn't.'

'Of course you couldn't,' Sara agreed.

Andy looked at her sharply. The contrition in his eyes had given way to surprise.

'Why would you have?' Sara continued. 'Andy, you're running a multi-million-pound company here. I would never expect you to jeopardise even one job on my behalf. In your position, I certainly wouldn't have challenged Gerrit Vos.'

And it was true. Sara did understand the circumstances that led to Andy withdrawing his support for the clinic. What Sara would *not* have done, she knew, was reveal the details of their private conversation to Vos in the first place. That was a way in which she and Andy differed. Sara didn't blame him for being indiscreet. She'd been both his friend and therapist; she understood he couldn't help himself.

Sara realised they were standing awkwardly in the centre of the room. In his embarrassment, Andy had not thought to ask her to sit. Sara gestured to the chair behind Andy's steel desk, then sat immediately on the one that faced it. Andy took his cue and slid behind the desk.

'You're being so understanding,' he breathed. 'It's far more than I expected, and, frankly, more than I had any right to expect.'

Sara was jarred by an involuntary shudder. Andy's choice of words sounded too much like the ones Rhodri used to use in one of his cloyingly contrite moods. That tone had always left Sara feeling manipulated. 'Let's face it,' she said to Andy, 'at the moment, we're all dancing to Gerrit Vos's tune.'

'You don't need to anymore,' Andy said reassuringly. 'I may still have to deal with Gerrit, but he's no longer your concern.'

Sara smiled. Sometimes, Andy's emphatic naiveté was endearing, even in the gravest circumstance. Of course Vos was her concern. Technically, Jamie may have worked for Andy, but they both understood he answered to Vos. Sara wondered whether Andy even knew Jamie had stormed out of their flat. If he didn't, she had no intention of telling him.

It was undeniable that Vos had Jamie in his thrall. He also had those screen grabs of Sara in Rhodri's house. As Jamie said, it was unlikely Sara could be charged over such circumstantial evidence. But the tabloid headlines that would come from such exposure would make her life bloody awkward. Sara had no desire to be a target of the tabloids again. And Vos was not leaving things there. He had now engineered the loss of her job. What more might he attempt?

Andy thumped his desk with renewed vigour, startling Sara from her reverie. 'Anyway – not to worry,' he pressed on with a motivational ring, 'I've been thinking long and hard about all this, and I have a plan. I am going to find you another position. An even better one. Since hooking you up with that support scheme in London Fields, I've come across so many better options -'

'Relax, Andy,' Sara interrupted. 'I don't want another position. Not now, anyway.'

'Why not?'

'When you sponsored me at the London Fields Support Service,' Sara went on, 'I needed it. I felt so unsettled and rootless. That job gave me stability. I was doing something I knew how to do, and it allowed me to blot out the things I needed to forget. I can't thank you enough for that – but I just don't feel that way anymore. Now I need time to myself.'

'What will you do?' Andy asked.

'Enjoy the summer,' Sara lied. She looked out Andy's moulded Georgian windows – so incongruous when contrasted with the modernism of the glass cube that surrounded them – and perused the grey sky that hung low over the square. 'They say the weather's going to improve,' she added.

'We can only hope,' Andy said.

'If you hadn't withdrawn the funding, I would have stayed in that clinic out of guilt,' Sara said. 'The fact that they had to sack me – well, it took off the pressure.'

'I hadn't thought of it that way,' Andy said.

'On top of all that, Ceri's asked me to go on holiday with her. I had told her I couldn't. Now, there'll be nothing to stop me.'

'Where are you going?' Andy asked.

'Mallorca.'

'What an excellent idea,' Andy said, trying to sound excited, but managing only to sound relieved.

Sara rose. 'When I got here, your receptionist said you were in a meeting.'

Andy waved a hand airily. 'Only with staff,' he said. 'They're paid to wait.'

'Maybe so,' Sara said, 'but they shouldn't have to wait for this. Thanks for seeing me, Andy.'

'I am sorry,' he said. 'I hope you realise that.' He smiled. 'So, when are you leaving?'

Sara cocked her head. 'Leaving?'

'For Mallorca.'

'Oh,' Sara said, and shrugged. 'Maybe soon.'

'Then I'll see you when I see you,' Andy said, moving from behind the desk to offer Sara another hug.

'That you will,' Sara agreed, hugging him back.

Sara walked from St James's Square to Piccadilly and turned in the direction of Green Park tube station. She was just approaching the Ritz hotel when her mobile rang. Next to the steady whoosh of traffic, Sara could not hear her Take That ring tone, but she felt the phone's vibration.

'Miss Jones?' The voice's tone was solicitous, but also

197

guarded. 'My name is Philip Berger. We met last Saturday evening.'

Sara's heart began to thump wildly. 'Mr Berger, of course,' she said, wincing at the traffic. It was too loud for this kind of conversation. 'Can you hold on a minute?'

Sara ducked into a patisserie. She waved away a waiter who tried to seat her. 'Thank you for calling back,' she went on. 'I have to apologise if I upset you when we met. It wasn't the ideal way to approach you.'

'That's perfectly OK,' Philip said in a flat tone that implied it wasn't. 'This call won't take long. I've spoken to Tim about what you said –'

At once, Sara felt as though she'd been kicked in the chest. 'Hold on, Mr Berger,' she said. 'You've told Tim that we'd spoken?'

'I had to,' Berger said. 'I needed to clarify some of the claims you made.'

'I specifically asked you not to do that,' Sara said as calmly as she could.

There was a prickly pause on the other end of the line. 'Miss Jones,' Philip Berger continued, 'I don't know what you think I owe you –'

'Nothing,' Sara interrupted, conscious that her voice was growing shrill, 'You don't owe me anything. I'm simply trying to help you.'

'I checked with Tim about the things you said. He seems to be under the impression that you're colluding with his social worker to discredit him.'

'That's not true,' Sara said.

The waiter approached again. 'Would you like a table, ma'am?'

Sara shook her head. 'I'm leaving,' she mouthed.

'You told me yourself you're affiliated with Tim's social worker,' Berger reminded her.

'I'm a psychiatrist,' Sara said.

An unemployed one, she thought.

'Tim's told me all about the incidents that brought him to the attention of the Social Services,' Berger said. 'To me it sounds like nothing more than youthful folly. Tim has explained how difficult it is to get shot of a social worker once one latches onto you. Someone's decided he's trouble, and so they brought in a psychiatrist to confirm he's also crazy.'

'I am not saying he's crazy,' Sara protested. 'I'm telling you he's prone to violence.'

'Tim said he asked you to leave him alone.'

'Tim tried to strangle me.'

Berger's voice grew sharper. 'If that's true,' he said, 'I'm willing to bet he had very good cause. Miss Jones, I don't know what deal you've got going with the Council, but I am asking you, quite formally, not to contact me again. Do you understand? Tim has made a similar request. If you bother either of us, I will lodge an official complaint.'

'With whom?' Sara said.

'Social Services, for one,' said Berger. 'Then the NHS and the General Medical Council.'

Sara felt herself swoon with helpless frustration. This stupid, stupid man was collaborating in his own murder. At the other side of the patisserie, the waiter had huddled with a woman who might have been his manager. He gestured towards Sara.

'Mr Berger,' she said, 'please listen to me. You are in terrible danger –'

The manager bustled towards Sara with a determined expression. Sara backed out onto the street. On the other end of the line, the quality of the silence had changed.

Philip Berger had ended the call.

SIXTEEN

It was Thursday morning, and Vos sat at his desk. He toyed absently with one of Nicole's camera pens as he thought about Sara Jones. It seemed like more than three days ago since they'd had their confrontation at Highgate. So much had happened since then. When Vos had met Sara over Rhodri Jones's grave, he'd hoped to win her over with promises about Jamie's future. Sara had stymied him by revealing her knowledge about the events in South Africa. After that, Vos had been forced to play his one ace-in-the-hole – those damning security photos. But, it turned out, Sara wasn't just resolute, she was crazy. It was true that the photos would not be enough to send her to prison – but they certainly could damage her reputation. And yet she hadn't budged. Vos knew that enticing Jamie to leave her was spiteful – as was having Andy terminate Sara's contract. Yet, he hoped both ploys would work to unnerve her. Vos wanted to make Sara Jones wonder what else he might do. At least that would slow her down and give him time to think.

Vos set down the camera pen. *And with one of Nicole's trackers under her car,* he thought, *I'll always know where she's going.*

Vos's office phone buzzed. He glanced at it, but decided he did not want to be bothered. He stabbed a button and silenced it.

He really did need time to consider his options. Maybe he'd been able to damage Sara Jones's career, but it was a damn certainty she could put an end to his. Nobody would question Sara's take on the events in South Africa. Vos knew his next move would need to be decisive.

The phone buzzed again. With irritated impatience, he picked up the receiver and barked his own name. Taking the verbal cue, Rashid from the front desk apologised profusely for the interruption, then informed Vos he had a visitor.

Vos frowned. 'In the lobby? Who?'

'Not down here, sir,' Rashid said. 'The gentleman is being retained at the front gate.'

Vos frowned. 'Hang on, Rash,' he said, and set down the receiver. He swivelled in his chair, jogged his computer's mouse, and clicked on the icon that linked him to the cameras. An image taken from the side of the redbrick security hut showed a new-model Ford sitting before the barrier. The long corporate road stretched behind it. A figure walked into the frame and opened the driver's door. From this high angle, the man's bald head was prominent. Vos's lips tightened.

Shit.

It was Levi fucking Rootenberg – here, in the one place he knew he shouldn't be, trying to see the one man he shouldn't be seen with.

Vos picked up the handset. 'Rash,' he said. 'Who's on the gate?'

'Ruth, sir.'

'Tell her to send our visitor to the Hollybush car park. He won't need a pass – he's not coming in.'

If Rashid was surprised by this order, he did not show it. 'Of course, sir,' he said.

Vos watched the image of Rootenberg. Now he was

slumped behind the wheel, waiting. Vos saw Ruth enter the frame, bend to the driver's window and gesticulate, indicating the campus's one-way system. Vos stared down at the items arrayed on his desk. Next to the security equipment and a number of toy soldiers sat a stack of folders, a box of tissues, some bottled water, pens, and a letter opener. Vos thought of several ways to kill Rootenberg with them.

By the time he'd made it to the lobby, Vos could see the shiny new Ford backing into a parking space. Rashid was already on his feet and opening one of the smoky glass doors. 'Do you require any assistance, sir?' he asked.

Vos offered the slightest shake of his head. 'As I said, our guest won't be staying.'

Rashid eyed the car. 'I'll linger anyway,' he said softly. 'If you need me, just wave your arms.'

Vos smirked. Rashid was a good bloke. Although, considering that Rootenberg looked like a blancmange, Vos wasn't certain whether to be insulted by Rashid's offer of support.

Did the man really think he couldn't deal with *that*?

Outside, Vos saw Rootenberg clamouring from the driver's seat. 'Get back in!' he bellowed.

Rootenberg looked up and made an exaggerated shrug. He gestured to the car. *In here?*

Striding forwards, Vos jerked his hand impatiently. *Yes, in there*. His irritated scowl managed to add the words, *you idiot*.

Vos noticed the car was a rental and wondered whether Rootenberg had hired it especially for today. It seemed likely, which meant this wasn't a casual visit. The fact that Rootenberg had chosen to bypass Jamie Harding and come straight to Vos – even though he knew it would make Vos furious – suggested it was something important. And yet, Rootenberg hadn't given any advance warning. That couldn't be good news.

Vos jerked open the passenger's door and slid inside. The car smelled new. 'What the fuck, Lee?'

'A charming greeting,' Rootenberg replied.

'Cut the shit. Do you know how many security cameras we're on?'

'I wouldn't have come if it weren't serious.'

'Serious or not, you aren't supposed to talk to me. Didn't I make that clear enough?'

Rootenberg released a huff of air. 'Jamie Harding seems like a pleasant fellow,' he said, 'but you haven't exactly empowered him to take decisions on your behalf. You use him like voicemail – except it takes longer for the message to get through.'

'I use him in the way I want to. It's not your business.' Vos stared bitterly at the grey rectangle of Hollybush House. He could see Rashid strolling near its far end, unobtrusive but available. 'I guess you've got something to tell me,' he said, 'so spit it out.'

Rootenberg sucked his lower lip, then smiled reassuringly. 'We've had a setback,' he said, 'but only a slight one. It's not something that will stop us in the long run …'

Levi Rootenberg told Vos that his Zimbabwean connections were no longer viable. He wasn't sure exactly what had happened, he said, but these were turbulent times in Zimbabwe. Maybe the cadre of high-ranking generals he had cultivated had fallen out of favour with the new leadership, or suffered a factional split. Maybe they'd been imprisoned or even died. Who could tell? The long and short of it was, Rootenberg no longer had the connections he had boasted of.

Once the arms broker had relayed his news, Vos drew

in a sharp breath. Before he could say anything, Rootenberg raised his hands in a gesture meant to calm. 'The only thing this means,' he said with exaggerated patience, 'is that we have to delay our shipment of fifteen-millimetre shells. And, even then, only for the moment. I'm working on some other assets I have in the Zimbabwean military, and I'm sure they'll take our goods in due course.'

Vos's eyes narrowed. He stared at his former colleague coldly. 'I really fucking doubt that,' he said.

'Gerrit,' Rootenberg replied in a wounded tone, 'after all these years, you should trust me more.'

'Your pitch,' Vos said, articulating every syllable, 'was that you had assets ready and waiting. The shells were not the issue – they were a calling card to get us in with these people. If your contacts are gone, why would anyone else come forward?' He looked his old acquaintance up and down with distaste. 'To you of all people. They've already got the Russians, for fuck's sake. Strategic Ballistics can sell them everything they need – and legally. The entire logic of this deal was based on your special friendship with these big-shots.'

Rootenberg shook his head like a stubborn chid. 'The logic of this deal is, you need to get into the country now, before embargoes are lifted. Zimbabwe is crying out for military hardware – not to mention software and training. If we don't act, then eventually Germany will – or some other country currently prohibited from trading.'

Vos looked away from Rootenberg and closed his eyes. He had never believed in his former colleague's grandiose plan. It was a pie-in-the-sky smokescreen to make Rootenberg some quick cash. This man sweated desperation like a gambler playing his last card.

And that card, Vos thought, *is me*.

'Lee,' Vos sighed, 'we go way back. But I have to be

honest – without any contacts, you're no more than a liability to me. Thorndike Aerospace has friends in Whitehall, and they're starting to see us as a potential prime contractor. If we keep them onside, and Zimbabwe does open up, then the Minister for Trade will do our lobbying for us.'

Vos opened the passenger's door.

'Wait a minute!' Rootenberg said. 'There's got to be something we can do together.'

Vos exhaled loudly. 'You can't force these things,' he said. 'For now, we need to accept we've hit a roadblock.'

Vos moved to climb from the car. Rootenberg's hand shot out and grabbed the sleeve of his jacket. 'You owe me,' he growled.

Vos fought to control himself.

'We did a terrible thing in Rustenburg,' Rootenberg said with firm conviction, 'but I have kept quiet for you.'

Vos stared ahead, eyes averted from the heavy breather in the driver's seat.

'Not for my sake, Gerrit,' Rootenberg went on, 'but for yours. I've been keeping schtum about the biggest secret you've ever had in your life.'

Vos forced his gaze to the windshield mirror. He stared sharply into Rootenberg's reflected eyes. 'You did that because it gave you a hold over me,' he drawled. 'And I've always helped you, haven't I? Without me, you'd be in prison.'

'I've never denied that,' Rootenberg said. 'But remember – with everything I know, *you* could end up being the one in prison.'

'And you'd go right with me,' Vos snarled, baring his teeth.

Suddenly, Rootenberg's patina of strength cracked. 'I don't care anymore,' he moaned. 'I feel like you've abandoned me, Gerrit. Friends don't do that.'

'We aren't exactly friends.'

'Maybe not,' Rootenberg said. 'We're bound by something deeper – guilt.'

Vos drew a short breath. He felt his cheek twitch. 'What do you want, Lee?'

Rootenberg stared at Vos in the mirror. 'Reparation,' he said.

'And what might that involve?'

'Put me on the payroll,' Rootenberg said cautiously. 'A regular income – that's what I want. You can call me a consultant, like you do with Harding.'

Vos's face tightened. Without warning, he bellowed, 'You're asking for regular fucking bribes?'

'It wouldn't be a bribe,' Rootenberg shouted back. His gaze fell away from the mirror, and he whimpered, 'I need money, Gerrit.'

Vos remained silent and stared ahead. This man, he thought, was like an unstable explosive device. He could go off at any time, and take Vos with him.

Vos had always known this, but today it was made crystal clear. Rootenberg would always be a threat ... until the day he was silenced.

To Rootenberg, Vos spoke with what sounded like quiet compassion. 'Lee, I can't just put someone on Thorndike's payroll,' he said. 'You know that. But here's what I suggest. Go away and think about what else you can offer the company. When you come up with a plan that's viable, we'll talk again.'

Rootenberg twitched with hope. 'Another deal?' he asked.

Vos pursed his lips noncommittally. 'Bring me some proposals. Who knows?'

Rootenberg hesitated. 'It'd have to be soon,' he said.

'Sure.'

Rootenberg sighed like a man released from a tight

grip. He began to giggle. 'What can I say? Thank you, Gerrit.'

Vos patted Rootenberg on the arm. He climbed from the car, and softly shut the door. With a final, conspiratorial nod, Rootenberg backed out of the parking space.

Gerrit Vos did not think of himself as a violent man. But as he watched Levi Rootenberg drive away, he reflected on what his years in the defence industry had taught him.

An unstable device always required a controlled explosion.

Vos had left orders not to be disturbed. He paced his office, keeping his eye on the tranquil view of the North Downs out the window. The view towards the ridge known as the Hog's Back usually had the power to soothe him and give him perspective. But if he could gain perspective on this mess, he thought, it would be a bloody miracle.

Vos picked up one of the metal soldiers that lined the back of his desk – the Foreign Legionnaire – and decided that it would represent his first problem, Levi Rootenberg. He placed it on the left-hand side of his desk blotter. Rootenberg had been a thorn in Vos's side ever since South Africa. However, until now he had been bought off with relative ease. When Rootenberg still possessed a Trade Control Licence, Vos had been able to placate him with small-but-lucrative brokerage contracts. When Rootenberg had lost his licence, Vos had pulled strings to keep him out of prison.

Vos stared at the Legionnaire. White hat, blue coat, red trousers, brown rifle. It was a good choice for Lee. They were known for their tenacity, these fighters. Like them, Rootenberg always came back for more. This time, the man had raised his expectations, as well as the threats that came with them. Vos knew enough about extortion to understand that Levi Rootenberg would be an increasingly costly problem if Vos gave in to his demands. But if he didn't, Rootenberg would grow even more desperate, and might reveal their mutual secret.

Sara Jones presented Vos with his second problem. To represent her, he chose the red-jacketed Welsh Fusilier, and placed it on the right side of the blotter. Vos had thrown every weapon he had at his problem with Sara. He had shown her incriminating photos of herself. He had isolated her from her boyfriend. He'd got her sacked from a job she loved. Yet, if Vos had been hoping that Sara would lay down her arms in surrender, he'd been disappointed. The problem persisted; Sara Jones would not back down. She knew about his past, and seemed willing to use it against him.

Vos looked down at the two figures on opposite sides of the blotter and wondered if he hadn't positioned them wrongly. Actually, they represented the exact same problem. In each case, their roots lay deep in the events of his past. These two small soldiers represented the only two people who could endanger his freedom. With Rootenberg, the problem was purely logistical. He needed to find a way to get rid of the man without being caught. With Sara Jones, the situation was different. Vos had already determined that Sara could not be got rid of. To do so would be stupidly risky and would devastate Jamie Harding. Vos may have managed to separate the couple temporarily, but their estrangement wouldn't last for ever. He had done it to give himself time to have exactly the thoughts he was having now. Vos hoped to have a long association with Jamie Harding, and Jamie still loved Sara.

And, he admitted to himself, if Vos had the woman

killed, he would loathe himself even more than he already did.

So where did that leave him? Vos studied the Legionnaire and Fusilier, and from somewhere in the depths of his mind, a thought twigged and caused him to flush with something like … what?

Fear?

Excitement?

The thought was this: Vos needed to eliminate Rootenberg, and at the same time silence Sara. Perhaps he could do both by introducing a third figure onto the blotter. Vos picked up the Royal Marine and stared at it. His thoughts turned to Jamie Harding. By showing both Sara and Jamie those incriminating security photos, and later by separating the couple, Vos had been trying to influence Sara's actions. Now, he realised there might be a better way to achieve that outcome. What if Vos were able to tie Jamie Harding so tightly, so irrevocably, into his world that Sara would never dare try to pry him away?

Like a kid at play, Vos placed the Marine on the blotter and walked it towards the Legionnaire. With a single whack, he caused the Marine to topple the Legionnaire, sending it flying to the back of the desk. It crashed against one of Nicole's surveillance devices. Then, happily, Vos walked the Marine over to the Fusilier, where they stood side-by-side, looking up at Vos with abject loyalty.

SEVENTEEN

Ever since she had spoken to Ken Salter, Sara had been thinking about Clients Two and Three, Ellie Giddings and Conor Lowe. As she made her way to that pub in Hackney, she had made herself a half-promise. When the insanity in her life had sorted itself out, she would pay them long-overdue follow-up visits.

Since Philip Berger's call last night, Sara realised that life would not sort itself out anytime soon. However, that was all the more reason to undertake a pilgrimage to see those former clients immediately. She dared not approach Wilson again, and his good-hearted boyfriend seemed intent on collaborating in his own violent death. The only avenues of research Sara had left were Ellie and Conor. Sara told herself that a conversation with each of them may just provide the clue she had been missing.

Sara left her blue Mini parked outside the flat. It seemed appropriate to travel on foot, like a penitent. Sara's pilgrimage took her across Brixton Hill and through Brockwell Park. Soon, she was surrounded by the boutiques of Dulwich Village, whose well-dressed professionals seldom thought about psychic powers or grotesque murders.

As Dulwich gave way to Peckham Rye, Sara neared her first destination: a small flat above a hair salon, where

Ellie Giddings lived. Ellie had been Sara's second special client, her second big success, her second proof that Eldon Carson's approach was not the only response to unsettling visions.

Sara had spotted Ellie just over a year ago in a supermarket on Dog Kennel Hill – a woman in her mid-twenties with a young toddler in the child's seat of her trolley. The first thing Sara noticed was that Ellie had been drinking; the woman wasn't falling-down drunk, but she sported that functional bleariness with which some alcoholics went about their day. The very next moment, Sara had swooned. She'd pushed her own trolley against a freezer and leant on it for support.

Sara could recall the series of impressions that had battered her mind. *A bathtub. The young woman kneeling. The toddler standing in the water, crying. Wanting out. But Ellie's too drunk – and she's angry. She lashes out, smacks the child. The child reels backwards. There's impact against the tiles; a splash. Bubbles in the water and the toddler does not surface. Ellie slumps to the bath mat, insensible, and wakes some minutes later to a very different set of circumstances.*

Even today, Sara felt sure about the veracity of that vision. It had felt so definite. So much like the others she had known to be true, such as the mass-killing in Shrewsbury that Carson had made her experience. Or that awful moment in Islington when she had psychically witnessed teenage Rhodri murdering their parents.

Sara took a breath and pressed the buzzer next to the door. Around the corner on Rye Lane, a passing bus driver shouted out to a friend on a market stall. She waited, then buzzed again. Such a delay wasn't unusual; Sara had learned to expect it with this client. Sara wondered what Carson would have done with someone like Ellie Giddings. After all, Ellie was no common

211

murderer, driven by fury or lust. The woman had been ill. But even if the young American had understood her disease, Sara doubted it would have stopped him from doing what he'd always done. Knowing this, Sara felt vindicated in her own, more subtle approach – she had convinced the woman to accept counselling, a full medical assessment, and ultimately a prescription for naltrexone to manage her dependence on alcohol.

Above her, over the salon's large plastic sign, Sara heard a window creak open. A familiar voice yelled, 'What is it?'

'Ellie, this is Sara,' she called, and waited for the door keys to clank onto the pavement. This morning, however, no keys fell; instead, the window shut with a *thunk*.

Sara stepped back and squinted upwards. Maybe Ellie was coming down. Sara realised she was anxious to see the progress her client had made without her. When Sara first counselled Ellie, she'd learned that the woman had once been referred to Social Services, back when her daughter was a baby. 'Shopped by a nosy neighbour,' she had explained.

Ellie had been investigated, but despite her heavy drinking, social workers determined no further action needed to be taken. Sara was surprised that nobody had tried to get Ellie to attend Alcoholics Anonymous meetings. This was something Sara had finally managed to do, and those regular sessions at AA had such a positive effect that Ellie had ended her counselling with Sara. 'My sponsor understands me better than you do,' she'd said.

In truth, Sara had not thought Ellie was ready to quit therapy, with or without an AA sponsor. But she took her leave anyway, because she knew at a deeper level that her task had been accomplished. In those final days with her client, Sara sensed that the gears of the future had shifted.

Whenever she put herself into a trance, she could find no sign that Ellie's daughter was any longer in danger.

Through the door, Sara heard heavy footsteps thudding down the stairs. A bolt slid back and the warped wood wrenched open. Ellie stood before Sara, still in her dressing gown at eleven in the morning. 'Why are you here?' Ellie said too loudly, and a strong waft of gin stung Sara's nostrils.

'Ellie?' Sara whispered.

Ellie hung her head. 'Fuck you,' she whispered.

Although Sara's ex-client was partly obscured by the door, Sara could tell she had gained weight. Ellie also seemed to have aged years in the seven months since Sara had seen her last. Her skin was sallow and blotched with broken capillaries.

'It's your fault,' Ellie muttered. She clutched the door to stay upright.

Suddenly, a sickening thought occurred to Sara. 'Ellie,' she said in a hushed voice, 'where's your daughter?'

'Your fault,' Ellie repeated, and tried to slam the door. The hinges were rusty; they slowed the swing and gave Sara time to raise a knee and shove it back.

'Who are you, anyway?' Ellie cried out. 'Why did you fuck up my life?'

A choking panic constricted Sara's throat and pulsed downwards into her chest. She knocked Ellie aside and dashed up the stairs.

'Hey!' Ellie yelped.

On the first-floor landing, Sara leapt into the flat's small living room. Knocking open the bedroom door, she scanned the room. It was a mess of laundry, empty bottles and dirty dishes on moth-eaten carpets. There was no cot, no child's bed. There were no toys and no toddler. Sara's stomach lurched and she turned to see Ellie, weaving and

213

sweating heavily, emerge from the stairs.

'Get out!'

'Where is your daughter?' Sara demanded.

'She's gone,' Ellie replied bitterly.

'Ellie – tell me what happened.'

'Leave my home!'

Sara reached forwards and grabbed her former client by the lapel of her terrycloth gown. She yanked her into the room and thrust her against a wall. Ellie released a guttural huff. Pressing herself close enough to feel the sag of Ellie's stomach, Sara spoke in a voice calmer than she felt. 'Tell me she's not dead.'

Ellie blinked: 'Huh?'

'Tell me your daughter is OK.'

'Fuck off.'

Suddenly, the room seemed to have lost all its air. Sara took rapid, shallow breaths and shook her head helplessly. 'Ellie,' she said, 'I tried to help you. I need to know what went wrong.'

'I got sober, that's what went wrong,' Ellie muttered. 'Sober enough to make a stupid choice. I was all responsible, you see. You told me to be responsible, remember? So I gave her up.'

Relief flooded through Sara. She filled her lungs deeply. 'To Social Services?'

Ellie shrugged.

'An interim care order?'

Ellie acknowledged this with a grudging nod. 'Just so I could get on my feet. We made a plan. When I'd be allowed to visit, when I might get her back ...' Her voice trailed away and she shuddered.

'But you fell off the wagon,' Sara speculated.

'It was awful,' Ellie whimpered. 'Without my daughter. Long days. Everything was so empty. I went off those meds you gave me. Stopped seeing my sponsor.

More than once, I ended up in hospital.' Ellie's face contorted and she doubled over, knocking Sara backwards. 'They took her away from me!' she howled. 'For ever!'

Sara helped Ellie ease to the floor.

'They got a placement order,' Ellie sobbed. 'Now she's going to be adopted.'

Sara kneeled down and *shushed* softly. She stroked Ellie's arm as the young woman's chest heaved. Sara felt genuine pity for this poor woman who had been so close to besting her disease. 'I can help you again,' she said. 'You can beat this problem. I'll keep visiting.'

Ellie rolled onto her back and drew a steadying breath. 'Fuck that,' she said. 'You were the problem. The only reason I let you come here and spout your shit was, you threatened me.'

Sara felt as though she'd been slapped. 'Ellie,' she said softly, 'I never threatened you.'

'You did,' Ellie countered. 'When we first met. You said if I didn't stop drinking, you'd see to it they took away my daughter for ever.'

Sara started. She had no clear memory of saying this – but she might have. Faced with the knowledge that Ellie's child would otherwise drown, she might have said anything. If Ellie` was telling the truth, and Sara had threatened to use her pull as a medical doctor with Social Services, it answered one question she had come here with. At least she knew why Ellie had continued to see her.

It had been fear.

'I used to drink, but I had a daughter,' Ellie said. 'Now I drink and I've got nobody.' She added bitterly, 'If I never met you, I'd still have my child.'

No, you wouldn't, Sara thought, quite certain of herself. *By now, she'd be dead.*

'I asked you to get out,' Ellie whispered. 'Now please leave.'

Sara passed the African food shops of Rye Lane. She did not pay attention to the burble of languages and accents, nor notice the smells of fresh fish, uncooked chicken, and spices that wafted along the pavement. She was wrapped in the heavy insulation that comes with grief and pushes the focus inward. Sara knew that part of the numbness was simply after-shock: any emotional confrontation was bound to leave a person hyper-aroused. But she could not blame the whole of her reaction on adrenaline. Sara had been horrified to see the state of her former client. The sight of what Ellie had become pushed her into a familiar state of self-recrimination – she should not have ended this client's care simply because she'd known the toddler was now safe. Sara had been too willing to accept Ellie's reassurances that she was on the path to recovery.

Sara was also taken aback by Ellie's reminder of how she'd ensured the woman's cooperation. She had threatened Ellie. In her practice, Sara had employed all kinds of emotional tactics for her clients' greater good – but she was disturbed by the fact that she had so readily erased the memory from all but her deepest mind. Sara wanted to think of herself as the good guy. She didn't like having to admit the lengths she would go to in order to achieve a goal.

But, damn it, Ellie's behaviour today was proof that such a tactic could be justified. *You saved the child*, she told herself. *Maybe that's enough – maybe Ellie was always beyond redemption.*

Sara had one further realisation, too, quicker than it could be silenced.

This is the way Eldon Carson thought.

And Eldon Carson had always been certain about what

216

to do with people who were beyond redemption.

Sara took a train from Peckham Rye to Victoria, then rode the underground to Acton in West London. She made her way to a terraced house on a pleasant, tree-lined street.

This is where the most recent of her special clients lived – or, at least, the most recent until Tim Wilson had thundered onto the scene. Like Wilson, Conor Lowe was a young man in his mid-twenties. Conor shared the Acton house with two mates. By the time Sara first met him, she was already working at the clinic in East London, in the position created for her by Andy Turner's largesse. Conor had already been languishing on the waiting list for psychiatric treatment in the borough of Ealing when a kindly GP pointed him towards the London Fields clinic. Conor had started to see Sara regularly to combat his depression. Sara treated him the way she would have treated any depressed client, but there was an added urgency to Conor's case. Shortly after meeting the young man, Sara had suffered a terrible premonition of his suicide. In that vision, Sara witnessed Conor driving along the North Circular road at night, up towards Wembley and his job at a 24-hour superstore. In her trance, Sara could feel Conor's emotional numbness give way to a sudden, overwhelming despair. Before he had time to process this new grief, Conor had jerked the wheel and swerved his car into the headlights of an oncoming lorry. The subsequent pile-up took not only Conor's life but those of eight others.

Conor had seen Sara twice a week. The young man was aware that he suffered from a certain amount of suicidal ideation, but he'd never actually tried to end his life. Without her psychic preview, Sara wouldn't have worried overmuch for his safety. However, week after week, that dreadful vision had recurred – a pile-up, just south of the Hangar Lane Gyratory, caused by Conor Lowe.

The solution had come from a source beyond Sara's control. Conor's uncle was a carpenter, hand-crafting bespoke furniture from rough-hewn wood for the middle-class rustic. Sara learned that this uncle had asked Conor to join him as an apprentice. Each time the uncle made this offer, Conor had refused it. This had not surprised Sara: it was hard for a depressed person to commit to active change.

Slowly, as Conor's mood responded to both drugs and therapy, Sara had been able to introduce this change as a real possibility. Her reason was simple: if Conor was no longer driving to Wembley, he would not be on the North Circular on the night he otherwise would have ploughed into a lorry and caused his own and eight other deaths. With Sara's encouragement, Conor quit his job at the superstore – and Sara's visions stopped. The timeline that lead to mass fatalities had been erased.

Conor's house turned out to be a well-maintained two-storey place on a suburban street. When Sara knocked, the door was answered by a tall lad with skin so white it was almost translucent. He wore sweat shorts and nothing else; his chest was pebble-dashed with freckles. He stared at Sara expectantly.

'I'm looking for Conor,' Sara explained.

The lad stared at her silently for a little too long.

'I suppose he might be with his uncle,' Sara went on. 'If he's still working as a carpenter.'

'Mark!' the lad called over his shoulder, cutting Sara short. 'Someone's looking for Conor.'

A muffled shout came down the stairs, and the tall boy repeated, 'Conor! Someone's asking for him.'

'Does he still live here?' Sara asked.

'Mark'll be right down,' the lad said, and retreated into

the house. A moment later, she could hear the babble of a YouTube video. For Sara, being left standing at doors was the theme of the day.

Mark turned out to be a pudgy, dark-haired young man with olive skin and a wary expression. Unlike his half-naked housemate, Mark was well-dressed, in a button-down Oxford shirt and pressed chinos. Only his lack of socks spoiled the effect. 'Good afternoon,' he said in an upbeat voice that was contradicted by his eyes. 'I'd apologise for Kevin's behaviour, but actually, you caught him on a good day. Normally, he doesn't even answer the door.'

From the living room, the tall lad named Kevin made a rude noise.

'He didn't tell me your name,' Mark said.

'I'm Sara Jones,' she said, and wondered whether Conor's housemates knew he had once seen a psychiatrist. She thought it best not to betray confidences. 'I'm a family friend. I haven't visited Conor in a while.'

In the living room, the YouTube video paused, and Kevin called, 'If she's a friend, why doesn't she know?'

Mark winced; Sara gave him a quizzical look.

The young man stepped out of the house and led Sara across the front garden. He stopped near the pavement. 'I'm sorry to have to tell you,' he said quietly, 'but Conor killed himself.'

Sara released a breath. 'When?'

'Couple months ago.'

She drew in a deeper lungful of air and failed to release it. It occurred to Sara that she wasn't even surprised by the news. She hadn't known that Conor was dead – not in the way she had foreseen his other suicide, the one she had prevented – but some part of her had understood it was a possibility. For the second time today, Sara condemned herself for giving up on a client too soon.

Why couldn't she have called him at least? Made sure he was feeling OK?

Because, a voice in her head told her, *you never cared about Conor. You only cared about stopping him from killing those other people. Just like you didn't care about Ellie – only about her daughter. That's why you abandoned them both, as soon as their victims were safe.*

It was an unsettling thought – but, Sara had to admit, it was at least partly true. As soon as she had foreseen Conor's potential act of murderous suicide, she'd stopped seeing him as a patient. Instead, he became a problem to be solved, a criminal plot to be thwarted. And once Sara had accomplished that task, she had mentally placed him in a file labelled 'job done.'

'How well did you know him?' Mark was asking.

'Oh,' Sara replied, 'not well. Sometimes we had coffee.' She remembered to breathe, and to offer Mark her condolences. 'How did he do it?' she asked.

'It was stupid, really,' Mark said. 'He jumped off Beachy Head.' The young man snorted bleakly. 'Can you believe it? The most unimaginative way to top yourself. After the funeral, Kevin started calling him *The Cliché*.'

Sara must have looked shocked, because Mark added, 'Yeah, Kev can be a real prick.'

She thought. 'Do you know whether Conor drove or took the train?' she asked.

Mark frowned, surprised. 'Sorry?'

'To Eastbourne. To the cliffs.'

'Oh,' Mark said. 'They found his car on Beachy Head Road.'

'That makes sense,' she mused, more to herself than to him. 'That requires less planning than catching a train. It's easier to do. Still, even driving takes effort – it's not something you'd do if you were deeply depressed, is it?'

'Was he depressed?' Mark asked.

Sara started; she had just revealed something she shouldn't have. She supposed the truth could no longer have an effect on Conor, but it was still relevant to Sara. For some reason, she remained reluctant to disclose her true connection to the dead boy.

'He must have been depressed, don't you think?' she asked with a shrug. 'Considering what he did.'

EIGHTEEN

By the time Sara turned the corner onto her Brixton street, her emotions were flatlining. Today's visits had taught her nothing that would help with her current predicament, and instead served only to cast an unpleasant shadow over her previous successes. It was still true that, in both cases over the last couple of years, she had achieved what she'd set out to do. Ellie Giddings had not drowned her daughter. Conor Lowe had not killed others in a deliberate act of vehicular homicide. Sara's interventions had been successes. But, beyond this truth, both her clients' stories had unhappy endings. Sara felt numb guilt for not having known, or not caring to have known.

Maybe I didn't want to know, she thought. *Maybe these were the outcomes I feared.*

Maybe that's why I stayed away.

As she got closer to the house, Sara's attention was drawn to her Mini, parked in her favourite space right outside her low garden wall. The first thing she noticed was that, in this burnished sunset, the car's blue paint looked a sickly green. Then she looked over the car's black roof and saw the back of someone's head. From this angle, it looked as though a person were sitting on the bonnet. Sara quickened her pace. Yes – someone had definitely perched on her car. Longish brown hair and a red-checked shirt.

'Excuse me,' she called. 'Could you get off there, please?'

The figure lowered its head slightly, but otherwise did not move. Sara reached the passenger's side and stopped, leaving most of the vehicle between herself and whoever was using her Countryman as a couch.

'Deep breath,' a man's voice said. 'I only want to talk.'

He slid off the car, and as he moved around, Sara saw past the stringy hair and into the bearded face of Tim Wilson. She caught her breath. Her first thought was to leap inside the car and lock the door, but realised she didn't have her keys. And once again, her medical bag was in the car.

Sara swivelled towards her front door. 'Easy, now – don't run,' Tim commanded, and grasped her wrist.

'Let go of me!'

'I only want to talk,' he repeated. 'If I let go, will you talk to me?'

Tim took Sara's silence as agreement and allowed his hand to slide from her wrist. 'I thought about coming to your office,' he stated. 'I know where it is – you gave me your card. But I thought it would be better to talk here.'

He meant, *where there was no security*.

'How did you get this address?' Sara said.

'You gave Phil your mobile number,' Wilson said. 'I noticed it was different from the one on your card, so I knew it was for your personal phone. I tried the reverse directories online. You weren't there. But there are companies that can trace mobile numbers. You cost me twenty quid.'

He grinned. It was the same grin he'd graced her with in Chalk Farm, not long before turning rabid. Once again, Sara noticed how sweet he looked when he smiled.

223

Wilson was even more boyish with his hair down – without the silly topknot. 'You owe me a couple of drinks, I reckon,' he said.

Sara tried to smile back. She was afraid the expression came out as a nervous simper. 'I could have bought them for you at the pub,' she said.

Wilson nodded. 'Would have been more honest,' he noted, his tone sharpening. 'I guess Phil rang you?'

'He did.'

'He said he would. I like him,' Wilson stated simply. 'Guys my own age have nothing to offer me, you know? It's like looking in a mirror. Phil's different.' Wilson shrugged wistfully. 'I give him something, too. He's only just come out. He's still coming to terms with everything. I can make him feel …'

He groped for the appropriate word. 'I make him feel comfortable,' he said finally.

This is good, Sara thought. *He's opening up.*

She tried to tell herself that Wilson's visit here this evening was a good thing. After all, he wouldn't have come unless he wanted to make amends. Maybe Tim Wilson could still become Success Number Four.

Wilson stared at Sara meaningfully. 'Why would you want to stop me from helping him?' he asked earnestly. 'Why would you go out of your way to come to a pub and tell him to be afraid of me?'

Because you're going to kill him, Sara thought.

'That wasn't my purpose,' she said.

'How did you know we'd meet there?' Wilson asked. 'I didn't tell you about it. I didn't tell you anything.'

'I found out because I needed to,' Sara said. 'We got off on the wrong foot, you and I, but I think maybe we –'

'Don't you think I deserve happiness?' Wilson demanded.

'I do. That's exactly why I'd like to –'

Sara noticed a change in Tim Wilson's breathing. It was becoming more regular, heavier. It was then that Sara noticed that he stood between her and her front door. 'If you want me to be happy, then leave me alone,' he said. 'It's pretty fucking simple, when you think about it.'

'I'm going inside now,' Sara said. 'You're frightening me.'

'You should be frightened,' Wilson said. He cocked his head, thought for a moment, and then gave her a clumsy shove. Sara stumbled backwards. The back of her knees connected with the low garden wall, and she fought to keep them from buckling. 'Maybe if you were scared, you wouldn't stick your nose into other people's lives.'

'I get the message,' Sara said.

Wilson moved towards her. 'I thought you got the message at my flat,' he said, his voice starting to strain. 'I thought you got the message when I let Stanley loose at this fucking car.' He banged the Mini's side for emphasis. 'And yet there you were again, trying to fuck with my life.'

'I'll leave you alone!' Sara blurted.

Without further warning, Wilson punched her. It was a sharp jab to the ribs, and it sent a shockwave through Sara's torso. She staggered backwards. Gasped for air. Wilson moved forwards.

Despite being winded, Sara cried out as loudly as she could. 'Help! It's Dr Jones. I'm being attacked!'

'Shut up!' Wilson yelped and made a grab for her hair. It was too short to grasp, but he managed to pinch a tuft of spikes between his thumb and forefinger. He yanked; Sara felt her neck wrench and her ears pop. With his other hand, Wilson covered her face and shoved. As Sara fell, her perceptions sharpened. It was as though she were moving in slow motion. She connected with the edge of the low garden wall. The bricks cleaved the small of her back like a hatchet. Sara couldn't tell if she was bleeding as she rolled onto the pavement, but her garbled thoughts told her that she'd have one hell of a bruise. She squinted upwards. Wilson advanced, blocking the dying sun, kicking out, his sneaker connecting clumsily with her abdomen. Sara felt herself double over on the pavement. She heard herself release a whoosh of air and gasped to replace it. Her lungs felt like a vacuum, unable to draw the next breath.

'You think I'm going to kill you,' Wilson growled. 'Maybe I should. Haven't decided yet.'

Suddenly, Sara's lungs cooperated, and she sucked in deeply. Pain exploded in her ribcage. At the same time, Wilson stomped downwards, his foot landing on her right thigh. Sara used her newly drawn breath to release a wail.

Then, suddenly, she heard a car in the distance. It roared towards them, then screeched to a halt. *Jamie!* she thought wildly. *It's Jamie and he's come to rescue me.*

'Stop it!' someone cried.

The voice was not Jamie's.

Still looming over Sara, Tim Wilson froze.

'What are you doing?' the voice cried shrilly. 'You promised you wouldn't hurt her!'

Sara twisted her head, feeling the muscles in her neck ring like high-tension wire. In a blaze of pain, she peered upwards and saw Philip Berger staring down at her.

'Oh, Christ,' he said. Without looking at his new boyfriend, Berger commanded, 'Get in the car.'

Wilson looked at the older man, then turned his gaze back down to Sara. 'Maybe next time, yeah?' he said, then lurched away without further comment.

As soon as he moved, a blast of low orange sun blinded Sara's eyes. She squeezed them shut. 'Help me up, please,' she whispered. 'Take my arm. Gently, though. Then I'll try to grab the wall …'

Berger did not reply. The next sound Sara heard was his car door clunking somewhere over there, on the street. The engine of Philip Berger's car roared, and then trailed into the distance, as he drove Tim Wilson away from the scene of his latest violent crime.

Tim Wilson is going to kill me.

Sara lay in a deep bath of cold water. It made her shiver badly but numbed the contusions to her abdomen, back and right thigh. She also had neck strain by hyperextension – probably caused when Wilson had pulled her hair – and may have suffered fractured ribs, too. It hurt to inhale.

Sara forced herself to take short, frequent breaths. In the air was the mild aroma of cinnamon; despite the piercing pain, Sara had searched her drawers for an old scented candle as her bathwater ran. She'd set it on the edge of the tub. Now, the flickering flame made shadows dance against the white tile walls. Once, Sara had surrounded herself constantly with this dim glow, this warm scent. It had always soothed her with memories of her early childhood, a time before the upheaval of her parents' deaths. But after Eldon Carson had been killed and Rhodri revealed as their parents' murderer, the smell of cinnamon had taken on very different associations. It had made Sara think only of her time in Penweddig, and of death after death, and of her own culpability.

But now – alone, beaten, shaking, and without Jamie to comfort her – Sara once again desired that scent, and what it used to stand for. It was like the return of an old friend.

He said 'maybe next time,' she reminded herself. *Wilson's decided that killing me is an acceptable option. If Philip Berger hadn't intervened, I could be dead right now.*

And there it was, she told herself – yet another blind spot in Sara Jones's psychic powers. She had foreseen Berger's murder, but not her own. She had been a psychiatrist for long enough to know when someone was telling the unvarnished truth. Tim Wilson had not been speaking rashly when he'd threatened to kill her. He was revealing his *to do* list.

Before easing gingerly into the frigid water, Sara had thought about ringing Jamie. She knew he'd have come home if she had. He might even be here now, she thought, depending on where he'd been hiding. But what, Sara had asked herself, could she tell him? If Jamie learned that the client who'd previously attacked her had come here, to her home, and beaten her again – not to mention threatened murder – he would have rung the police. Without knowing the whole story, it would seem the sensible thing to do.

But the whole story was something Sara could not tell him.

I'll have to stop Tim Wilson alone, she thought. *And the ways I've tried to protect myself so far aren't going to be enough.*

Sara had always relied on her secret syringe of pentobarbital for a feeling of safety. The truth was, it had seldom done her any good. She had failed to have it to hand for either of Wilson's attacks, and it would not solve her current predicament either. Sending someone into a thick slumber might halt one out-of-control moment, but it would not deter a psychopath who kept coming back. As Sara lay in the tub, gently running her fingertips over her contusions and the goose bumps that covered them, she allowed her imagination to wander.

If I can't use pentobarbital, then what? she wondered. *How? And to what end?*

By the time Sara drained the water and climbed slowly

from the tub, she had devised an impossible plan. In truth, it was less of a plan and more of a daydream – a ridiculous notion she would never entertain seriously in any other situation. And yet, this was not a circumstance Sara had ever experienced before. After towelling herself gingerly, she found a ball of gauze and set about wrapping her ribs. It was safer to leave fractured ribs unbound, but she needed to be able to move. Sara found a summer dress she could easily wriggle into, and sandals she was able to slip on without bending. She picked up her purse and car keys and left the flat.

In the hallway, Sara caught a glimpse of herself in the mirror. Her clothes were inappropriate for the time of year, she looked haggard and pale, and moved in a staccato shuffle. She wondered whether her dreadful appearance might actually help her with the conversation she needed to have next.

It was a short drive down Brixton Hill to Coldharbour Lane, where Sara parked on a side road. She baby-stepped her way to the fringes of Brixton Market, her head swooning, hoping to stay upright. She stopped in front of a burger bar and scanned the street life. Soon, she'd found her man standing on a corner across the street. He looked for all the world like someone with time on his hands, a dawdler enjoying the passing parade. Sara watched him carefully for several minutes. She needed to make sure she wasn't mistaken about who he was. But, really, she'd known from the moment she saw him. Sara wasn't blind enough to overlook the sharp focus of his thoughts.

The man noticed her, too, and after a while made direct eye contact. 'The fuck you want?' he shouted at her.

She smiled and moved cautiously across the road. He took in her inappropriate clothing, her fresh bruises and shuffling gate.

'I think you know exactly what I want,' she said.

Sara was already suffering from a form of buyer's regret. She looked at the baggie of white powder nestling in her palm. What exactly did she intend to do with this bloody stuff? In desperation, she had concocted a bold and reckless plan. It was one she knew she didn't have the backbone to carry out. And even if she were able to summon up the foolhardy courage required, she would have to wait until her bruised body had healed. She was not cut out for this, she told herself.

Flush it, Sara. Get rid of it now.

Sara's mind flitted back to the vision she'd had on the night Rhodri died ... her brother murdering their parents, revealed to her as though through Rhoddo's own thoughts. What had he felt? At that moment, there had seemed an inevitability to his actions. A grim logic. Daddy had to go, and Mummy – in the wrong place, at the wrong time – couldn't witness what had happened. Then again, Rhoddo had been stoned, and young, and under the sway of a bolder personality. On the other hand, Sara was sober, mature and ...

And threatened by a deranged young man who plans to beat me to death.

Sara's mobile rang. Its light cast a pale glow over the ceiling and walls of the bedroom; Sara realised she had not even switched on a lamp when she'd arrived home with her illicit package. She found herself both hoping and fearing it was Jamie. She picked up the phone and checked the screen. Then she tapped it and said, 'Nos da, Ceri.'

'Are you hungry?' her friend asked.

'Now?' Sara said. For a panicked moment, she worried that Ceri had arrived unexpectedly in town, and would soon come over and see her like this.

'I mean, hungry in general.'

Sara hesitated. 'I don't even understand the question.'

'Well,' Ceri said, 'I just learned there are three and a half thousand restaurants on the island of Mallorca. So, if you're hungry, it's definitely a good place to go.'

Sara sighed. 'You've been Googling facts about Mallorca.'

Ceri chortled. 'The first foreign settler there was the novelist Robert Graves,' she said in confirmation. 'You liked *I, Claudius*, didn't you?'

'Never read it,' Sara said. 'I know *The White Goddess*, but that has nothing to do with Mallorca.'

Ceri snorted. 'Neither does *I, Claudius*,' she said. 'Are you absolutely sure you can't get time off work?'

A pang of shame pulsed through Sara, as though she had been caught in a lie. Everything had happened so fast, she had not yet told Ceri about losing her job. How to break this news remained a concern, and one that Sara had not yet given thought to. Certainly, she did not want to reveal Vos's attempt at blackmail, since that would require admitting things about the night of Rhoddo's death. However, Sara could probably share her concerns regarding Jamie and his association with Thorndike. Maybe she could tell Ceri about how she had confronted Vos over his dark past, and how Vos had forced Andy Turner to withdraw funding from the clinic -

'Sara? Are you still there?'

'Sorry; I was thinking,' Sara replied. Suddenly, she surprised herself by adding, 'Ceri, I really don't know about Mallorca, but I could probably take enough time off for a quick visit to Wales.'

'Sara, that's wonderful!' Ceri said. 'When?'

'Err – I'm not sure.'

'But soon?'

Sara calculated. She did not want Ceri to see her in this condition. But, she wondered for the second time in minutes, how long would it take her wounds to heal? If Sara stayed in London, the chances were greater of confronting Tim Wilson again. Maybe running to Wales was the safest thing she could do.

Sara knew she tended to be obstinate, and usually liked to see things through to the bitter end. She had a nose-to-the-grindstone perfectionism common to all Type A personalities. But there was a rarer, perhaps wiser, side to Sara that could sense when a situation was unwinnable. It tended to announce itself whenever the act of pressing ahead might actually push her further behind. That is what had happened a few years back, when a single altercation with Rhodri had led her to sell her Pimlico flat and flee London. That spur-of-the moment decision had been taken during another telephone call to Ceri.

'Oh, hell, why not?' Sara heard herself say. 'I'll leave late tomorrow morning.'

Still on the line to Ceri, Sara moved decisively to the bathroom and dumped the contents of the small baggie into the lavatory.

'I should be with you in time for dinner,' she said.

NINETEEN

On Friday afternoon, Gerrit Vos sat next to Nicole at a table in the main bar of the Royal Festival Hall. They had come for a lunchtime concert. Vos had already had a meeting today, and had arranged more for the afternoon. He needed to hang around anyway; this evening Thorndike's Investor Team was holding what they called a *mingle* at a wine bar in the City. Vos was expected to be there and make pleasantries with the company's investors. These ranged from people who managed pension funds right down to financially savvy individuals. The evening was relatively informal, so Vos had suggested that Nicole come too. Pretty wives tended to charm a certain type of shareholder. Plus, Nicole would keep him from getting too bored or too drunk.

Vos stared at a piano, which sat alone in the performance space. The instrument, and all those who watched it, waited for the arrival of a Croatian composer whom Vos had never heard of. As far as he was aware, the star of the show would be sharing his own composition about the Adriatic. Or at least something like that; Vos had forgotten precisely what Nicole had told him. Still, he mused, the performance couldn't be any more excruciating than the Norwegian dance troupe she'd made him sit through last January, or that Turkish poet whose reading he'd endured at Conway Hall. That guy had insisted on writing in English, even though he couldn't make his couplets rhyme.

'Check the app for me, would you?' he said to Nicole.

'I checked it when we got here,' she reminded him.

'Do it again. Keep checking.'

Resignedly, Nicole withdrew her mobile. 'You do know Sara hasn't used her car since she was sacked, don't you?'

'Humour me,' Vos insisted. 'Do you want me to enjoy the performance or not?'

Nicole smirked. 'You won't enjoy it anyway,' she said. 'You're a Philistine.' She thumbed the app, which was linked to the tracker under Sara's car.

A handsome man with a mane of curly dark hair strolled towards the piano to polite applause. 'My God,' Nicole breathed.

'What?'

'Sara.'

'Sara *what?*' he repeated.

At the next table, a woman in a Salvation Army uniform cleared her throat and twitched her hand towards the stage. Vos half-turned and offered her an apologetic smile, mouthing the words, *Fuck yourself.*

'She's on the move.'

'Sara?' Vos snapped. 'Shit! Where?'

The pianist opened his set with a slow rising glissando that might have been meant to sound like a wave, or perhaps a leaping fish. Nicole focused on the screen. Her eyes widened. 'She's at Reading Services,' she said.

The Salvation Army woman sighed and looked towards heaven. The music began to roil and crash.

'On the M4?'

'Westbound,' Nicole confirmed.

'Fuck. She's heading to Wales,' Vos said. Their

234

constant checking of the tracker app had paid off, and also changed everything. Suddenly, things were serious. Vos leapt to his feet. 'Come on,' he barked.

'What? Where –'

'Sorry,' Vos said aloud to people at the surrounding tables and headed towards the exit. Nicole rose and scurried after him.

'Gerrit,' she called, 'you're getting worked up over nothing. If Sara's going to Wales, surely that's a good thing. She'll be out of your hair. You'll have Jamie all to yourself.'

Vos stopped at the glass doors. 'Don't you see?' he snapped. 'She's going straight to her friend. That cop, Inspector Lloyd.'

'I suspect she is,' Nicole agreed. 'Who else would she visit?'

'It's not social,' Vos stated flatly. 'She's up to something. She's chosen the cop she trusts most.'

'For what?'

Vos looked at her with a frown of contempt. 'She's going after me.'

He pushed his way out the doors and onto the walkway that paralleled the river. From behind him, Nicole said, 'You've been working too hard. It's making you paranoid.'

Vos turned. 'Nicole, this is serious. I told you what Sara believes about me – about what happened in South Africa. She's plotting a way to use it against me.'

'Why would she do that?' Nicole asked. 'What you're saying doesn't make sense.'

Vos shook his head stubbornly and said, 'It makes perfect sense.' His expression tightened. 'There are things I haven't told you.'

Nicole narrowed her eyes. 'What things?'

Vos gazed out across the river. 'I'm pretty sure Sara

Jones murdered her brother,' he said.

Nicole stared at him, eyes widening. 'That's crazy.'

'You think?' Vos asked. He took her arm and led her towards a bench. From his leather case, he retrieved his iPad. He called up the file with the security images from nearly three years before. 'These are from the night Rhodri Jones died,' he said. 'He was still alive when they were taken.'

Nicole peered down at the screen. Her lips parted. 'Sara was there?' she gasped.

'She was indeed.'

'But Rhodri Jones killed himself,' Nicole stated.

Vos shrugged. 'Then Sara watched him do it,' he concluded. 'Think of that ... she watched her own brother die. Didn't bandage his wounds, didn't even ring 999.'

Nicole's frown deepened and she stared at Vos appraisingly. Then her expression hardened. 'You showed her those photos, didn't you? When you were there this week.'

Vos inclined his head. *Maybe.*

'And Jamie too, I'll bet. Is that why he left her?'

'You're asking the wrong question,' Vos insisted. 'You should be asking, what the hell was Sara up to in her dying brother's house? Did he know a secret she wanted to conceal? Or maybe it was just the prospect of a fat inheritance.' He gestured towards the iPad. 'Sara Jones has a very big skeleton in her closet, and the only person who can prove it is me. She needs to silence me.'

That was as much as Vos could tell Nicole. He hoped it was enough to convince her of the seriousness of their plight. Things were even worse than Vos could let on. Nicole still believed Sara was misinformed. From her point of view, the worst thing Sara could do was spread false rumours. Vos knew that Sara was dead right, and all the more dangerous for it. Maybe she couldn't prove anything herself – in that sense, it would be her word against his – but it wouldn't take an intrepid investigator too long to confirm her story. Maybe one of those Afrikaaners might talk, with the right offer of immunity. For that matter, maybe Rootenberg would, too.

Nicole shook her head softly. 'I can't believe it,' she said. 'Sara wouldn't let her own brother die. It's not like her.'

'Look at the pictures,' Vos said. 'I know it's not easy to think of her that way, but it's true.'

'If you've been threatening her with those photos, then she must be desperate,' Nicole observed.

'That's why she's going to her cop friend,' Vos agreed. 'Her lies about South Africa are the only weapons she's got to use against me. She must know that, at the very least, I'll be interviewed by the Met. That will ruin my reputation. Then, anything I say about Sara Jones will sound like bullshit.' Vos slid his hand along the bench, until he gently touched Nicole's fingers. 'You have to take this seriously,' he said. 'I'm in danger ... and I need you.'

Slowly, Nicole's expression shifted. Incredulity gave way to steely resolve. 'So what do I do?' she asked finally.

'You have to stop her.'

'How?'

'Follow her,' he said. 'Do whatever you have to do to keep her from reaching her friend.'

Nicole offered a bemused half-smile. 'Follow her in the Porsche?' she mocked. 'Sara wouldn't need to be a trained spy to notice that.'

Vos nodded, conceding the point. 'I'll drive you to the airport,' he said.

'The airport?'

'Heathrow. It's on the way to Wales. It'll be the easiest

237

place to hire a car. We'll need to leave now, though – you have a lot of time to make up.'

'Gerrit,' Nicole said, 'even if I can catch up to her – even if I find a way to delay her – we can't keep Sara from talking for ever.'

'We don't need to,' Vos replied. 'We just have to stall her until I get to Jamie.'

'What are you going to do?'

Vos stood. 'Something desperate,' he said.

Two hours later, Vos was home. He had left Nicole at the airport and followed the M4 as far as the turning to Wokingham. On the way, he cancelled his afternoon meetings. The he made reservations for an early dinner at a City restaurant – the fourth he tried – and rang Levi Rootenberg. An opportunity had arisen, he explained to his old colleague, but it was time-sensitive and they needed to discuss it right away. Vos told Rootenberg when and where to meet and rang off before the man had finished spouting his profuse thanks. Vos's call to Jamie Harding was even shorter. Do not leave the Green Street flat, he'd said. Put on a suit. Wait for me.

Vos had just returned from a visit to the first floor of the barn when Nicole rang. She had passed Swindon, she said, and had been monitoring Sara's progress all along the M4. Sara had stopped more than once already, and Nicole had shortened the distance between them. By the time Sara reached the Severn Bridge, Nicole may well have caught up. 'What will I do once I've got a visual on her?' she asked.

'Keep following,' Vos said. 'If she stops, wait till she's walked away, then puncture her tyres.'

'What if she doesn't stop?' Nicole asked.

'Ring me,' Vos replied. He went downstairs and slipped on his shoes. 'But whatever you do,' he said, 'don't let her get to the inspector's house. At the very least, not until tomorrow morning.'

'What's so special about tomorrow morning?' Nicole asked.

Vos fingered the small bag that nestled in his suit jacket. 'By then,' he said, 'Sara Jones's world will look very different.'

Sara hadn't been able to drive for long without stopping. Despite the relative comfort of her Mini, the dull throb of her injuries meant she needed regular breaks. Along the M4, she had stopped at three motorway service areas. She knew from long experience that, once she crossed the Severn Bridge, opportunities to rest anywhere other than the side of the road would be severely curtailed.

Sara understood she should be thinking about what she would tell Ceri. Although it was true that most of her bruises were hidden under clothing, her old friend would surely notice her stiff gait, and the way she winced when she turned her neck. Sara needed to come up with an explanation. Still, it was not Ceri whom Sara was thinking about, but Jamie. She found herself replaying their final conversation in her mind, searching for the words she could have said to him to make him stay. Sara couldn't tell him about her psychic powers, but surely, she could have said something. It was that damned pendant, she thought – the fact that Jamie produced it had derailed their conversation. Sara had been forced to lie about having made it, simply to justify its presence. That had sent her into a spiral of fabrication that had only alienated him further, making him leave, sinking him deeper into Vos's clutches. That had endangered Jamie, of course, but his absence had also put Sara in harm's way. Would things have been different if Jamie had been home yesterday when Tim Wilson had attacked?

Of course they would have.

Sara crossed the Severn still torturing herself with these recriminations. She felt a powerful urge to ring her partner. She had made previous attempts, of course – on Tuesday evening when he left, and also on Wednesday. On each occasion, he had refused to answer.

Soon, Sara was heading towards Newport. There were two ways to drive to Ceri's house from south Wales. Sara had anticipated taking the A487 coastal road, which was relatively straight and a sensible choice for someone with injuries. But, despite its offer of occasional panoramas of Cardigan Bay, the journey was also drearily dull. Especially if she were unlucky enough to get stuck behind a slow-moving farm vehicle. This had happened to her more often than she cared to remember. It wasn't until Sara saw the sign for Merthyr Tydfil that she decided to change her plans. She checked the clock. It was just after five pm, which meant there were more than two hours of daylight left. That would be enough for her to take the A470 through the mountain range just to the north. The Brecon Beacons offered beautiful scenery and far less traffic. Sara could cross Wales diagonally and join the coastal road at Llanrhystud, just south of Penweddig. There wouldn't be much difference in terms of time. Although the mountain route was longer, Sara was less likely to have to endure tractors for any great distance.

She swung north, deciding to make a quick call to Ceri to give her time of arrival, and then to try Jamie.

Vos was back on the two-lane road that led up to the M4. In front of him, a lorry rumbled along, much too slowly. In the next lane, a Ford Fiesta kept pace with it, forming a barrier of metal that held back his progress. Vos cursed, jerked the wheel and weaved in right behind the Fiesta, leaning on his horn as he did. The car sped up, and Vos remained on its tail until it pulled into the left lane, in front of the lorry.

Vos's phone trilled, and he thumbed a button. 'You see her?' he said.

'I'm right behind her,' Nicole replied. 'Looks like she's going to cross the Brecon Beacons.'

Vos glared at the driver of the Fiesta, who didn't seem to notice. How easy it would be, he thought, to give that car a nudge and send it careering into the trees at the side of the road. 'She won't stop now until she's at her friend's house,' he told Nicole.

'Maybe for petrol,' she suggested. 'When she's on the other side of the mountains.'

'We can't rely on that happening.'

'I don't know what else I can do,' Nicole said.

Vos sighed as he pulled back into the left-hand lane. He pressed heavily on the accelerator. 'I think you know perfectly well what to do,' he replied.

There was a silence on the other end of the line. Finally, Nicole said, 'What are you suggesting?'

In his mirror, Vos watched the Fiesta disappear behind him. 'Find a spot with a decent slope, and run her off the road,' he said.

'Gerrit!' Nicole cried. 'I can't do that.'

'For God's sake, I'm not asking you to kill her,' he snapped. 'Just find a remote place where she'll slide down the bank. It'll take hours for a rescue truck to get to her.'

'And you're sure that'll be enough?' Nicole asked.

'It has to be,' he replied.

Nicole was silent for several seconds. 'Gerrit, please reassure me you have a plan.'

'Trust me,' he replied.

Another pause. 'I don't like this,' she said finally.

Then I'd better not tell you the plan, Vos thought. *You'd really hate that.*

But all he said was, 'Who does?'

Sara's phone sat in its cradle on the dashboard. She opened the FaceTime app, and selected Jamie's number. Quickly, his image appeared on the screen, and something in Sara's chest sparked. Jamie was sitting on a chair, dressed in a jacket and tie. 'Err – hi,' he said.

'You look nice,' she replied. 'New?'

Jamie nodded. 'The tailor Andy recommended. Just picked it up.' He tilted his camera so Sara could take in the whole suit, then leaned towards the screen. His brows knitted. 'Are you driving?' he asked.

Sara made a grunt of confirmation.

'Do you think that's safe?'

Sara stared ahead at the narrow road, and saw oak, ash and yew trees flash by. 'Don't worry,' she said. 'I'm keeping my eyes on the road.'

Jamie shrugged. 'Where are you?'

'Wales. Going to see Ceri.'

'Ah.'

Sara had already decided she would not allow the call to be awkward. She had things to tell her partner. 'Jamie,' she said. 'Tuesday evening. I really should have –'

He cut her off. 'You don't need to say anything.'

'No,' Sara interrupted, 'I want to. I didn't tell you everything then, because I didn't know how. Then you showed me that pendant, and ... well, we got off track.'

'OK,' Jamie said. 'What didn't you tell me?'

She began haltingly. 'The night at Rhodri's, when I went to his house. I said I was in shock, and that's why I didn't ring 999.' Sara drew in a breath. It was a relief that she had to keep her eyes on the road, so she didn't have to look at Jamie. 'What I told you wasn't true,' she went on. 'I mean, maybe I was in shock ... but that's not why I left.'

'So then, why did you leave?'

'Because of what Rhodri told me. When I got there, he was still conscious. He said he'd changed his mind about dying. He begged me to save his life.'

Sara felt tears dampening her eyes. She blinked and forced herself to keep focusing on the tarmac ahead. She had left behind the tunnel of trees; the road now fell away into steep ravines on either side, with mountains in the distance. The sun had disappeared behind the distant slopes on the left, leaving them in stark silhouette. 'Rhoddo also ... well, he made a confession,' she said.

'A confession?'

'He told me that, when we were teenagers –'

Suddenly, Sara felt her throat thicken. She shuddered and started to tremble. More tears welled. 'Jamie,' she blurted, 'it was him! Glyn Thomas did not kill our parents. Rhodri did.'

'What?' Jamie gasped.

'He murdered them. Rhoddo. He was high on drugs. Daddy had been treating him badly. He'd locked him in his room. So Rhoddo slipped out the window, and he got a shotgun from the shed ...'

'My God, Sara,' Jamie said. For several moments, Sara heard nothing more, save for the hum of her tyres on the tarmac. Finally, Jamie added, 'No wonder you couldn't tell me that.'

'Once Rhodri had confessed,' Sara went on, 'it seemed ... well, almost a sin to let him live.' Her voice rose in volume. 'I'm sure he would have acted contrite for the courts and appeared all repentant. But he wouldn't have changed, not really. People like Rhodri don't.'

Jamie tried to shush her with soothing noises.

'And to be honest, Jamie,' Sara said, her voice trembling, 'I still don't feel I was wrong.' A sob tore through her chest. 'He didn't deserve to live!'

'Sara, we can't talk on the phone,' Jamie said. 'Please turn the car around. Come home. I'll meet you there.'

'No,' Sara cried, 'I told Ceri I'd –'

'Ceri will understand.'

'Jamie, I promised.' She fought to control her tears. 'She's been after me to go on holiday and I've been putting her off and ...'

Sara sniffed and steeled herself. 'Listen,' she said. 'I'll stay in Penweddig until Monday morning. How's that? I can be home in the afternoon. We'll talk then.'

'Sure,' Jamie agreed. 'OK.' He paused awkwardly. 'Sara, I can't even begin –'

'I know,' she interrupted.

'We'll talk about it,' Jamie said. 'Monday. When you come home.'

Sara cleared her throat. 'Why are you in a suit, anyway?' she asked.

Jamie laughed in relief. 'To be honest I don't really know. Vos told me to wear one. A meeting, I suppose.'

'Oh, Jamie – be careful,' Sara warned. 'You know I don't trust that man.'

'I know,' Jamie said. 'And I will.'

They said goodbye, and Sara reached over and touched the button that ended the call. Her eyes were off the road for barely a second, but in that time a dark-coloured Skoda had gunned its engine and roared up behind her. Sara's eyes darted sharply to the wing mirror. She clocked the approaching car, then looked ahead at the narrow road. She could see there wasn't enough room for the car to overtake. Sara leaned on her horn, but the Skoda persisted, trying to pull alongside the Mini. Sara pumped the brakes to let it pass, but suddenly the Skoda slammed into Sara's door. She felt the impact before hearing the crunch of metal. The other driver continued to bear left, forcing her close to the verge. Sara jerked her wheel to the

244

right, pressing her car into the Skoda, and fishtailed as her rear tyres spun on gravel. This drove her assailant back into the other lane. The car shot off ahead as Sara's Mini continued to turn, arcing off the road and thumping down the incline. Something on the undercarriage clunked. Every tender spot on Sara's body screamed as her head jerked forwards and impacted with the steering wheel. The airbag exploded open.

Sara blacked out. She did not feel the car slide to a halt in the ravine below the road. Nor did she hear the thudding and crunching of ripping metal several dozen yards ahead, as the other driver's Skoda barrel-rolled down the opposite side of the hill.

TWENTY

Sara woke up in a hospital ward. Oxygen tubes protruded from her nose, and an IV drip had been inserted into a vein in her hand. Her head was spinning. She felt woozy.

'Dr Jones?' a nurse said.

I seem to have my own nurse, Sara thought. *She's been sitting beside me.* That meant she was in an Intensive Care unit. Sara tried to remember what had happened. There had been a car trying to overtake. No – not trying to overtake, but deliberately running her off the road. Suddenly, Sara's stomach lurched.

'I'm going to vomit,' she said.

Quickly, the nurse placed a paper-pulp vomit bowl under Sara's chin. There wasn't much to expel; despite having stopped at three roadside services, Sara had eaten little. When she had finished, the nurse handed her a tissue, then kneeled at a locker at Sara's bedside. She produced another vomit bowl, a bottle of water, a small tube of toothpaste and a disposable toothbrush. 'You'll want to freshen up,' she suggested.

Sara accepted the items and set them next to her.

'Do you know why you're here?' the nurse asked.

'Of course. I was in an accident on the Brecon Beacons,' Sara said.

'You collided with a rented Skoda Octavia.'

'And how am I?' Sara asked.

'As well as can be expected,' the nurse said, with every intention of leaving it at that.

Sara sighed. 'You've obviously seen my details,' she said, 'so you know I'm a doctor. You can be more specific. I assume you've X-rayed me?'

'There are no skull fractures,' the nurse said, 'but you took a nasty blow to the head. You've been unconscious for a couple of hours. I suppose you'll know what that means.'

'It's a long time to be out,' Sara admitted. 'There'll be a danger of swelling to my brain, and it's going to take a few months before I've fully recovered. I assume you're going to keep me in for observation, and when I get home I'll need to rest for a week or so. Is that about it?'

'More or less,' the nurse agreed. 'How's your vision?'

'Blurry.'

'Are the lights bothering you?'

'Not overly.'

'Good,' she said. 'Still, you'll probably have headaches, fatigue, memory problems and a bit of good, old-fashioned pain.'

'I'm sure I will,' Sara agreed. She glanced blearily at her surroundings. They offered little to see, save for the curtains around her bed. There was a small gap where two of the curtain panels should have met, revealing a sliver of the Intensive Care ward beyond.

'Where am I, anyway?' she asked.

'You're at Heath Hospital in Cardiff,' the nurse said. 'They got you here in a search and rescue helicopter. Your car was in a ravine.'

An elderly woman led by a nurse shuffled past the gap between the curtain panels. She peered in, making eye contact with Sara. Sara's nurse followed her gaze, then rolled the panels closer together.

'Where's my car?' Sara asked.

The nurse shook her head. 'The police will have to tell you that. Chances are, it was recovered by a local garage and they're holding it for you. When you're able, dial 101 and ask for the Dyfed-Powys police headquarters.' The nurse slid a plastic chair up to Sara's bedside. 'You'll need to pay the towing charges, and authorise repairs. You'll want to liaise with your insurance company.'

The nurse sat. She was lower than the mattress, and had to look up to see Sara. 'But that can wait until you're better,' she concluded. Then her voice lowered. 'Since we're talking, though, do you want to tell me about your other bruises?'

Sara paused. She knew immediately what the nurse meant, but made sure to adopt a carefree tone. 'I assume I have lots of them,' she said. 'After all, I was just in an accident.'

'Dr Jones,' the nurse said, 'I think you know what I'm asking. Those older bruises. The ones that weren't caused today. On your legs, and on your back, and your ribs. What happened there?'

Sara closed her eyes. 'They're not relevant,' she said. 'They have nothing to do with this.'

'You don't have to tell me,' the nurse sighed, 'but the police might ask about them when they question you.'

Sara nodded. She had expected as much. 'Will they come here to the hospital?'

'Probably not,' the nurse said, 'unless there just happens to be a constable free. They'll let you get better first, and talk to you at home in London.' She stood. 'They're willing to wait when it's only an accident, rather than a criminal investigation.'

They don't know I was run off the road deliberately, Sara thought.

'In the meantime, if you'd like to chat with the

chaplain –'

'Who was driving?' Sara interrupted.

The nurse's forehead creased. 'I'm sorry?'

'The other car. Who was the driver?'

'I suppose I can have a look.' She thumbed through her papers. 'Let's see … her name was Odera. Nicole Odera.'

Sara's head seemed to grow lighter. *Nicole?* She thought. She pressed her skull more firmly into the pillow as though trying to ground her thoughts. Sara had never learned Vos's partner's last name … but could it have been Odera? Surely Nicole wouldn't have run Sara off the road … would she?

'What does she look like?' Sara asked.

'I'm afraid I didn't see her,' the nurse replied.

'How old is she?'

The nurse reached up and laid a hand softly on Sara's wrist, as if humouring a delirious patient. 'You really shouldn't get worked up about this right now.'

'Please.'

'Late twenties, I think. Why do you ask?'

'And she's here in the hospital, too?'

'Well …' The nurse hesitated. 'I'm afraid the injuries Ms Odera suffered were far worse than yours,' she said.

A pang of grief closed Sara's eyes. 'Is she …?'

'I'm afraid so,' the nurse said. 'The poor woman died at the scene.'

Vos was taking ages to arrive, and with every minute the Green Street flat felt as though it were shrinking just a little bit more. Even the air seemed to grow denser as Jamie waited. It pressed in on him, making him sweat through his shirt into the fabric of his new suit. He paced the small floor, unable to stop thinking about how little he'd understood Sara. These thoughts had no progression, no rational order. Tiny vignettes twined around Jamie's self-recrimination – Sara explaining how she had made the Eye-in-the-Pyramid pendant to dampen her grief, and telling him why she'd let her brother die. How could Jamie have walked out on her when she was staggering under such a weight? Of course he'd been blind to her true burden – but why hadn't he seen?

He was insensitive.

Sara needed him.

He'd failed her.

He loved her.

A loop of thoughts, repeating.

Jamie was relieved he'd commissioned the jewellery from the shop down the street. It lay coiled in his pocket now. He planned to keep it there, like the talisman of a better future, until he gave it to Sara on Monday.

The white door swished open almost silently, and Jamie turned to see Vos standing in the doorframe, eyeing him narrowly. 'I hope you feel better than you look,' Vos said, 'because you look like shit.'

Jamie blinked. 'Come in,' he said.

Vos closed the door and gestured to the sofa. 'Sit down,' he said. 'What we do today is going to decide our futures. The stakes are incredibly fucking high.'

Vos was always blunt, but Jamie had never seen him this urgent. He moved to the sofa and sat. 'What's wrong?' he asked.

Vos dropped into the chair opposite and leant forward, elbows on his bony knees. 'It's Rootenberg,' he replied solemnly. 'I've just found out that our friend cannot be trusted.'

'Why?'

'He's been playing both ends against the middle. He hasn't only been trying to shill his Zimbabwean contacts to us. Turns out, he's also been working on Strategic

Ballistics – that Russian government firm.'

'He's been in contact with the Russians?' Jamie asked. He searched his memory for any clue Rootenberg might have offered in their meetings. 'Since when?'

'At least since the fall of Mugabe. Maybe longer.'

'Before he came to Thorndike?'

Vos sneered. 'I suppose the little shit finally realised the Russians already have plenty of contacts in Zimbabwe. That's when he called on me. He'd have been better off starting here and sticking with Thorndike alone.' Vos raised his eyebrows. 'What can I say? The guy's a greedy prick. And, let's face it, he's not the sharpest tool in the shed.'

Vos looked so agitated, Jamie imagined he must feel torn apart by the betrayal. 'It can be difficult when friendship and business collide,' he said. 'Why did you ever work with him?'

'I owed him a favour,' Vos replied.

'Well, I'm sorry,' Jamie said. 'I take it you've cut ties with him? It's likely for the best.'

Vos glared at Jamie as though he were an especially thick child. 'You're not hearing me,' he snapped. 'Russians are involved. What Rootenberg's done has left us all in a shit-ton of trouble.'

'How?' Jamie asked.

'They found out about his double-dealing, that's how. A couple of days ago, Rootenberg was contacted by someone he thinks is an arms procurer. Now the idiot believes he's back in Moscow's good books.'

'I take it this guy isn't what Rootenberg thinks he is,' Jamie ventured.

'Nope,' Vos agreed grimly. 'He's an agent of Russian Foreign Intelligence. They're called the SVR. Specifically, he's with the part that deals with illegal operations, known as Directorate S.'

Jamie shook his head. 'Why would Russian Intelligence get involved? The sale of a few mortar shells isn't high-level politics.'

Vos lolled his head onto the back of the chair and stared at the ceiling. 'The answer is business,' he replied. 'It's one of the things that keep the Russians spying. International espionage isn't just about politics any more, it's also about money. Trouble is, the Russians' tactics have stayed the same since the Cold War. It doesn't matter whether the motives are politics or business.' He lifted his head and leaned forwards. 'Listen, kiddo – Directorate S has two jobs. First, they conduct false flag operations, where they recruit stooges who never know they're working for the Russians. Second, they kill people.'

Jamie paused as he considered the implication of Vos's intelligence. 'But Rootenberg knew he was working with the Russian government,' he pointed out.

Vos smiled grimly. 'So we can rule out a false flag operation.'

'You mean, they're going to kill him?'

Vos angled his head equivocally. 'On balance, my guess is not. You ask me, they'll use him to do their bidding for the rest of his life.' He raised his thin eyebrows. 'But if I'm right,' he went on, 'they're sure as shit going to kill somebody.'

'Who?'

Vos stared at Jamie blankly. 'You and me, chum,' he said. 'Maybe Sara and Nicole, too.'

'What?' Jamie cried.

'It's how these people operate,' Vos said. 'How better to get Rootenberg on side? They kill the Westerners he was trying to do business with and frighten him into cooperating with them for ever. A spineless shit like Rootenberg would do anything for them after that.'

'Do they know who we are?' Jamie stammered.

'They'll know the company,' Vos replied.

'But us as individuals?'

'I'd say, not yet,' Vos said, 'but they will soon. My intelligence indicates an agent from Directorate S is due to land at Heathrow tonight. By tomorrow morning, he'll have met with Rootenberg and extracted our names.' Vos leaned back and stretched out his lanky legs. 'They won't do anything to us immediately. The Russians are careful in their planning. We'll die soon enough, but at a time least likely to arouse suspicion.'

'What can we do?' Jamie stammered. 'Have you called the police?'

'You mean, your old alma mater?' Vos sneered. 'The Met will be of no help to us, matey,' he said. 'This is out of their league.'

'MI6, then.'

Vos snorted. 'Thorndike Aerospace has contacts, sure – but by the time anyone took us seriously, we'd most likely be dead.' He shook his head slowly. 'Nope,' he said, 'you and I are going to have to deal with this problem tonight.'

'How?'

Vos stared at Jamie levelly. After what seemed like minutes, he asked, 'Are you ready to do the worst thing you've ever done in your life?'

253

TWENTY-ONE

Nicole is dead, Sara thought. *Nicole tried to run me off the road and now she's dead.*

But, Sara reminded herself, she didn't know that for a fact. It hadn't been confirmed. All she had been given was a name. It might not be the same Nicole. Sara was not sure whether the Nicole she knew was named Odera or not. The grim suspicion that was causing her stomach to lurch might be completely unfounded.

But I know it's not, she insisted to herself. *I know it's true.*

But how exactly did Sara know that? Was her certainty founded on a mere premonition? And, if so, could she even trust it? *I've been out of touch with my psychic side for too long*, she thought. The bonds between Sara's sense of self and her visions had been loosening for weeks. That dissolution had begun with those unsettling visions of the Kapadia family. *Navid kicks Jamila and she's still; Navid tosses the petrol-soaked newspaper to Yusuf.* Since then, Sara's abilities had taken on a sour quality. Not long after her premonitions of Tim Wilson bludgeoning his lover to death, her confidence had been knocked sideways by those contradictory visions of Rachel Poole. Even after confirming all she'd suspected about Wilson and Berger, Sara's relationship with her abilities had been uneasy. As it turned out, avoiding her visions had been as dangerous as having them. If Sara had allowed more of her second sight into her life recently, she might have foreseen this evening's altercation on the Brecon Beacons. Maybe Nicole would still be alive.

Sara adjusted her head on the pillow and took a deep breath. She needed answers – and for that to happen, she had to trust herself. She turned her head gingerly, looking for her nurse.

'Excuse me?' she called.

The nurse popped her head between the panels. 'What can I do for you?'

'I think I'll rest for a while,' Sara told her. 'Is it possible not to be disturbed?'

The nurse's eyes smiled. 'I will have to check on you,' she said, 'but of course. You try to get some sleep.'

When the nurse had retreated and rearranged the panels, Sara closed her eyes and forced herself to think of Nicole. Nicole Odera. She pictured the woman's thin, intelligent face, framed by hair plaited so perfectly into cornrows. Sara also thought of Vos, and Jamie, and Thorndike Aerospace, and South Africa.

And of danger; she couldn't help but think of danger.

Then, from a corner of her mind, Sara could hear echoes of Eldon Carson's voice. They bounced against her other thoughts, flooding her consciousness.

OK, Miss Sara, she heard Eldon say, *here are your coordinates ...*

Immediately, fragments of colour and shape began to collect. Slowly, Sara made out the form of Gerrit Vos. She envisioned him strolling into some sort of public space. Outwardly, Vos's set features, his sunken eyes, formed a mask of complete calm. But Sara could also feel his nerves jangling like the vibration of shrill music. Whatever she was witnessing, it was not an image from the past ... this was about to happen, and soon.

And it felt *wrong*.

A figure walked at Vos's side. Sara strained to tune into the image more clearly. She yearned for it to be Nicole. That would mean she'd been mistaken about her assailant, and that Nicole was still alive.

Sara forced herself deeper into the trance. As the images grew sharper, the sense of menace became even more palpable. These two people were walking into danger. Sara could almost make out the figure next to Vos now. She strained, focused ... and her chest hollowed as she realised it was not Nicole.

It was Jamie.

Jamie could feel his pulse racing, his breath thickening. It was difficult to think, and the thoughts that wanted to push through were impossible. The situation seemed so unreal.

Jamie reminded himself that, unlike Vos, he did not have access to intelligence briefings. There might well be a bigger, deadlier picture that Jamie could not see. The only things he was able to focus on with certainty were his thoughts of Sara.

Sara – now driving blithely through her beloved hills to visit her oldest friend. So unaware of any danger.

'How would we deal with the problem?' Jamie asked.

Vos released a grunt of approval. He sat up straight and dug into his jacket pocket. He withdrew a small zip-lock bag of white powder and tossed it onto the coffee table.

'This,' he said, 'is thallium sulphate. When it's ingested, it mimics the effects of a viral infection – vomiting, convulsions, that kind of thing. Assuming you use enough – and by that, I only mean a quarter of a teaspoon full – its effects are fatal. And the cause of death will be listed as *natural*.'

Vos grinned. 'You see, thallium is seldom tested for in autopsies. Now, there's always a slim chance that it would be found. So let's just say, for example, that Levi Rootenberg ingested this and died. If it were ever discovered in his body … well, two facts would soon emerge. One, that Rootenberg had been working with the Russians. And two, that thallium is known to be a poison much loved by the KGB. Put those two facts together, and the conclusion is obvious – Levi Rootenberg was assassinated by Russian intelligence.'

Jamie's brow knitted closer together. He blinked. 'Levi Rootenberg?' he said.

Vos shrugged. 'For example.'

'No,' Jamie breathed.

'No what?'

Jamie shook his head so lightly it looked like a tremble. 'You're suggesting we commit murder,' he whispered.

'I'm suggesting we save our skins while we have the chance.'

Jamie threw himself back defiantly. 'Not in that way,' he said. He stared at the bag of white crystals on the coffee table, and added, 'We can't solve this problem like that.'

'Why not?'

'For all the reasons people don't commit murder,' Jamie shouted. 'I just won't do it.'

Vos grimaced and suddenly kicked out, shoving the coffee table. 'Matey,' he bellowed, 'what aren't you understanding here? You don't have a choice!' His sunken eyes glared. 'This situation is literally kill-or-be-killed. Maybe you want to be a martyr and take the ultimate hit for your morals, but remember, it's not only you and me who'll go down. It's Nicole, too … and it's

Sara.'

Jamie couldn't think. He could barely breathe. Vos sat straighter but lowered his gaze. 'Rootenberg's a piece of shit,' he muttered. 'For one, he's a murderer. He killed people in South Africa. Don't ask how I know that, but it's an iron-clad fact. Do you think he deserves to live while all of us die?'

From the paralysis of Jamie's thoughts, snippets of his conversation with Sara surfaced. How she had let her brother die, and still did not think what she'd done was wrong. Rhodri Jones hadn't deserved to live. Jamie even thought of his father, and how he had risked his good name for the sake of his family's comfort.

Sometimes you do the wrong thing for the right reasons, he'd told Jamie.

But this was different. This was murder. 'I don't want to spend my life in prison,' he said, his voice trembling.

'You won't,' Vos replied with conviction.

He reached out and picked up the bag of powder. 'Think of the safeguards,' he repeated. 'This thallium is almost certain not to be detected. It'll be logged as a death by natural causes. And even if the coroner does detect it, the government is going to blame the Russians.'

Jamie shut his eyes so hard they sparkled. Something behind his right eye twinged. His chest burned, and he could feel bile creeping up his throat. He silently apologised to Sara for not having heeded her warnings. Sara had told him to reject Vos from the very start. Sara hadn't wanted him to have anything to do with Thorndike Aerospace. But Jamie had not listened and, now, here he was … in a Thorndike flat, discussing murder.

'I shit you not,' Vos said quietly. 'We do it, or we all die.'

As Jamie opened his eyes, he noticed that his cheeks tickled. Tears were dribbling down them.

'But how?' he asked dully. 'The thallium, I mean.
How could we even get Rootenberg to take it?'

Vos grinned slyly, and held out the small bag for Jamie
to take. He said, 'That, my friend, is a wonderful
question.'

The sounds of the Intensive Care ward are long gone now.
Sara is no longer in Cardiff. She is not even a physical
presence. She is Spirit, floating behind Jamie and Vos as
they stroll into a narrow room with floor-to-ceiling
windows on two sides. Beyond the glass, the sky over
London is dimming into twilight, and the skyline is
lighting up. Inside, the restaurant's high-end starkness
telegraphs the price customers will pay, just to be here.
Both men are on edge, all senses twitching.
Unconsciously, Jamie brushes his hand against his right
jacket pocket. Sara can feel danger there, and also a deep,
deep wrongness. The men stand behind a well-dressed
couple, waiting to speak to the maître d'. In a barely
perceptible mutter, Vos says, 'Centre of the ceiling. See
the dome camera? Likely pointed this way. Whether that's
a threat depends on where we sit.'

'There was one outside the lift, too,' Jamie observes
quietly.

'Inside it as well,' Vos adds. 'Concealed.' He masks
his tension by smiling wolfishly and knocking Jamie on
the arm. 'Surprised you didn't notice that, Detective
Inspector,' he says aloud. 'Can't let your game slip now.'

Jamie widens his eyes a fraction. Vos shouldn't be
saying these things aloud. Vos snorts at his protégé's
visible skittishness but returns to his soft murmuring.
'Don't sweat it, kid. They're irrelevant. Couldn't deny
we've been here, anyway. It's any cameras close to the
table we'll need to worry about.'

The couple in front glide away, shepherded by a

waiter, and the maître d' bows her head in greeting to Vos and Jamie. Vos stops muttering and offers his name.

'Of course, sir,' she says, looking down at the screen on her desk. 'Your other guest has already arrived.'

A waiter appears and leads Vos and Jamie down a thin aisle between tables towards the back. Each of them spies Rootenberg at the same time. He sits in the far corner; his back is to the aisle, and he faces the window and the London skyline beyond. 'Oh, look at that,' Vos says aloud, 'he's chosen the best view for himself.' Quietly, he adds, 'Sit in that chair closest to us, and I'll squeeze in by the wall. Unless there's a camera above the table or in the corner, you're concealed. Check before you do it.'

They arrive at the table. Rootenberg half-rises, and the men exchange greetings. Vos frowns at a bottle of Carling that sits in front of Rootenberg. 'You classless son of a whore,' he says good-naturedly. 'Here's more proof you were raised in a brothel. I was about to order wine.'

'That's because you're a toffee-nosed ponce,' Rootenberg says with equal cheer. He's confident tonight; the call from Vos has made him feel part of the in-crowd again. Rootenberg upends the last of the bottle into his glass. 'They probably served Beaujolais Nouveau with your school dinners, you elitist prick. Give me a cold South African brew any day.'

'Well, you can take the engineer out of the mines ...' Vos says. Although his lips smile, his eyes frown in Jamie's direction. Their plan requires wine.

Jamie shakes his head slightly. *We can do it with beer.* His eyes flit up to the ceiling and over to the wall, and he shrugs almost imperceptibly. *No cameras that I can see.*

Vos nods slightly. He agrees. He raises his hand for the waiter, and gestures to Rootenberg's beer. 'What's the largest bottle you've got of this yak's piss?' he asks.

'750 millilitres, sir,' the waiter says.

'Three of those then,' Vos decides. 'We're slumming tonight.'

'It's good beer,' Rootenberg protests.

Vos glances at him from the corner of his eye. 'You know it's not actually South African, don't you?'

Rootenberg shrugs. 'Still tastes like Africa to me.' He drains his glass, then changes his posture and rubs his hands with a get-down-to-business air. 'So, Gerrit,' he continues, 'what's this business opportunity you mentioned on the phone?'

'No, no, no,' Vos counters with a raised finger. 'Not till we toast. We may be drinking fucking beer, but we're still going to do this with some panache.'

Rootenberg's disappointment, not to mention the trembling pressure of his anticipation, are palpable. The three men make strained conversation as they wait for their bottles to arrive. Sara hurries along this lull in the action in the same way she'd fast-forward a video file. She stops as the waiter leaves three bottles of Carling on the linen tablecloth and departs.

'Well then,' Vos says pointedly, with a sharp look at Jamie, 'I guess there's no time like the present.'

Immediately, Rootenberg tries to grab one of the bottles. *'Black Label sê die bybel'*, he quotes.

Vos's hand lashes out and grasps him by the wrist. 'Not so fast, you backwoods oik. Young Jamie here will be our sommelier.' He bows to Jamie with comic formality, and a dagger-sharp gleam in his eye. 'Inspector Harding?' he says. 'Please do the honours.'

Jamie stands, making sure his back is to any unseen camera that may be behind him. He picks up the first bottle. *It's the same drill*, he tells himself, *just as though this were wine*. He pours beer into Vos's glass as Vos moves to distract Rootenberg. 'Lee, get out your phone,' he orders. 'I want you to take down this number ...'

Rootenberg reaches into his pocket. Relief washes over Jamie as he notices the man's attention is entirely focused on Vos – then his hope deadens as Jamie sees Vos's glass. Beer does not behave like wine, and the foam expands within; it nearly overflows onto the table. Jamie knows if he waits for it to settle, it will be too late – Vos will have distracted Rootenberg for as long as he can. Jamie abandons Vos's glass, even though it still has more head than beer. He sets down the bottle and picks up Rootenberg's. His other hand reaches into his right pocket and unobtrusively withdraws the small bag of white crystals. Deftly, his fingers pry open the zip-lock, and he moves to transfer the bag into the same hand as the bottle. All Jamie will have to do now is ensure the thallium falls into the glass as he pours. His pass with the small bag, however, is clumsy, and Jamie feels his left hand slip along the cold bottle's sweat-beaded surface. He jerks his palm to keep his grip, but the bottle drops to the table in a shower of suds. At the same time, the crystalline thallium cascades in front of Rootenberg, like sugar from a diner's dispenser.

Rootenberg looks down. He is not a stupid man, and immediately sizes up the situation. He releases an anguished bellow and leaps backwards. Guests at the surrounding tables swivel their heads.

Rootenberg stands and swipes at his trouser legs with a linen napkin. 'You cunts!' he cries.

TWENTY-TWO

Sara sensed a figure looming beside her, but did not open her eyes. A part of her mind thought, *It's only the nurse, checking the heart monitor.* She fought to keep her focus on that table in London, on the danger. The images were blurring.

'Lee,' she heard Vos shout, 'just calm down.'

Sara's bed juddered. She felt it lower. The figure next to her leaned over. *Now she's checking the blood oximeter... Damn it, Sara, focus!*

'You absolute fuckers!' she heard Rootenberg cry. His voice was fainter now, his image almost gone. 'You're trying to poison me!'

Sara felt the nurse grip her hand. She pressed into Sara's wrist, taking her pulse. The vision faded more, and then disappeared altogether. Its absence left Sara with nothing but panic and anguish. Somehow, she told herself, Vos had coerced Jamie into ...

Into what? Poisoning someone?

Not just someone. Levi Rootenberg, the one Vos called Lee. Sara had recognised him from her earlier vision. He was paunchier and balder, but still obviously the man who had done Vos's South African dirty work. It all seemed clear to Sara now: this was what Vos had been grooming Jamie to do. To clear up a loose end. To carry out this remaining piece of dirty work.

When was this going to happen? Sara fought through her panic and tried to reconnect with the source of the vision. A sense of immediacy tingled through her. It was going to happen soon. Or it was happening now.

I have to leave here, Sara thought, and opened her eyes. The brightness of the fluorescent lighting stung.

'Well, well, *noswaith dda*,' said the nurse in greeting. She set Sara's hand back on her stomach. 'How are you feeling?'

'Where's my phone?' Sara demanded.

'I'm sorry?'

Sara realised the urgency of her tone must have made her sound like a madwoman. She shut her eyes for a moment, so hard her forehead wrinkled. Sara took a deep breath and released it. Forcing herself to ease her voice, she opened her eyes and said, 'I need to make a call. May I have my phone, please?'

The nurse considered this. 'I believe it's locked up with the valuables,' she said. 'I could get it for you.'

'Please, as soon as you can.' Sara looked around the small rectangle formed by the curtain panels. 'And where are my clothes?'

'We disposed of them,' the nurse replied. 'Some of them were cut off you when you arrived.'

Sara's chest grew heavy. If she didn't have any clothes, how could she get out of here? She started to think wildly. Were there any shops near the Heath Hospital? How could she even visit one in a hospital gown? Her face must have shown her dismay, because the nurse added, 'But don't worry – the police brought a travel bag from your car. I assume you have clothes in that.'

Giddy relief flooded over Sara. 'Yes,' she said. 'Is my medical bag there, as well?'

'Small, leather?' the nurse said. 'Yes, it's there.'

'Thank you,' Sara sighed. 'Could you bring both of them to me, please?'

'I could,' the nurse said haltingly, 'but why would you need them?'

'Because I have to go,' Sara said. 'I'd like to self-discharge.'

The nurse looked genuinely shocked. 'That's not advisable,' she said.

'I know that,' Sara said calmly.

'You, of all people, should.'

Sara spoke reassuringly, choosing her words with extra care. 'I recognise I'm doing this against medical advice,' she said. 'Please prepare the form and I'll sign it. But I do need you to go quickly.'

'Why?'

Sara waved her hands vaguely. 'Responsibilities,' she said.

'People always think things can't wait,' the nurse replied. 'But they can.' She raised her finger and spoke briskly. 'I'll make you a deal,' she said. 'I'll prepare the form and bring it with your bag and phone – if you'll agree to speak to a doctor first.'

'I am a doctor,' Sara reminded her. 'There's no need.'

'I have to do everything I can to make sure you know the risks,' the nurse explained. 'You wouldn't want me to get into trouble, would you?'

Sara sighed. 'If you can get a doctor right away, and hurry with the form, then I agree,' she said.

'Good.' The nurse stared at her with resignation. 'But you're not going to change your mind about leaving,' she added, 'are you?'

Vos led Jamie from the car park through the murky yellow light under the Cannon Street railway bridge. A steady stream of traffic whisked past them. 'Have you spoken to Sara?' Vos asked.

'No,' Jamie replied tightly, not looking at him. 'She's away.'

Jamie's voice was so quiet, Vos could hardly hear him over the street noise. Vos nodded. He had been sure to keep Jamie with him ever since he'd unveiled the Russia story. The last thing Vos wanted was for Jamie to ring his partner – at least not until the evening was over. Once Rootenberg was dead by Jamie's hand, the only protection Jamie would have would be Vos. Even someone as stubborn as Sara Jones would have to understand that. Both Harding and his partner would be securely under his thumb.

'Do you remember what you've got to do?' he asked Jamie.

Jamie brushed against his jacket pocket. 'Add the thallium to the wine,' he said dully.

Vos nodded. 'That's it. Pour them together, just as we practiced. It's best we get the business over with quickly, so do it as soon as the first bottle comes to the table.'

'What are you going to tell him?' Jamie asked quietly. 'I mean, about why we've met.'

Vos could barely hear Jamie's wavering voice. He glanced across at him, but read nothing in Jamie's fixed expression. The poor guy trying to mask how shit-scared he was. 'Don't worry, I'll feed him some bullshit,' Vos said. 'It only needs to sound convincing over dinner. It won't matter after that.'

Jamie tongued his lower lip. 'He won't ... in the restaurant, I mean ... Rootenberg won't keel over or anything, will he?'

'Relax, it won't affect him right away,' Vos reassured him. 'Our friend will make it through dinner alright. Later this evening, he may imagine he's caught the flu. By the time he's throwing up, it'll be too late for him.'

They turned onto King William Street and headed towards the Monument. The giant pillar glowed under floodlights. 'Back in the nineteenth century,' Vos told Jamie casually, 'suicides used to swan-dive off of that thing. Somewhere around 1850, they put up wire mesh to stop it.' He shook his head. 'Death,' he mused. 'It's everywhere. You just can't avoid the fucker.'

Jamie didn't appear to be listening. He stared straight ahead and walked at a robotic pace.

'After this,' Vos went on, 'you'll come with me to the Thorndike Investors' Mingle. I had asked Nicole to come, before this Rootenberg shit blew up. We can say you were always going to attend, and that's why we scheduled a meeting with Rootenberg just before it.'

Jamie nodded unthinkingly and Vos grimaced. It was understandable the kid would be nervous, but the sheer level of Jamie's current paralysis was worrying. Vos was placing a lot of trust in this ex-cop's ability to swallow his moral qualms and do the necessary. He found himself wondering whether Jamie had completely bought his fairy-tale about the Russians. Vos had seen no signs of doubt at the time – but then, the poor guy had been walloped hard by the sheer weight of the news. Now, that shock may have been giving way to some heavy soul-searching, and nothing would fuck up the plan like Jamie getting wobbly at the wrong time.

So far, Vos had been nice. He'd done his best to create a *we're-all-in-this-together* sense of urgency. But if Harding was having second thoughts, Vos knew he would have to try a different tack to keep him on board.

They were walking up Gracechurch Street when Vos finally came out and said, 'Kiddo ... your silence is spooking me. Are you sure you can do this?'

Jamie nodded curtly but did not look at him.

'I mean, totally certain.'

Jamie stopped. He reached out a hand to steady himself on the stone wall of a shop front. 'I think so,' he said.

'Right now,' Vos told him, 'you're not exactly convincing me.'

A range of emotions crossed Jamie's face. 'I just wonder if there's another way,' he said finally.

'What?' Vos said starkly.

'I'm thinking,' Jamie said. 'If the Russians are coming for us anyway, then what will – you know – killing Rootenberg do to stop that?'

'I told you,' Vos said. 'They don't have our names yet. If we don't get to Rootenberg tonight, you'd better believe they will. And after that, they'll know exactly where to find us.'

'Let's hide Rootenberg away,' Jamie suggested. 'If we told him the danger he was in, he'd come with us. He could lay low in Green Street. They wouldn't find him there.'

Without warning, Vos smacked his hand against the building. 'Harding, you don't seem to get it,' he shouted. 'Rootenberg's been playing us! He wouldn't stay hidden, even if we tried. He's a weasel. He'd run straight to the Russians.'

'But why?' Jamie persisted. 'Why would he do that?'

'Because he thinks he can get something from them! That sneaky little shit would betray us in a second if he thought it would advance his interests. And he is stupid enough to think that.'

Jamie released a hard sigh. His implacable expression had given way to contortions of distress. His eyes were focused on the pavement. He was thinking things through. When Jamie began to shake his head subtly, Vos knew he had to act. 'Think about Sara,' he urged. 'If you don't do this, you know what'll happen. The Russians will kill her.'

Jamie shook his head more vehemently. 'I'm not sure if that's … I mean, I can't –'

'And even if they don't,' Vos added, his voice growing harsher now, 'things will never be the same for her. If she lives, the best she can hope for is to be investigated by the police. Her career will be ruined.'

Jamie looked at Vos, his eyes widening. 'What do you mean?'

Vos offered a small shrug. 'Remember,' he said, 'I still have those photos of her. I'm doing my best to keep them under wraps, but hell, man – if I'm in danger myself, I can't guarantee they won't leak.' He angled his head. 'I don't want to sound cruel, kid, but I'm trying to point out that we're better off working as a team.'

Jamie stared at him, wide-eyed. 'Sara was right,' he whispered. 'She said you were trying to blackmail her, and I didn't believe it.'

'Blackmail?' Vos spat. 'What bullshit. I could have released those photos any time I wanted, and your missus would have found herself in a police interview room. I didn't do that because I thought we were on the same side.' He shot Jamie a disgusted look and added, 'Tell me how helping a colleague cover up a potential crime is blackmail.'

Jamie was trembling. Vos felt a stab of shame pierce him. He hated what he was doing to the kid right now, and he hated himself for doing it. He was deliberately corrupting someone he actually liked. What kind of a person did that?

He knew the answer of course: a person who didn't want to go to prison. Still, Vos hadn't felt quite like this since the years immediately following the events in South Africa. He hadn't felt bad when he and Rootenberg had planned their attack on Bakone and his boys. In fact, he'd felt rather powerful. It was only in the aftermath of the deed, when Vos was being lauded by the upper echelons at Thorndike Aerospace, that he'd begun to judge himself. The more successful he became in the company, the guiltier he had felt.

That was also when he'd started making good his never-ending debt to Rootenberg. Eventually Vos had learned to tamp down the bile that was ever rising in his throat. And he'd kept it down, more or less, until now.

Vos wondered what he would do if the kid bottled it. He had just about concluded that he might have to abort the operation and take Jamie back to the Green Street flat, when Jamie took a deep breath. 'I'm sorry,' he said. 'It's just overwhelming, you know?'

Vos released an inner sigh of relief. 'Believe me, I understand. But you know how important this is.'

'Yes,' Jamie said.

Vos placed a hand on his shoulder and steered him away from the shop front. 'And you can do it?'

Jamie steeled himself. 'I can do it.'

'Good man.'

His debt to Rootenberg, Vos thought, would end tonight. He and Jamie began to walk. 'The restaurant's just over there,' Vos said, waving his hand. 'When we get in, we'll need to check out the security cameras.'

Jamie nodded. 'And then?'

Vos clapped him on the shoulder and said, 'Then just do what we rehearsed. It'll be over before you know it.'

TWENTY-THREE

Two hours later, Jamie arrived with Vos at the Thorndike Investors' Mingle. The event was being held in a basement wine bar in the City, not far from the high-rise eatery they had just left. Jamie and Vos had parted from their dinner companion on the street outside, Rootenberg heading one way, the two of them another. A wash of pathos had passed through Jamie as he watched Vos looking at Rootenberg. Their prey had seemed on edge during the dinner. Even Vos's elaborate confection of lies, half-truths and promises had done little to ease the man's tense shoulders, to soften his chary gaze.

Unlike more heavily regimented investor events, the atmosphere at the Thorndike Mingle was relaxed – a chance for shareholders to drink and chat with the company brass in a low-pressure environment. There were no placard-waving protesters outside the venue, and no strict agenda inside. Jamie and Vos were among the last to arrive. As they climbed down the shabby-chic wooden stairway into the basement, they were met with a rumble of polite conversation and the soft clinking of empty glasses being whisked away by staff.

'You OK?' Vos asked.

'Yeah,' Jamie breathed.

'You did great,' Vos assured Jamie under his breath.

271

'Nobody saw a thing. Your life's going to be a lot better from now on, trust me.' He laid a hand on Jamie's shoulder. 'Tomorrow morning, I'll come round to the flat, and we'll get our story straight.'

'Our story?' Jamie whispered. 'You said we wouldn't be suspects.'

'Don't sweat it, kiddo, we won't. But when someone dies, there are always questions. It's important to have the right answers.' Vos patted Jamie as they entered the bar. 'Have a drink. This event's called a mingle – so go ahead and mingle.'

Jamie noticed Andy Turner across the room, chatting animatedly to a well-dressed woman in late middle-age. Andy clocked the two men coming in and raised his arm in greeting. Before long, Vos was approached by someone looking every inch a Thorndike executive. Vos introduced him to Jamie, who did not catch his name, and the two execs drifted away. Jamie watched Vos's back as he folded into the crowd. He wondered how the man could appear so calm.

Jamie hoisted a glass of champagne from a passing tray and edged towards the bar. On it was arrayed a selection of nibbles: bowls of upmarket crisps, rustic-looking crackers, and a cheese plate from which several guests had already carved chunks of cheddar and brie. Jamie tried to stand unobtrusively; the last thing he wanted was to smile his way through a conversation. He was happy to be left to his own thoughts; he needed to puzzle over his predicament. Jamie could recall each moment in the restaurant. He and Vos had noted the surveillance cameras as they arrived. They found Rootenberg at a back table. He'd already asked for a bottle of beer, but Vos had flagged down the waiter and changed the order to a white Meursault. When the wine arrived, the waiter had uncorked its bottle and tipped a small amount into Vos's glass.

'Leave it,' Vos had grunted. 'My colleague will pour.'

The waiter deferred. Vos distracted Rootenberg as Jamie stood, reached for the wine, and felt his world slow to a crawl.

His right hand had slid into his pocket. He pinioned the plastic pouch between his index and middle fingers. As he did, he thought, *Vos threatened Sara. No matter how he explained it away, it was a threat. He has those photos. He'll use them if he doesn't get his way.*

Something about that had seemed … off. Why had it been necessary for Vos to mention the photos? Surely the fact that their lives were in danger from the Russian government should have been enough to convince Jamie to act. Still, Vos chose to overplay his hand.

Had he been lying?

In those few slow-motion seconds, doubt had washed over Jamie. Maybe Vos had other reasons to want Rootenberg dead. Maybe Jamie was being used. Maybe the real threat to Jamie and Sara was Vos himself, with his incriminating photos and wild tales of intrigue whose solution was murder. For one giddy moment, a whole new possibility surged through Jamie's mind. The thallium, he'd told himself, could just as easily be slipped into Vos's glass as Rootenberg's. If its symptoms were as unremarkable as a viral infection, he was just as likely to get away with Vos's murder as Rootenberg's. Then, the threat to Sara would go away. As would his increasingly uncomfortable ties to Thorndike Acrospace.

It all depended on whether – or how much – Jamie believed the story about the Russians …

Jamie's memories were interrupted by a commotion on the other side of the room. He could hear Vos's voice barking, 'Jesus Christ – are you sure?'

He peered over. Vos was partly hidden by the crowd of

investors, but Jamie could see he was on his mobile. His voice was thick, marbled with distress. 'When? Oh, Jesus Christ.'

Vos listened with an expression Jamie had never seen him wear before. His normally hooded eyes were round with shock, his mouth had curled in a gape of grief. With growing awareness, the people clustered around Vos understood something was very wrong. They shushed each other.

'Tell me exactly – where?' Vos cried.

He listened intently and snapped his fingers at a low-ranking Thorndike staffer. 'You – get my car.' He handed over keys and a ticket. 'NCP, Thames Exchange. Run!'

The staffer grabbed Vos's keys and fled. Vos threw his head back, hyperventilating. The circle of minglers widened to give the executive space. People began to murmur.

'Gerrit – are you alright?'

'Call a doctor!'

'It was the phone call.'

'Something about his partner.'

Jamie's thoughts, still ticking over methodically, appraised the situation. He peered at Vos, and Vos's hollow eyes made contact. He began to move, softly parting the circle of concern that surrounded him. He approached Jamie unsteadily.

'Nicole,' Vos whispered. 'Sara.'

'Gerrit,' Jamie asked, 'what's happened?'

'I told her to do it,' Vos said. 'It was my fault.' His face contorted, and his shoulders began to shudder. 'All my fault,' he repeated.

'What's your fault?' Jamie said. 'Someone said it's about Nicole.'

'She's dead,' Vos told him.

Jamie felt himself blanche. 'What?' he asked.

274

'I sent her there, in that car,' Vos went on. 'Told her to do it.' He shuddered. 'It's my fault. I killed her.'

'My God,' Jamie said. 'What car, Gerrit? What did you tell Nicole to do?'

Gerrit Vos blinked, and something in his eyes shifted. A gleam that came from grief hardening into shock. Vos peered over Jamie's left shoulder, his brows knitting.

A voice rang from behind Jamie. 'Vos!' it cried. 'You and me, we need to talk.'

Vos blinked, and allowed his gaze to return to Jamie. 'Christ almighty,' he shuddered.

A member of the bar staff scurried past Jamie, calling, 'Sir, this is a private function. I'll have to ask you to leave.'

Jamie turned away from Vos, swivelling towards the source of the commotion. There, standing on the bottom stair under the glowing-red Exit sign, was Levi Rootenberg.

Rootenberg shouldered past the barman and weaved between the few well-dressed bodies that separated him from his quarry. 'I don't trust you, you fucker,' he yelled towards Vos as he walked. Someone from Thorndike security made a beeline towards Rootenberg, but Vos stopped him with a small shake of his head. Vos had managed to tamp down his own private grief in the face of a potentially calamitous new problem. 'I'll placate him,' Vos muttered to Jamie. 'We don't want a scene. We need to get him out the door before he starts puking.'

Jamie looked at the wine bar's gnarled floorboards. 'Gerrit, I need to –'

Before Jamie could finish, Rootenberg was on them. He glowered at Vos and said, 'I want to know what's really going on. I tried that number you gave me. The message said it wasn't in service.'

Vos held up his hands. 'Easy, Lee,' he said. 'I must have got it wrong.'

'And you,' Rootenberg said to Jamie. 'Why were you so nervous? All the way through dinner. You were jumpy and couldn't make eye contact.' His gaze flicked between the two men. 'There's something you're not telling me, and I want to know what it is.'

'Levi,' Jamie said, 'This is a bad time. Mr Vos has just received some terrible news.'

'I don't give a shit, I want to know what's up,' Rootenberg insisted.

'Do you know his partner, Nicole?' Jamie said quietly. 'She's been ...'

Vos placed a hand on Jamie's arm. 'Leave it,' he said. 'This fucker doesn't deserve an explanation.'

Vos turned his hooded gaze onto Levi Rootenberg. 'The number I gave you was false,' he said. 'There's nobody for you to call, because everyone knows what a clown you are. I was your only friend, and you stretched that privilege to snapping point.'

Rootenberg started trembling angrily. 'What are you saying?'

'I'm saying that everything I told you at dinner was bullshit. There's no new contract. There's not even the prospect of one. You're finished, Lee.'

'No,' Rootenberg said.

'Yep,' Vos replied.

'I'll tell everybody,' Rootenberg gasped. 'You know I will. Everything I know about you. You'll be finished, you bastard.'

Vos pondered this, and grimly shook his head. 'Don't think you'll have time,' he said. 'Pretty soon, you're going to start vomiting.'

'What?'

'Gerrit!' Jamie warned.

'Then you'll get confused. You'll start having blackouts. Then you know what's going to happen?' Vos raised his hand to Rootenberg's stubbly chin and held it firmly. 'You'll die,' he continued. 'Pretty fucking soon, too, Lee. You're going to die, and it's too late for anyone to stop it.'

Jamie could hear his own blood pulsing in his neck. Why was Vos doing this? It had to be grief. Maybe some sort of displacement, an angry cry after the terrible news about Nicole. Whatever the reason, he was making a terrible mistake.

'I don't believe you,' Rootenberg said levelly. 'You're lying.'

'I shit you not,' Vos said with a bleak grin. 'I tried to warn you not to push things, Lee, but you were too thick to see this coming.'

Jamie was almost swooning. He had to fix this. 'Levi,' he said, 'I'll explain this. Let's go outside. Mr Vos isn't in his right head.'

He moved towards Rootenberg, trying to take his elbow. Rootenberg leapt backwards towards the bar. 'You stay away from me!' he cried.

Vos grabbed Jamie's shoulder and wheeled him around. 'Leave him,' he snapped. 'This fucker will be dead soon enough.'

'No,' Jamie said urgently. 'No, he won't.'

Vos blinked. 'What?'

'I couldn't do it,' Jamie breathed.

Vos's eyes widened. He plunged his hand into the right pocket of Jamie's suit jacket and fingered the full pouch of thallium sulphate that still nestled within. Vos withdrew his fingers as though they had been burned. 'You gutless bastard,' he cried.

'Gerrit –'

Behind Vos, Rootenberg moved so quickly he was a

blur. He snatched up a knife from the cheese board. Throwing himself forwards, Rootenberg plunged it just under Vos's right ear. When he pulled the weapon out, Vos's blood spurted, and Rootenberg drove the knife in again, stabbing it swiftly and repeatedly until Vos dropped.

Two Thorndike security officers piled onto Rootenberg. The three men crashed in a scrum at Jamie's feet.

Sara took the morning's first London-bound train from Cardiff Central. It was scheduled to leave just before five o'clock. Standing in the chill of the outdoor platform, as the sky morphed from purple to crimson, Sara rang the Dyfed-Powys police. She ignored the hours-old flurry of messages and missed calls from Ceri. She knew her friend must be going mad with worry, but she wasn't thinking clearly enough to concoct a convincing story. The mixture of truth and calming fiction required a clearer head than Sara's right now. Sara worried she would reach someone at Carmarthen who knew her. After all, she was not a stranger at headquarters. Mercifully, she talked to a young woman who didn't recognise her name. The operator simply told her that her car was in a garage in Brecon and supplied the contact number. Sara wrote it down and slipped the note into her bag. It was something for later – nobody would be at the garage now, and the Mini wasn't going anywhere.

When the train doors unlocked, Sara settled into a seat and wriggled with discomfort. Her body had taken an awful battering over the last couple of days, and the lack of ergonomic seating did not help her now. Had the designers of train seats ever actually seen a human body? Sara forced herself to breathe deeply. For the first time since the kerfuffle of discharging herself from the hospital, she had time to reflect. Sara knew from experience she was now in danger of latent panic swelling up and overtaking her. She fought to quell the rising overwhelm. Now more than ever, Sara needed to think rationally. She tried to focus. What had she seen in her vision at the Heath Hospital?

She had seen Jamie trying to poison Levi Rootenberg.

It was that simple – Sara had witnessed her partner attempting murder.

How many hours ago had she foreseen this? Seven or more? At the time, Sara's sense had been that the act was imminent. If that were true, then Jamie would have tried it by now. Which meant he would be …

What?

Arrested? In hiding?

No, Sara thought, the whole notion was ridiculous. She stared out at the crimson-streaked sky on the border between Wales and England. Jamie may be under Vos's sway, but he wasn't brainwashed enough to try to kill a man. Once again, she asked herself the question that had dogged her this entire spring – how did she know if what she had seen was true?

Sara followed that trail of thought. *And what if it were? Why would Jamie have done such a thing? Would he be caught? Good heavens, shouldn't he be?*

Sara squeezed her eyes together so tightly her face flushed; she could feel her features sting as they scrunched. She tried to wish away the tide of questions. Sara felt traitorous even to think of Jamie deserving prison. Hypocritical. Her own morality had taken so many twists in the past few years, Sara had no right to judge Jamie for whatever had happened.

If it had happened.

Because she could be wrong.

Stop it, Sara.

The train had left Newport and was approaching Bristol Parkway. Sara would be in this carriage for the next hour and a half, regardless of what unsettling twists her life had just taken. There was nothing she could do except wait.

Well, she thought, there was one thing she could do. Sara kept her eyes closed and focused on relaxing her face. She took a further deep breath.

OK, Miss Sara, here are your coordinates ...

Look for Jamie, she told herself. *Tune in. Find him.*

Immediately, Sara felt a thrust of pressure, like a reservoir bursting its barrier. A sudden breaking-through of emotion, once held in check, but now escaping in one great torrent. It was Jamie, and he was quivering with emotional exhaustion. But safe! Jamie was safe.

Sara could feel her eyeballs moving under her closed lids as she surveyed her vision. Was Jamie at home? She reached out in one particular direction and felt around. Yes, he was. But he was agitated. Jamie's mind swirled like the foam-flecked eddy of a teeming river. Blasts of overwhelm knocked Sara. She needed to pull away or be consumed by them.

Sara forced open her eyes. The train had stopped at Bristol. Boarding passengers knocked past her, jolting her shoulder and arm. However, nobody asked her to remove her things – the overnight case and medical bag the police had returned – from the seat next to her. Sara was breathing heavily. She sweated in a way not justified by the weak train radiator pressing against her ankle.

She would have answers soon, Sara told herself. For now, it was enough to know that Jamie was safe and at home.

And with that, she shut her eyes again. Quickly, she succumbed to the overwhelming fatigue that had threatened to engulf her since she'd regained consciousness in Cardiff. Before the train had left Parkway, Sara was asleep.

Sara took a black cab from Paddington. It was just before 9:30 when she charged into the Brixton flat. She found Jamie sprawled on the leather sofa, one leg dangling onto the floor. He still wore the suit she'd first seen on FaceTime fifteen hours earlier. As Ego tried to wrap himself around her ankles, Sara set down her bags and perched on the chair next to the sofa. She reached out a hand and brushed Jamie's sweat-soaked copper fringe from his forehead. He stirred and opened his eyes.

'Sara,' he croaked. 'I'm so sorry.'

'Me, too,' she replied.

Jamie radiated anguish like a black aura. Sara pulled her eyes away from his and found herself staring at one of her tribal masks. That one had been in the Pimlico flat, hanging just over her favourite cane armchair. Next to it was the print of Abaddon, angel of death.

'Things have been … bad,' Jamie began. 'I can't even tell you what's happened.'

'Does it involve Levi Rootenberg?' Sara asked.

A flash somewhere between surprise and panic shot through her partner's eyes. Jamie's lips worked subtly, trying to form sounds, before he said, 'How do you know about him?'

Sara breathed once, shallowly. 'I know about Vos,' she replied. 'About South Africa. Of course I'd know about Levi Rootenberg.'

'But last night,' Jamie whispered. 'I was with him last night.'

Sara nodded. Ego bounded into her lap; absently, she scratched his forehead with her middle finger. Adrenaline pumped through her, but she forced her voice to stay level. 'Did you kill him?' she asked.

Jamie's eyes widened, and his lower lip trembled. 'God – no!' he breathed. 'How did you even – I mean ...'

Sara felt her chest tingle with relief. Her vision had been wrong. It was the first time she'd been grateful for that.

Jamie shook his head softly. 'How did you know?' he asked.

'Know what?'

Jamie rolled into a sitting position and groped in his jacket pocket. He withdrew a small pouch of powder and tossed it onto the coffee table. 'That Vos wanted me to.'

Sara eyed the poison and fought to keep her expression neutral. Jamie had not tried to kill Rootenberg – but Vos had wanted him to. Her vision had not been entirely inaccurate. It had been one of Eldon Carson's probabilities – something that might have happened, but didn't. Sara offered Jamie an enigmatic shrug. 'Intuition,' she said. 'I told you I didn't trust Gerrit Vos.'

Jamie furrowed his brow. Sara knew that such a flippant response was not going to satisfy him for ever. She might steamroller over Jamie's puzzlement while he was in anguish, but soon she'd have to offer a more plausible explanation.

Jamie's features remained contorted. He squeezed his eyes shut and suddenly became overwhelmed by tears. He raised his hands to his face, as though protecting himself from an invisible blow. 'Vos is dead,' he said, his breathing sharp and rapid. 'Rootenberg stabbed him.'

Sara gasped. Briefly, Jamie outlined the events of last evening, from his failure to act at the restaurant, to Vos's learning about Nicole's death, to Rootenberg's arrival. When he had finished, he mumbled, 'Rootenberg only did what I couldn't do. Back at the restaurant, when Vos expected me to poison Rootenberg, I had a sudden urge –'

'To kill Vos instead?'

Jamie breathed out heavily. 'I thought about what you said on FaceTime – that you didn't feel bad about letting Rhodri die. That he hadn't deserved to live.'

Sara nodded. 'But you didn't do it,' she said.

'No,' he sighed with relief. 'I didn't.'

Sara sucked a tooth and looked again at the powder on the table. 'You should have,' she said quietly.

Jamie had finally crawled off the sofa and staggered his way to the shower. The poor man was exhausted. After the horror of Vos's murder, Jamie had been forced by police to vacate the crime scene. He'd been made to wait in a nearby office lobby until called to give a witness statement. He had not got home until the wee hours of the morning, and had been sprawling on the sofa ever since. As it happened, Sara was tired too. So tired, in fact, she had said unwise things. Fortunately, Jamie had not asked her to explain why she thought he should have killed Vos. For that, she was grateful. It had probably been stupid to confess as much as she had in their FaceTime conversation, without also admitting a certain laxening of her attitudes towards murder.

Still, had Jamie's resolve been stronger – had he come home and admitted to killing Vos or even Rootenberg – what could she have said? Sara knew she had no right to have soul-searching conversations with Jamie that she hadn't even concluded with herself. Sara wondered if she could afford to waste any more time on further rationalisations regarding her own problem.

She was so deep in thought she had not heard the shower stop running. Sara jumped when Jamie appeared in his dressing gown. 'You need to rest,' she told him. 'So do I. Why don't we climb into bed and get some sleep?'

'I don't think I'll be able to.'

'Believe me, you will,' she said. 'Now, go.'

Jamie turned and walked robotically towards the bedroom. Sara rose stiffly. The adrenaline that had animated her since leaving Paddington had also dulled the pain from her injuries. Now, that pain was back in force, and she went to the kitchen and swallowed two paracetamol tablets. By the time she got to the bedroom, Jamie had slid into bed. 'I almost forgot,' he said. 'I got you something. When we were apart. It's been in my suit pocket this whole time.'

Sara smiled sadly. 'Thanks,' she said.

Jamie slid his hand from under the duvet. 'I have it here,' he said.

Dangling from Jamie's fingers on a silver chain was a disk, about the size of a fifty-pence piece. Gently, Sara accepted it from him. 'I had it made for you,' Jamie explained.

Sara looked at the pendant and began to shiver like the victim of a haunting. 'Jamie,' she gasped. 'Why on earth?'

'Because I broke your other one,' he said. 'Obviously, this thing is special to you. I don't have to understand your reasons to know that.'

Sara shook her head. On the pendant was a perfectly engraved replica of Eldon Carson's Eye-in-the-Pyramid symbol. She did not know what to say. 'Do you want to put it on me?' she asked.

Jamie took back the pendant and Sara lowered her head, ignoring the pulsing pain from her neck. Jamie slipped his arms around her and clasped the silver chain. Sara stood, and showed him the result.

'Well, I can't say it's beautiful,' he told her, 'but somehow, it looks OK.'

Sara bent down and kissed Jamie on the lips. 'Thank you,' she said. 'It means a lot.'

'God damn it, Sara,' Ceri yelled over the mobile line, 'I was worried half to death.'

'I know,' Sara said, 'and, Ceri, I'm so sorry. How did you find out?'

'When you didn't show, I tried to ring you.'

'A number of times,' Sara agreed.

She glanced at the clock on the kitchen microwave. It was now late afternoon. Although Jamie still slept, Sara had napped for no more than a couple of hours. She could have returned Ceri's calls sooner, but had been dreading the conversation they were now having.

'Anyway,' Ceri continued, 'I started having all those paranoid thoughts people have at a time like that. It must have been around ten thirty last night when I finally rang headquarters. That's when I found out. They didn't know your condition, but they knew where you were.'

Sara rooted around in the fridge and withdrew a package of meat. She tore a few sheets of paper towel from a roll attached to the wall and wrapped it snugly. 'So you rang the hospital in Cardiff?' she asked.

'Of course. They said you'd been out cold. Even I know how dangerous that can be.'

Sara placed the wrapped meat on the counter and knelt to open a drawer. This was where she kept various medical supplies.

Ceri paused for a deep drag on her cigarette. When she spoke again, it was on the exhale. 'What in hell did you think you were doing,' she went on, 'discharging yourself when your brain could swell to the size of a melon?'

'How did you know I self-discharged?' Sara said.

'What do you mean?'

'I'd have still been in the hospital when you rang. Did you call again later?'

'I wanted to,' Ceri admitted, 'but I knew what a nuisance I'd make of myself. So instead, I took a sleeping

285

pill and went to bed.'

'Sensible,' Sara said. She glanced around for a roll of masking tape.

'Then I got up this morning and drove all the way down here to see you,' Ceri concluded. 'I'm in Cardiff right now.'

'Oh, good heavens, Ceri,' Sara said.

'What in hell else did you think I'd do?' asked her old friend.

'I'm sorry,' Sara replied. 'If I had only rung you earlier, I could have saved you a trip.'

'True enough,' Ceri agreed. 'But listen ... since I've come this far, I figure I might as well get on the M4 and drive the rest of the way to Brixton. I could be there by early evening.'

'Ceri, no,' Sara said abruptly. 'Don't do that.' She tried to lighten her voice. 'I mean, I'd only bore you. I'm stiff – I really can't do much.'

'Then I'll nurse you,' Ceri said.

'I have Jamie for that.'

'But –'

'Please, Ceri,' Sara said insistently, 'just go home.'

On the other end of the line, Sara heard nothing but white noise and the sucking of a cigarette. Ceri was not happy.

Sara remembered – the masking tape was in the drawer below the cutlery. She opened it as she drew in a breath. 'I'll tell you what,' she added. 'When you get to Penweddig, go online and book us that trip to Mallorca.'

'What?' Ceri asked.

'I want to go with you,' Sara said.

'What about work?' Ceri asked.

'I've quit,' Sara said.

She gathered up her ragtag supplies and moved into the living room, where she lay them in her medical bag.

She whisked a small packet off the coffee table and dropped it in, too. 'Just give me a couple of weeks to recuperate. After that, I'm all yours. You decide where we'll stay and what we'll do. And I'll even pay. The whole trip will be my treat.'

'Well,' Ceri said. 'Shit.'

Still clutching her medical bag, Sara crept into the bedroom and gazed down at Jamie's twitching features. He was showing signs of restlessness and, left on his own, would wake up soon. 'I would like to ask one favour though,' Sara added quietly to Ceri. 'Would you be willing to book the trip for three? I think Jamie could use a break, too.'

Ceri hesitated. Sara knew this was not what she'd wanted to hear, even though she'd grown to like Jamie over the past few years. Despite Ceri's evident disappointment, it only took a few seconds for her to say, 'Oh, hell, why not? The more the merrier.'

'Lovely,' Sara said. She dipped into her medical bag and chose a sedative and syringe. 'Now, I have to get some rest,' she said, 'and you have a long drive home.'

'I suppose I do,' Ceri agreed. 'Give my love to Detective Inspector Harding.'

Sara agreed and rang off. She filled the syringe, strapped a tourniquet to Jamie's arm, and injected him with the sedative. He would sleep untroubled now. All Sara needed to do was to wait for the wee hours of tomorrow morning.

Then she would be ready to pay a visit to Tim Wilson.

EPILOGUE

The window was easy to spot – it was the one with a triangular shield of torn cardboard covering the wedge-shaped hole. Sara located a wheelie bin – dull orange in the amber glow of the estate's streetlamps – and rolled it up to the brick wall. The one she'd chosen stank of rotting meat, but it was all the more stable for being full. Despite its ballast, the bin's plastic wheels rumbled on the concrete, causing echoes to skitter between buildings. Sara took a breath, cocking her ear for sounds of any interested residents, then positioned the container directly under the window. Placing her medical bag on top of the closed lid, she gripped either side of the bin's rim. One balletic leap, and Sara was kneeling on the buckling plastic. She gritted her teeth as several shards of pain stabbed through her simultaneously.

One day, she thought, *I'll learn to recover from my injuries before doing the next reckless thing.*

Sara lay one hand against the bricks for support; with the other, she unclasped her bag and withdrew a bundle of kitchen towel; rolled inside was a large chunk of salami. Pulsing her leg muscles for balance, Sara stood and leaned forwards. Her leather-gloved hand shoved through the cardboard, ripping away the tape that secured it to the window. She listened again and heard only silence.

'Stanley?' she whispered. 'C'mon, mate. Yummy yum-yum. Come get it.'

She heard a heavy rustling from the bedroom next door, then the sound of large claws clacking on linoleum. She dropped the salami through the broken window and leapt from the bin. Landing ungracefully and with bright flashes of pain, she slid down the bricks – the still-tender small of her back screaming in protest – and huddled, straining to hear. The stench of decomposing meat nearly made her retch.

Sara was rewarded with sounds of wet smacking, coupled with deep, satisfied grunts. *He likes salami, does Stanley.*

And now she had to wait. She considered getting up and biding her time with a casual-seeming stroll ... but the thought of encountering security cameras kept her here, in the relative safety of this stinking shadow. So far this evening, Sara had done her best to avoid appearing on camera. That had been a hard-won lesson, courtesy of Gerrit Vos. She waited longer than was necessary, until the silence in the flat had held unabated for several minutes, then rose unsteadily to her feet.

It was harder climbing onto the bin the second time. Eventually, she stood atop the lid, wavering, and dug into her medical bag, withdrawing a roll of thick masking tape. As quietly as she could, Sara tore off a strip and smoothed it onto the glass, directly under the break. Then she tore another, and another. Finally, Sara took hold of the broken edge of the window and tugged, snapping off a large chunk of glass. Even muffled by adhesive paper, it made the sound of a gunshot, and she froze. Nobody had noticed; the night remained as silent as Chalk Farm ever got. Standing on tiptoe on the rocking bin, Sara pressed her arm through the hole in the glass, shoving it shoulder-deep, then reached downwards. She fumbled for the window's straight handle and, with extended fingers, managed to push down. She nearly fell as the window swung inwards. Catching herself and gingerly withdrawing her arm, Sara crouched on the sill and dropped to the living room floor, landing next to the drugged form of Stanley the Rottweiler.

The flat smelt of air freshener. Sara surveyed the small, darkened room. It was as tidy as it had been the first time she'd visited. There were the wooden chairs she and Tim Wilson had sat in, now arrayed side-by-side against the wall. She remembered Wilson's chair clattering to the floor as he leapt up to choke her. Unbidden, other images swam into Sara's mind, too – an onyx tea set, a Chobi rug, a brass wall plaque engraved with a picture of the Kaaba. They were items from the Kapadias's home in Aberystwyth; things that Eldon Carson would have seen in those horrible visions that launched his fatal career as a killer. Visions Sara herself had witnessed so many times only recently, and which had recurred night after night. These memories, flashing into her mind here, now, reminded Sara of why she had come – as if she'd forgotten.

Stealthily, Sara eased herself towards the bedroom door, and was struck by another awful thought. *What if Philip Berger is here?* Sara hadn't thought of that possibility. She hadn't thought of anything, really – she was reacting to a deep, subconscious impulse that told her now was the time, and her actions were inevitable.

She peered into the bedroom. Relief tingled down her chest. There was only one figure under the thin duvet. Tim Wilson lay rigidly on his back, his head centred on the pillow, a tattooed arm jutting at a right angle across the other side of the futon, hand off its edge, knuckles brushing the tatami mat. *He even sleeps neatly*, Sara thought.

She sank to the floor, inches away from Tim Wilson's dangling hand, and gazed upon his face, slackened by deep sleep, and appearing so angelic. There was no trace of the furious young man, his features contorted by rage, spittle flying from his sneering lips, that Sara had witnessed twice now. In these still, small hours, sleeping Tim seemed no more harmful than a baby.

A hollow cavity seemed to swell in Sara's chest, and her throat thickened. When she drew her next breath, it came in staccato waves, and her head lolled forwards. *I could leave now*, she told herself. *Straight out the front door, down to Regent's Park Road, over the railway bridge and straight to Jamie's Range Rover*. And she knew she would do precisely that – but not yet. Hot tears welled in Sara's eyes and she groped for her bag. She squeezed her eyes shut, then wiped them with a sleeve. She mustn't cry. And she didn't need to think. All that could come later.

Because the alternative was to allow Philip Berger's death.

And possibly her own.

With a last look at Tim Wilson, Sara stood, and eased from the bedroom. She stepped over Stanley's drugged body, moved into the kitchenette, and gently opened the refrigerator. The pale light cast a milky glow over the peeling linoleum on the floor. On a rack inside were several unopened bottles of Sunny D, and another in the door tray, half-full. That was the one she chose.

Sara set the bottle on the counter and unscrewed its orange plastic cap. Then she reached into her bag and withdrew Gerrit Vos's small pouch of thallium sulphate. As she did, Eldon Carson's words sounded in Sara's mind. 'The gift I have handed you is a poisoned chalice,' he had said, 'but I believe you will not run away from the responsibility.'

At least you got that one right, Eldon, Sara thought, as she upended the contents of the bag, and watched it dissolve into the fluorescent orange liquid.

DEAD IN TIME

When successful London psychiatrist Sara Jones's relationship breaks down, she returns to the remote part of Wales she grew up in, keen to clear her head and start afresh. But soon her former boyfriend, Metropolitan Police detective Jamie Harding, is back in her life – investigating a series of murders with links to the occult. Sara is drawn into assisting the investigation – much to the chagrin of her childhood friend, Ceri Lloyd, the detective in charge.

As more bodies are found, a series of clues makes Sara realise that the killer believes they have psychic powers. Soon, the killer confronts Sara and offers a shocking explanation for their crimes – one that could have a massive impact on her life and, crucially, allow her to come to terms with the tragedy that haunts her past…but at what price?

A sharp, clever thriller with a paranormal twist, Dead in Time is the first novel featuring Sara Jones by up-and-coming crime writer Terence Bailey.

Proudly published by Accent Press

www.accentpress.co.uk